D1519698

Praise for
CAPITOL GAINS

"If you have ever wondered how Washington, DC, really works and suspect that the federal government is broken, you do not want to miss this read. In *Capitol Gains*, Rick Spees has created a fascinating story about a lobbyist and his imaginative plan to climb to the top of his profession. This hilariously disturbing plot kept me reading, laughing until the end, and hungry for more. Buy the book. You'll enjoy it immensely . . . and unlike CATI, that's no scam."

—JOHN J JESSOP
Author of *Pleasuria: Take as Directed, Murder by Road Trip, The Realtor's Curse, Guardian Angel: Unforgiven, Guardian Angel: Indoctrination*

"With his spellbinding novel *Capitol Gains*, Rick Spees invites us into a world of intrigue and touching human drama: Washington, DC. The protagonist, a delightful family man and rising star lobbyist, becomes obsessed with desire to enrich himself in a forbidden way, and his story is captivating. A gifted craftsman, Spees is a skilled storyteller whose novel takes direct aim at the foibles of human conduct. In *Capitol Gains* he effectively combines the darkly humorous, tender, and sensual to create a memorable satire. Suspense builds throughout the novel, but there is never a clue to the denouement—until you get there, and the arrival will not disappoint."

—RAY CARSON RUSSELL
Author of *Philurius College Blues*

"Readers who want to know how Washington really works will turn to *Capital Gains*, the new novel from the amazing imagination of Rick Spees. Here a highly experienced but bored DC lobbyist invents Citizens Against Tax Injustice (CATI), which becomes the basis for a real-sounding story about the highest levers of government, even though the whole thing may be just a sexy charade. As a Washington veteran myself, and an inveterate reader, I became an increasingly hooked believer, and you will too.

—BARRY JAGODA
Author of *Journeys with Jimmy Carter and Other Adventures in the Media*

"*Capitol Gains* is a very funny novel. Rick Spees has taken his decades of lobbying experience to create a lovable but corrupt lobbyist in Richard Brewster—ambitious, willing to bend a few rules, never telling a direct lie but never quite conveying the whole truth, fast and loose with money. It all goes quite well until Brewster is on top of the world. Then reality sets in. I couldn't put it down until I saw how Brewster survived his roller-coaster ride."

—BUDDY DYER
Mayor of Orlando, Florida

"Rick Spees' novel will have you laughing out loud while you marvel at this riveting inside story of the incredible ways in which Washington really works. It would be hard to find a more sympathetic scam artist than Richard Brewster, or a better guide to the murky world of lobbyists and legislators that inhabit our capital city. I don't think I've ever learned so much about the world of politics while having so much fun!"

—LEONARDO A. VILLALÓN
Professor of Political Science at The University of Florida

Capitol Gains

By Rick Spees

Published by

köehlerbooks™

3705 Shore Drive
Virginia Beach, VA 23455
800–435–4811
www.koehlerbooks.com

CAPITOL GAINS

RICK SPEES

VIRGINIA BEACH
CAPE CHARLES

PROLOGUE

Imagine my surprise when I learned that my nephew Ryan's high school government class was studying the details of my scam. We were visiting my in-laws in Chapel Hill, North Carolina, when Ryan said to me, "Hey, Uncle Richard, I think they wrote about you in my textbook. At least, someone named Brewster who is a lobbyist in Washington. I wondered if it was you."

Though I tried to get more information, he was far more interested in making a *Duke Sucks* poster for the basketball game against North Carolina that night. But I did gather that my story was being used as a case study of the evils of the lobbying profession. My scam—or Home Alone 2, as it was called in the textbook—was described as the culmination of a carefully planned, ruthless manipulation of the American political system. Occurring years previously, it embarrassed a president, consumed the energies of Congress, and dominated the news media, for a brief period. The lurid descriptions of the scam were exaggerated, and the textbook was wrong about my motivations. It wasn't nearly as well thought out or organized as was reported. To be honest, I wasn't that smart. It just happened. It came together slowly, piece by piece, until I was in over my head.

I decided to correct the record and get the truth out. You understand, of course, that Ryan did not encourage me to do this. The East Chapel Hill High School government class had told my story as a bold morality tale. Any competing versions of the story, including the truth, would cause confusion. Later, when I tried to explain my side of the story to Ryan, he got a bored look on his face.

"I am sure you had cool reasons to do what you did, but knowing the truth won't really help in my class. We just need to give Mr. Roberts back the answers he wants so we can graduate. I want to hear all about it. Really. Sometime. Just not today."

Despite his lack of enthusiasm, I began to mine my memories to determine exactly when to begin my story, when to start the history of the biggest Washington scandal between Watergate and Monica. When did my scam really begin?

CHAPTER 1
THE GERMINATION

It was twenty-five years earlier, in the spring of 1994. I drove with my wife, Elizabeth, up Wisconsin Avenue in Georgetown, to an evening reception. I was a junior lobbyist at the law firm of Johnson, Woods & Hart. I had left government service in 1986 after serving eleven years on the Senate staff of Nevada senator Paul Laxalt. In the eight intervening years, I had risen in the ranks of the law firm and as a Washington lobbyist. Of course, I was not at the top of my profession. However, I was ambitious and hungry and fully intended to get there as soon as possible. But even at that stage of my career, within my sphere, I flattered myself that I was a force to be reckoned with. And this party would reinforce that view.

As for my profession in Washington, we ran the show. Washington lobbyists, during the last decade of the twentieth century, were the rulers of the American dream. The federal government's budget exceeded two trillion dollars. Legislation was passed that connected with every aspect of modern life. The American people looked to the government to solve problems they couldn't even define. The politicians were the nominal rulers of the city. But every two years, several disappeared, thanks to the whims of the voters. Only the lobbyists remained, hidden from view but pulling the strings. We were in control. We were the institutional memory, the glue that held American society together. But only in Washington were our skills acknowledged. We had money, power, and recognition.

Elizabeth and I arrived at the party fashionably late for two reasons. First, Elizabeth had spent far too much time at Tysons

Mall, purchasing the right outfit for the day. But more importantly, I wanted to make an appearance.

As we entered the home where the party was held, my good friend Sue Ellen Davies and her British husband, Niles, greeted us. Sue Ellen then fulfilled her role.

"Oh my God, it's Richard and Elizabeth Brewster," she said so the entire room could hear. "I am so glad you are here. Now the party can start."

Her husband chimed in with his thick accent, "Yes, it's nice to see you, Richard, along with your lovely wife. We always appreciate it when you leave your trendy suburban zip code to visit us here in town."

"We wouldn't have missed this party, Niles," I assured him. "You always have such an interesting mix of guests."

"Yes," said Sue Ellen, "but you are the most important person here." She took my hand and led me further into her house. "Look who's here," she said, making sure that everyone heard her. The room quieted. "Richard Brewster, my good friend and lobbyist. Without him I would be nowhere. And I am his favorite client." She squeezed my hand.

Sue Ellen ran a trade association that promoted international education. I had met her years ago in Egypt, when she was working as an archeologist on a US government–sponsored dig and I was on a congressional fact-finding trip. We hit it off immediately. When she returned to Washington years later, she was hired to run the association. By then I had left the government and started working as a lobbyist. She hired me to help her get federal funds. While our track record had been mixed, she always credited me for our successes and forgot our failures. She was my best advocate. Of course, as an archeologist, she really didn't understand Washington. She didn't need to. She just needed to appreciate me.

She led me around the room, introducing me to the other guests in very flattering phrases—"you need to hire him" . . . "he is just brilliant" . . . "he is the best lawyer in Washington." I caught a few guests rolling their eyes after we moved on. But I was the center of attention, thanks to Sue Ellen. I relished my role. After meeting all the other guests, I headed to the bar.

I sipped a drink and struck up a conversation with a striking woman. "I've certainly heard all about you," she said.

"Well," I said, smiling and trying to look humble. "Would it be better if we put it all that behind us and started fresh?"

"Oh no. That's not necessary. Sue Ellen only says great things about you," she reassured me. I enjoyed her attention. We exchanged small talk for a while, until Sue Ellen interrupted us again. She was standing back in the middle of the room.

"Everybody, this is James Jeffery Stills. He is the deputy assistant secretary of commerce for foreign trade promotion."

"The *principal* deputy assistant secretary of commerce for foreign trade promotion," he corrected her.

"The principal deputy assistant secretary of commerce for foreign trade promotion," she repeated, "just back from some very important trade mission overseas. I hope he will tell us all about it."

James Jeffery Stills began to ramble about how vital his work was. People crowded around to hear him, including the very striking woman who had been fascinated by me just a few moments ago. I concentrated on my drink.

A bit later, as I leaned against a doorsill, an elderly man approached me. Around his neck was a gold chain holding a red-and-gold medallion covered with Arabic writing.

"I see you were looking at my medal," he said. "It's the royal order of Moroccan Knights. It was given to me personally by the king of Morocco."

"Really?" I asked. "What did you do to earn it?"

"I negotiated the wheat deal between Morocco and the United States two years ago," he explained.

"You mean two years ago when there was a drought and famine in Morocco and a wheat surplus in the United States?"

He nodded, smiling, appearing happy that I knew about it.

"How hard could that have been?" I asked.

"It was a lot more complicated than that," he replied, clearly insulted. "There were many parties involved, and it was vital to American interests to not press our advantages too far."

"In other words, we gave away the store?"

He turned away at that and moved off to show his medal to more impressed guests, including my wife.

Niles made his way over to me. "What are you doing here, Richard, in the corner?"

"Well, it seems the best place for me," I said. "I seem to have been upstaged by the deputy assistant secretary of something and the guy with the Arab coin on his chest. Even Elizabeth seems interested in the advisor to the king of Morocco."

"Ahhhhh," he dragged out the word. "Not the undisputed top of the pile at this party? But why are you complaining? You had your five minutes. There are other sources of power, and they all deserve attention. This city is so complicated."

"No, it's not, not really. Those guys are just window dressing. Lobbyists run the show."

"Well, maybe. But you might get some disagreement from those two, at least."

"I am sure I would," I agreed. "Those two don't run anything or do anything important. In the government, big titles are a scam. And with academics, awards and medals are a scam."

"Don't be defensive, Richard," he said. "You are the big lobbyist. And you do make more money. Your wife is telling everyone you are looking for a bigger house in McLean."

I was surprised by that information. "That's news to me. We can't afford our current house." I sipped my drink as I watched my two competitors work the crowd. "Niles, maybe you're right. Maybe I am looking at the city in the wrong way. Maybe being a successful lobbyist is not enough. Maybe to climb the ladder of success in Washington, I need more than that. Maybe I need a title or a medal. Or something else."

"Like what?"

"Well, Niles, maybe I need to come up with my own scam."

───────────

The next afternoon, I returned to these thoughts of a scam. Not in detail, you understand, but as a way to remind the bureaucrats and the academics how important I was. And on that particular day, my work wasn't too interesting. I was bored.

The day hadn't started badly. Waking early, I got out of bed long before my wife or the children. Deciding to start the day with some physical exercise, I dressed quietly and went out to jog.

The summer weather had descended that morning. Spring had lasted precisely one week, sometime in early April. Washington thereafter rapidly progressed from the arctic cold of winter to melting heat and humidity. It looked like a long, hot, miserable summer was upon us.

The air was steamy and dirty. I was covered in sweat by the end of the second block. My running socks slipped down around my ankles as my soaked shirt clung to my body. My eyes were stinging. Later, I could shower, but I would never lose the clammy feeling on my skin. A bad summer Washington day is a constant companion.

Running that day was no fun, but I had to admit it gave me a feeling of quick accomplishment that I seldom felt at work. As a lobbyist, I could spend months, or even years, working on a project without knowing the outcome. When I ran, I battled the course, battled the heat, and battled my own body, but I would finish with a flourish.

To avoid dwelling on the heat, I thought about the day ahead. It was not going to be difficult. The president was riding high in the polls. Congress was not debating anything of relevance to my work. No clients were in town. It would be a day to tackle little projects. Phone calls to government bureaucrats. Doing some long-overdue reading and research. Low-key congressional staff calls. Insignificant things. Not very interesting. There was little promise of excitement. I was in the mood for more of a challenge.

Continuing, I turned off the road to go through a nature preserve. The trail twisted through the woods and up a hill. I leaned forward and charged up. Reaching the crest, I leaped over the top and, stretched in midair, looked down and spotted a large turtle lying on the path where I would land. He was speckled with bright-yellow spots. He froze when he heard me crashing through the underbrush. I almost crushed him with my foot, but, at the last second, I managed to extend my stride. I shot over the top of the hill and started slipping and sliding down the other side. I stumbled but never fell. As I looked back, I saw the turtle watching me, frozen in fright but safe.

It was a very minor incident, but it filled me with joy, a combination of runner's high and the satisfaction of avoiding a disaster. On most days I would have tripped, crushed the turtle, and skinned a knee or broken my wrist. My attitude improved immeasurably.

Returning home, the children were still asleep, but Elizabeth was beginning to stir. Her summer nightgown was sheer, and I could see her dark nipples through the fabric. I was instantly aroused, and my penis pressed against my jogging shorts. I moved towards the bed, hoping I was downwind, and whispered into her ear, "Hey, babe, it's nice to wake up to you. The children are still asleep, and it's just you and me."

Rolling over slowly, Elizabeth squinted at me in disbelief. I was covered in sweat and dust.

"Get a grip."

"I mean after I take a shower. Or you could take one with me."

"Get a grip," she repeated.

"Does that mean you're waiting until tonight?"

She groaned and rolled over.

"I'll take that as a good sign."

She pulled the pillow over her head. Okay, I was hot and sweaty and probably smelled like horse manure. But I was sexually frustrated.

Seven hours later my desk was covered with pink phone slips. Everyone had called me—but no one I wanted to talk to. Some clients wanted hand-holding. Some wanted to know what I was doing to justify my fees. Still other clients wanted some inside information from Washington so that later that night, at a cocktail party, they could drop in a conversation the line "I was talking to Washington today and I learned . . ." It did not matter that the information I gave them was from CNN or the *Washington Post*; just as long as they could say it came from a Washington insider.

Every time I left my office throughout the day, I came back to a bigger pile of pink slips. At one point as I walked past, my secretary, Kathryn Monroney, pointed out how many phone calls I had yet to return and how many reflected the second, third, or fourth call. To please her, I went back to my desk and laid them out. Going through them, I threw out the duplicates. Following that, I put them in priority order to return. By the time I was done, my motivation had vanished.

I flipped on the television. There was nothing of interest on any of the news channels. I turned to C-SPAN to see what was happening in the House and the Senate chambers. As usual, nothing of relevance was going on there either. For a brief moment, I was tempted to watch *Oprah*, but I was afraid that one of my partners would catch me. With regret, I turned the set off.

I scanned my office for something to read. There was a political journal in my in-box. I reached for it with rising interest. It was a dry academic journal published by the Great Basin Intergovernmental Center. The lead story was about voter attitudes on South Dakota. I decided to read it. I have an excellent memory, and later I would find a way to work the information into casual conversations with my clients. They would be impressed with my encyclopedic knowledge of politics.

Within minutes, my mind was wandering. I tried to refocus but was soon staring out the window. Again I looked down at the page. Moments later I caught myself listening to the traffic patterns, waiting for reckless drivers to run the red light in the street below my window. I was bored. And it was then that I thought, *I really do need a scam.*

It felt good to think about it for few minutes. With the proper scam, I could leapfrog the years of climbing up the ladder at the firm and gain the recognition of an ever larger circle of movers and shakers in DC. I just needed an idea. When I came up blank I resigned myself to getting back to work.

But first, I decided to get a soft drink, promising myself to buckle down once I got back from the kitchen. As I got up, I noticed that there was already a can on my computer table next to a half-full glass with melting ice floating on the surface. Then I tried to determine whether I had to go to the bathroom but decided that I really didn't. I was in serious trouble. My determination to do serious work kept faltering while in the back of my mind I kept thinking a scam would make life more interesting. It was only two in the afternoon.

I rose abruptly and left my office. Outside, Kathryn was at her desk, updating her Rolodex. She looked up and asked hopefully, "Do you have anything for me to type?" She, of course, knew that I had not written or dictated anything all day. She was hoping that her good intentions would motivate me into working.

"Soon," I promised, as I moved quickly away. I marched down to the end of the hall, looking for one of my partners to talk to. Most offices were empty, or the doors were closed. Only Walker Dudley was in his corner office. He was on the phone, but he smiled and waved me in.

Walker Dudley was one of the senior partners at Johnson, Woods &

Hart. He was also leader of the twenty attorneys in the firm's legislative law section, where I was employed. Despite the name, our section did no legal work whatsoever. We were full-time lobbyists. The rest of the attorneys in the firm, who did traditional legal work, looked down on us as incomplete practitioners of our profession. On the other hand, we found their work dull and enjoyed our continuing role in politics.

Dudley was the perfect leader for our group. He had come to Washington forty years earlier when a few powerful committee chairmen, all of them from the South, ruled the Senate. Dudley fit right in from the start. Family connections gave him entry to the staff of one of the most powerful senators, and he stayed there for years, rising in the ranks as more senior staffers either died or retired. Dudley hung on until the end, until his senator was found dead in his office, preparing his announcement to run for a ninth term.

Life had been kind to Dudley. His primary senatorial staff duties had been to see that the senator's friends were wined and dined whenever they were in town. On leaving government service, Dudley bounced from firm to firm. He always arrived with great fanfare and promise but left before the managing partners got to know him too well. He continued to move up to bigger firms, finally arriving at Johnson, Woods & Hart where he supervised nineteen bright, eager attorneys who knew all the answers. With that technical and legal backup, Dudley could focus on seeing that the clients had a good time. He was a great success as long as no one asked him exactly what was going on in Congress.

Dudley grew bigger every year. In a few years he would be considered fat, but at that time it was said that he was living large. His hair was thinning, and he smoked big, smelly cigars. He particularly enjoyed lighting up when opposing attorneys were meeting in the nonsmoking conference room adjoining his office. When he spoke, his points were always made with a smile and good-old-boy humor. When it suited his purposes, his Southern accent became so thick it was incomprehensible. He never finished a meal without spilling food on his shirt or tie. But just when you were ready to laugh him off as a sloppy has-been, he would land a big client or use his connections to pick up a crucial piece of information.

Behind Dudley hung the flags of Texas and Arkansas. He had grown up in the town of Texarkana, a small town that straddled the two states. I never learned which side of the town he really grew up in because when Bush was president, Dudley was a proud Texan. When Bill Clinton won, Dudley hailed from Arkansas. His flexibility was exceeded only by his total dedication to whichever state served as his current birthplace.

Dudley finished his call, looked at me, and said, "I'm setting up a meeting with the National Phone Operators, Richard. Are you around the next few days so you can help me when we pitch 'em?"

Dudley never handled a client pitch alone. He always made sure that some of his detail men were around in case he was asked to do something difficult, like explain how a law is passed.

"I'll be in town," I replied, "but why are we still chasing them?" We had spent four months chasing the phone operators, and I had lost all hope of ever landing them as clients. "I think they're only interested when we buy them lunches."

Dudley had invested too much effort chasing them to accept defeat. He dropped his gaze to his desk and shook his head. "You don't understand," he said, his accent growing thicker. "That is a fine organization, but they need help. Do you know what I mean?" That last phrase, which Dudley used to punctuate every point he made, was pronounced as one continuous word. *DewyouknowwotImean*?

"What do we need to do?" I asked.

"I think we just need to get them over here again and have them meet everyone. We could talk about their issues, show them our strengths, do you know what I mean?" As he talked, he stood and started putting on his coat. I noticed a stain that looked like soy sauce on his shirt cuff. He glanced at it and tugged his coat sleeve down to hide it.

"Well, we've only done that four times," I replied. "What have we got left to tell them, unless we want to bring them up to speed on voter attitudes in South Dakota?"

Dudley looked disappointed in my response. "I know we can get those guys. We could do a great job for them. It's unbelievable how well our skills match up against their special needs, do you know what I mean?"

I was impressed that Dudley had taken the time to match our firm's personnel with their needs. "What are their special needs?" I asked.

"I have no idea."

"But you figure we can handle anything, right?"

"Exactly. You know, this could be a big client. We can probably bill them a hundred hours just to figure out exactly what their issues are. Do you want to be part of this one or not?"

"I'm in."

"I knew I could count on you. If we get them over here, I'll ask them to tell us about their issues, and then you jump in and give them the details of how we can help them. A real one-two punch. It will work this time. Do you know what I mean?" he asked as he left the room.

"I know what you mean," I said to an empty room. I found it depressing that Dudley had more to do than I did, although for all I knew he was late for a drink with one of his buddies.

I headed back to my office and settled in my chair. I was still bored. I was bored. *I'm bored!* I needed a scam. Not really to do—just to think about. To carry me until the day was over. I would tackle real work tomorrow.

I pulled out a yellow legal pad to list all the elements of my plan. Across the top of the page I wrote, *Scam.* I looked at it for a long time. Then I underlined the word. I looked at it for another long time. Then I added three exclamation points. I felt better. Now the word had the level of emphasis I wanted to convey. I wrote with a dull pencil so the word was dark and smeared.

Underneath, I started my list. First I wrote, *Makes Money.* That seemed to be a prerequisite to any good scam. Next I added, *Minimal Effort.* I thought a short time, then added, *No Accountability.* This was important. I already had enough clients expecting results. Of course, this also limited the opportunities. Most people did not give you money without expecting something in return. Perhaps the way around this problem was to have a client that lived far, far away. Somewhere overseas—so far away that even phone calls were precluded by the time difference.

I considered creating a US–Far East friendship association. I could solicit monies from very rich Asian conglomerates. It was a good idea, but I had no way to get myself introduced to the right people.

Moving back to my list, I added the requirement that the project be *Legal*. That was a basic requirement. I had no intentions of getting snared in a scandal.

About that time, I heard Barbara Lehman coming down the hall, talking loudly to anyone who would listen. Lehman was not yet a partner in the firm, having just left government service only three months before. She was a tall woman with red hair, green eyes, and an infectious laugh. She had spent the previous five years raising campaign money for Congressman Conlin, the chairman of the House Ways and Means Committee.

Everyone loved her. She was funny and outrageous. She reeked of sexuality and had nearly every man in the firm convinced that they had a real chance to bed her. But to my knowledge, she had not yet done it with anyone. At least, no one was claiming credit for it. And at my firm, such information would be circulated quickly.

Peering in my door, Barbara noticed me and gave me a full blast of her considerable charm. "Richard Brewster, I hope I didn't disturb you." There was a twinkle in her eye.

"Not at all," I replied, smiling. "I need a break. I have been working hard all afternoon on important client matters. Where have you been?"

"I was at my class. I'm all certified," she announced. She explained that she had spent a day in classes required by the District of Columbia Bar Association, brushing up on her legal skills. These classes were usually very dull and always irrelevant to our work. Her class that day had focused on the statute of limitations on various crimes such as fraud. It amazed me that the governors of the bar association required attorneys to take refresher courses in the law. All the attorneys I knew were diligent at keeping up with their specialties. As for the other aspects of the law, you could always call a partner. Yet the courses were required to maintain our certifications.

The classes were well attended and expensive. *Now, that's a scam*, I thought. I hoped that whoever came up with the idea was living it up in Mexico.

"What a scam," I said, waving her into my office.

She came in and sat down. "Yeah, but I knew it would be a wasted day, so I went out drinking last night. It's better to nurse a hangover in class than to try to deal with clients when you have one." Determined to find success as a lobbyist, Barbara was learning to drink like a seasoned veteran. She also knew how to talk like a truck driver when the situation called for it.

"Yeah, but what a scam," I repeated. Actually, Barbara's use of the class to recover from some hard living the night before seemed relatively productive, particularly if they served free coffee. It was a great scam.

"The class was so boring I couldn't stay awake," she said. "I just put my head down, and the next thing I knew, the room was empty and the teacher was standing over me."

"What happened? "

"He threatened to withhold my certificate."

"I am sure you charmed your way out of that fiasco."

"I tried. At first, it didn't work. So I promised him a job interview at Johnson, Woods & Hart, and I got my certificate," she said, laughing. "He was very interested. He said our firm eventually hires everyone."

"He's right about that," I agreed.

She looked serious. "To be honest, I told him to call you to arrange it. I was going to tell you that he was a great prospect with good clients, but I am too tired to bullshit you. Will you accept the truth?" She raised her eyebrows, both questioning and promising.

I nodded. "I appreciate that you trust me enough to tell me the truth," I said, wondering if that also brought other benefits. "But I am still thinking about the classes. We should do the same thing. You know that bill going through Congress to regulate lobbyists? Why don't you get Congressman Conlin to add a requirement that lobbyists must take an ethics course? We could teach the only approved one. With seventeen thousand lobbyists in town, we would make a killing."

She got the point. "Yeah, we could really stick it to our competition. We'd charge $1,000 for a half day."

"And we wouldn't allow them to step out to make client calls."

"And we wouldn't give them the certificates until the end of the day so they couldn't leave early."

"Better yet, we could have a test and would flunk Charles Nagle, and make him take the class over and over." I was getting into the idea.

So was she. She sat up straight like she was lecturing, pointed a forceful finger, and said, "Sit down, Charlie, you unethical bastard!"

Charles E. Nagle was the premier lobbyist in Washington. You want proof? Just ask him. He was featured in every newspaper and every magazine published in the city. He had the largest corporate clients and charged the biggest retainers. He was a friend of the president, the vice president, Congressman Conlin, and all the important members of Congress. It was said that you could never predict who would win an election, but you could always predict that the winner would soon be playing golf with Charlie Nagle.

Barbara and I continued to humiliate Charlie for a short time. Barbara's smile was very broad and happy as we decided to schedule all the classes when Charlie was out of town. We decided to give the driver of Charlie's car bad directions. We decided to bounce his check and then sue him. We were having fun. It was good to laugh with her, and I got a look of warm appreciation. I figured it would help me in the sexual competition with my male partners. Not that I was really going to make a run at sleeping with her. After all, I was married. But then I thought about Elizabeth with the pillow over her head. I let that image roll around in my head along with the scam.

As for Barbara, I seemed to be on a roll with her. "Barbara, I have been thinking about starting a scam of my own all afternoon. You know, just thinking about it. If successful, it could be very lucrative. But even if I don't go through with it, it would be fun to think about during firm meetings."

"Or a DC bar certification class," she added.

"Exactly. But to make it work, we have to think small, not big."

"What do you mean?"

"Well, I was thinking about trying to land one big client and do nothing. But that's too hard to do. Your example today is along the right track. You pay $300 and don't expect much. Right?"

"I got a pretty good nap."

"But if you paid $3,000 or $3 million, you would have paid attention and expected the moon. But if the price was $30, your expectations would be even lower."

"I don't know. My expectations were pretty low to begin with," she said. She was being deliberately obtuse, and I found it very fetching. I am sure it was the reaction she wanted.

I went on. "The easiest way to get away with something is to keep it small. People raise the roof if they feel cheated out of $500. But they don't put up much of a fight to get back $40. But small numbers add up. See, here is what I mean."

I got a pocket calculator out of my desk drawer. Barbara came over to watch me. As I leaned over the calculator, she leaned over too, and put her hand on my back, presumably to keep her balance. Our heads almost touched. I could smell her perfume as the air got hot between us.

"Let's say we charge $25 and got twenty-five hundred people to pay us for something," I said as I typed in the numbers. The calculator blinked *$62,500.* "Not bad."

"Let's try $30 and thirty-five hundred people," she suggested. I typed those numbers. The answer flashed back: *$105,000.* "That's better," she said.

We spent the next half hour multiplying dollars and people in endless combinations, until we finally combined $50 and one million people and got $50 million. The implications of the number shocked us both. I raised my head and looked right into her eyes, which were two inches away from mine.

"I love your idea," she said, slowly and softly. "I think it shows real potential."

With my heart pounding through my ears, I smiled.

She pressed her hand on my back as she straightened up. "I'd better go. Thanks for sharing your vision with me." Her voice seemed huskier. As she left the room, she looked back and said, "Let me know what I can do to help. I'm in, you know, all the way. I mean it, too. For $50 million, I'm in all the way."

I leaned back, excited and flushed. It took me a few minutes to realize that we had done nothing more than dream up some fictional numbers. We never even decided how to get people to part with their money.

With my motivation enhanced, I returned to the task. How could I get masses of people to send us, or me, or Johnson, Woods & Hart, money? I knew that two emotions motivate people—greed and fear. I focused on fear. How could I scare people to send me money? As a lobbyist, I naturally thought about the federal government as a tool. I needed an agency that put the fear of God into people so that they would see a lobbyist as their savior. But what agency? The CIA? No, that concept was too overworked. The FBI? No, I was afraid of the FBI.

Still pondering, I got up and paced in my office. Looking out the window, I spotted three individuals standing in line at an automatic teller machine. I thought about money, and banks, and then it hit me. The Internal Revenue Service. No one liked the IRS. No one liked taxes. I would form a group dedicated to fighting IRS abuses. There were hundreds of horror stories around that I could draw on. Not the most creative idea, I admitted to myself, but it seemed dependable.

After thinking a bit more, I decided to call my group the Citizens Against Tax Injustice, or CATI, pronounced "Katie." It would focus on IRS abuses of power. Everyone feared a tax audit. CATI would turn that fear into an effective lobbying tool, raising tens of thousands of dollars to protect the little guy from the evil IRS.

I got another blank page of paper and started to write:

CITIZENS AGAINST TAX INJUSTICE

Do you know that there is an agency of the United States that can take away your house without a court order? Do you know that nothing is safe from those people—your bank account, your car, or your personal freedom? Do you know that they can wiretap your house to learn your most personal secrets? This agency is the Internal Revenue Service. And you pay this agency out of each and every one of your paychecks—pay them to hire investigators and to buy the world's most sophisticated computers, so they can turn around and hound you.

It is time to stop this madness. If you have not faced the wrath of the Internal Revenue Service, it is only a matter of time. You are not safe!! You must join with your fellow citizens (victims) to fight this agency. This is not the Soviet Union. Americans can get control of the IRS, but only if they stick together! The IRS can pursue any single taxpayer, but even the IRS is no match for the power of millions of Americans standing together for their basic rights.

Today, join the CITIZENS AGAINST TAX INJUSTICE (CATI). Join along with other hardworking Americans who are fighting to protect your rights, property, and liberty. Just sign the form below and send it in with $20, and you will be joining the great crusade for freedom. Once you are on the rolls of CITIZENS AGAINST TAX INJUSTICE, the IRS will fear you rather than victimize you. Join today. It may be your last chance . . .

Kathryn Monroney
Executive Director

The scam was born. It was clever. It was fun. But, oh my God, I wish it had gone away.

CHAPTER II
CONFEDERATES

I walked out of my office. There sat Kathryn Monroney, my secretary, at her desk. She was on the phone, talking to her latest boyfriend. She put him on hold and turned her attention to me.

"I got a new client," I announced.

She looked confused. She knew that I had not been in contact with anyone that day. It's hard to get new clients that way.

I handed her the paper with *CITIZENS AGAINST TAX INJUSTICE* across the top. "Please type this," I requested. She got off the phone and started typing while I watched her. At first she typed without reading. Then she stopped typing and just read. She looked more confused. When she reached the bottom, and saw her name as the executive director of the *CITIZENS AGAINST TAX INJUSTICE*, she slowly looked up at me.

"What is this?" she asked.

"My new client," I answered. "When you are done typing that, please create a file for it and fill out the necessary new-client forms."

I walked back into my office. She followed me.

"What is going on here?" she asked.

It was a fair question. I should not have involved her. I should have torn up the paper and thrown it away. But I was having fun and I didn't want to end the scam quite yet.

"It's time for us to look beyond our selfish interests and do something for the good of the country," I started. "Our clients are important, but we cannot forget our responsibility to make the world a better place. The Internal Revenue Service is a menace to the freedoms we hold sacred in our country."

She wasn't convinced. "Why are you playing games when you have so many phone calls to return?"

"I'm serious. I want to start my own lobbying group."

"Then why am I the executive director?"

"You are just the figurehead. It will allow me more freedom to act if I can say I'm representing someone else."

"Do you intend to discuss this at the next partners' meeting?"

Without thinking I said, "Sure."

"Everything about it?"

"Not in its entirety."

"Why not?"

"I don't want anyone objecting to it until it's up and running. Once we're bringing in millions of dollars, no one will object."

"I don't like it. Do you want me to go get you a frozen yogurt with M&M's on top while you return calls?"

"Do you think I can be bought off with a frozen yogurt?"

She smiled. "I thought I'd try. I don't want you to do anything wrong."

"Don't worry. We'll do this one step at a time. I can stop it at any time. Okay?"

"I don't want to be the executive director."

"Fine, no problem. You pick a name."

"No. You pick one." She was reluctant to have anything to do with the idea.

I thought and suggested the name of her ex-husband. She smiled again. "If things go in the tank, we'll throw him to the wolves," I joked.

Her smile faded. "What could go wrong?"

"Nothing. I was kidding. Everything will be fine." I needed to get past this issue quickly. I looked down and saw a popular magazine on her desk with an ad for Ford trucks on the back cover. "How about the name of Warren Ford as the executive director?" I asked, pointing at the ad.

With relief in her face, she agreed. "Okay."

So the scam had a name, a purpose, and an executive director. It was taking on a life of its own.

I was still thinking about the scam later that night at home. To pass the time while waiting for dinner in the kitchen, I brought it up. My conversation with my wife went differently than with Kathryn. While Kathryn always assumed that I would do things that I discussed, Elizabeth believed, from experience, that I would lose interest in any idea I had within three days.

"I have a new career idea," I announced as I opened a bottle of wine and Elizabeth cooked.

"Good. I'm getting tired of hearing that you're going to write a book."

"I want to form a citizens group to fight IRS abuses."

"Is this before or after you open the brewpub?" she asked. Years before, I had decided that Washington needed its own brewpub that featured beers brewed in the back. I had discussed the idea extensively with my circle of friends. But while I was busy talking, a brewpub opened four blocks from my office. It was called the Potomac Pub, and featured beer brewed with Potomac River water. It was a huge success.

"Before. After I save the country from the IRS, I'll buy the Potomac Pub with the profits."

"We'll see," she said skeptically. I could not tell whether her tone was due to doubt that any of my ideas would pan out or determination that if any of them did succeed, the profits would go instead to purchases at Bloomingdale's, Macy's, Nordstrom, and other trendy stores in Northern Virginia.

"Besides, what happened to the health club?" she asked. Another idea of mine. I would bring exercise and health to Capitol Hill, where it was needed.

"That's still a good idea," I said defensively. "In fact, I am still pursuing it."

"Before or after the citizens group to fight whatever it is?"

"The IRS."

A pot boiling over on the stove drew her attention away. Her skepticism was getting under my skin.

"So, do you support my idea?"

"What? What?" She was wiping up the mess. "Of course. I support all your ideas. Except the one where you want to teach Civil War history at a small college."

"That's an old idea. I've deferred on it for now. I'll do that when I retire."

She stirred some meat sauce in another pan. "So, tell me again. Just what does this citizens group idea entail?"

"I want to start a group dedicated to fighting IRS abuses."

"You told me that already. Is that as far along with this idea as you are?"

"No. Of course not. I've actually got a written plan. I'll advertise for members. I'll sign up interested people and charge them $20 a year, and use the proceeds to highlight IRS abuses."

"Such as?"

"Such as warrantless searches, seized bank accounts, abusive auditors."

"Do you have any proof those things have occurred?"

"I am sure I can find some. I don't have any specific cases yet."

"So, based on rumors, you want to create a public interest group?"

"Yes. One that will shake up this town."

"Sounds good, Richard. I can't wait to see this town all shaken up by one of your ideas."

"You don't think I'm going to do it, do you?" I asked.

She turned from the stove and looked right at me. "No, I don't."

Despite the fact that I never really intended to take the idea very far, I got annoyed. "Just watch me," I said, staring back at her.

She reached for her glass of wine. She didn't want an argument, so she smiled and said, "Well, if you do, I'll be very proud of you."

The conversation was ending when my attention was diverted to our three-year-old son, David, who entered the kitchen and announced, "My squirt gun needs water." He was soaking wet. He came over to me and said, "Dad, I need more water for my squirt gun. I need to get Matthew back."

"In a minute, David," I said, sipping my wine.

"Dad, I need it now. I need to whip Matt's butt."

"Don't say that," Elizabeth said. She turned to me. "Their language is getting worse every day. Earlier today, David told his brother he was dead meat. Yesterday, he called one of the neighborhood kids a butthead."

"I hope you are not implying that I taught him those words," I said.

"Well, I don't know where they learn them. We need to be more careful in front of them."

"I agree." I filled David's gun and handed it back to him. "Just remember the name Citizens Against Tax Injustice, Elizabeth. It will be a big deal someday."

David took the gun. He looked up at me and said, "Daddy, you're dead meat."

———————

The next few days passed quickly. Having created my scam, I found it easier to concentrate on my usual work. I knew the scam would be a huge success if I ever wanted to activate it. I was so convinced, in fact, that I didn't really need to prove anything by going further, even if it meant that Elizabeth's skepticism was justified.

But about a week later, I returned from a series of meetings out of the office and got on the elevator in the lobby of our building. Just before the door closed, Barbara Lehman slipped in. We were alone. As we started to ascend, she turned to me, put her hand on my elbow, and asked, "How is our multimillion-dollar plan going?" Then she rubbed her hand further up my arm. Maybe it was the motion of the elevator.

"I am working on it," I said, shifting my weight.

"Let me know when you want to proceed," she said softly. "I still want to be a part of it."

We reached our floor and went our separate ways.

That encounter was still on my mind a few hours later when I attended the biweekly partners' meeting.

Johnson, Woods & Hart was one of the fastest-growing firms in the country. Started only eight years before, the firm had 300 attorneys located in seventeen cities. There were over 120 partners, with more added every week. One never knew if the strange person looking lost in the lobby was a client or a new partner.

The firm made up for its youth with extravagance. Lacking sixty-year-old traditions, we tried to buy some. The firm was located in one of the premier addresses in Georgetown. The offices were large, with highly polished oak floors covered by Oriental rugs. Original artwork hung from the walls. The tea service was silver, the dishes china. The city's best caterer handled all our events. There was a car and a driver for the partners. Fresh flowers were delivered every Monday.

The antiques were matched by state-of-the-art office equipment. The phones, fax machines, copiers, printers, and computers were the latest models and did everything but land clients. Partnership meetings were particularly impressive, with seventeen-way audio teleconferencing equipment tying together the offices from across the country. It was the perfect blend of the old and the new.

But above all, the firm's greatest asset was its founder and managing partner, Jason Douglas Johnson. Jason was underutilized as a lawyer. He should have been pope, or Secretary General of the United Nations.

Tall, gray, and very distinguished looking, Jason reeked of respectability. He always managed to mention in conversations that his middle name was the same as a famous Supreme Court justice. The implication, of course, was that they were related. No one ever bothered to check. He never wore a short-sleeved shirt. He never took off his jacket outside the office, no matter how hot the day. His office was big enough to hold a basketball game. At one end, next to windows that overlooked the Potomac River, was an informal seating area on a raised platform. There, in four overstuffed chairs around a coffee table, the real decisions of the firm were made. Junior members of the firm knew they were on the fast track when they were invited there to discuss an idea with our leader.

Jason flew first class because the airlines didn't allow passengers in the cockpit. His monthly American Express bill rivaled the debt of some third-world nations. Charles E. Nagle may have reigned as the city's top lobbyist, but the Nagle firm was smaller, located only in Washington, and limited itself to lobbying. Jason Douglas Johnson was the city's ultimate legal professional.

Jason ran all the important partnership meetings. Things were not worth knowing until Jason told us. His approval of an idea guaranteed its success. On the other hand, if he expressed the slightest doubt about a proposal, it never happened. Jason would never explicitly criticize an idea put forth by one of his people, but there was a pack of followers that would move in for the kill when he seemed to want it. All the associates and most of the junior partners, including me, were in awe of Jason. We competed for his favor.

Today, as usual, the partners' meeting started when Jason entered and took his place at the center of the large conference table. The rest of us filled the lesser seats. With a nod from Jason, Bill Meyer, the office manager, called the roll of the firm's seventeen offices. Surprisingly, halfway through, the phone erupted with a loud squeal. I was surprised that any equipment the firm purchased would fail, but as I watched the office manager yell instructions and flip switches, I realized Bill was the problem, not the machinery. He had no idea what he was doing. Eventually, he did something right, and the noises ended. Throughout the disturbance, Jason conversed quietly with the partners lucky enough to be sitting near him. Flattered by his attention, two junior partners kept nodding in agreement to everything he said.

When the roll call was complete, Jason began.

"The financial reports are in from last month," he said. "We had an outstanding month. We collected $4.5 million in receivables for our services. Our expenses, including our own salaries, totaled $5.8 million. This results in a deficit of $1.3 million. However, our unpaid accounts receivable increased by $2 million. I have checked with our accounting department, and I believe we will eventually collect over $1.8 million from those bills. This would give us a net profit of over a half million dollars. That would be outstanding. So, to reward everyone for all their hard work, and to facilitate our collections, I recommend to the partners, for their approval, that we draw down on the firm's line of credit at the bank and pay each partner a bonus of ten to twenty-five thousand dollars, based on the number of years of service. Of course, this would be in addition to your full draws for the month."

The room exploded in joy. We had assumed that we would get a lecture for failing to bring in enough money to cover our salaries and expenses. Instead, we got an unexpected cash bonus. There had been rumblings of concern from some partners about financial trouble, but this certainly proved that everything was okay. Jason would never threaten our solvency.

The payments were quickly approved. A few partners objected, pointing out that it was unwise to distribute money we had not collected. But the overwhelming majority of us shouted them down. Jason waited for us to finish, then moved on to other items on his agenda.

"As you know, firm travel is up. Between traveling on firm business and visiting our clients, attorneys are in the air every day. This is costing us money we could save if we brought this function in-house. I have reviewed the figures, and I calculate that we could save up to $84,000 per year if we had our own plane, with a pilot."

No one could argue with that. It saved money. Of course, no one had seen the numbers except Jason. But it was the recommendation of Jason Douglas Johnson, our leader, who ran the firm so well that we all got a midyear bonus. We agreed to the plane.

Other items were quickly covered. We extended offers of partnership to three attorneys only Jason had met. We agreed to the plans for the firm's Fourth of July party. We made contributions to Jason's favorite charities.

Then Jason brought up his latest idea. He wanted to open an office in Paris. Although we had no clients and no business there, Jason described all the untapped potential that existed for our firm in France. It was the next logical step in the firm's long-range growth plans, Jason told us. On the subject of growth, Jason was an evangelical. He would describe our future as one vast, worldwide firm, with offices in every major city, handling the work of multinational corporations. Within ten years, six or seven huge law firms would dominate the legal business of the world, he told us. And Johnson, Woods & Hart would be one of those firms.

Then, to reassure us that it was not a personal whim, Jason proposed to hire a consulting firm to review the idea. He told us that he was convinced opening the office was the right thing to do, but he wanted an outside firm to make an objective appraisal of the idea. He would engage the consultants tomorrow.

"So, all I am asking from you today is permission to study the proposal. Nothing more. Is that agreeable?"

He looked around the room. Most of us were nodding silently. Then, over the phone, came a voice from one of the field offices. Some irrelevant partner, I can't remember who, suggested that we shouldn't be expanding until our monthly income exceeded our expenses. A few other voices expressed the same concern. Jason listened to them, but we could see that he was suppressing a smile. None of the firm's section leaders or major rainmakers raised an objection. The objections were localized outside Washington, in the smaller offices. Theoretically, all the offices were equal, just as theoretically all the partners were equal to Jason. But those of us who worked in Washington knew, deep down, that our office was the head and the other sixteen offices were the tail of the brilliant comet that was Johnson, Woods & Hart.

As the voices of dissent ran out of steam, Jason's loyal soldiers moved in for the kill. Junior partners, like me, competed for the opportunity to argue for Jason's plans. We addressed our partners but kept our eyes on Jason. We discussed the need for growth, the need for European offices, and the new clients we would land. Besides, we argued, we were only approving a feasibility study. We would look at the results and decide later whether to actually open the Paris office. The debate was over quickly, and the partners overwhelmingly approved the study.

Of course, every feasibility study we ever did recommended exactly what Jason had proposed. Jason picked the same consulting firm to conduct the review, and it always reported back that each additional office would be very profitable. So we would proceed, and new cities were be added to the firm's letterhead, even though over half of our existing offices were losing money. We justified the losses with the thought that if we were going to be one of the surviving firms in ten years, there would be growing pains.

It was late. We grew restless. But Jason kept moving. "Next," he said, "there is the matter of public relations and advertising. I think the firm deserves a higher profile. I recommend that we appoint a team of partners to review the matter. They can report back on ways we can further enhance our image."

I nodded. I couldn't have agreed more. I thought, *Who is Charlie Nagle to get all the press?* His firm was one-tenth the size of our firm. There were rumors all over town that his firm had financial trouble, that he couldn't keep his costs in line. Yet, every day, his name was in some press story. On the other hand, Jason had been featured in the *Washington Post* only once that year. For the sake of the firm, I wanted to see his name, and his picture, in the papers all the time. Apparently, he agreed. Jason told us that he valued his privacy but was willing to sacrifice it for the sake of the firm.

Jason said he would appoint seven people to the public relations task force, under the direction of Dudley Walker. I ignored the names on the panel until mine was called out. I was surprised. I knew nothing about public relations. I glanced at Jason. He nodded back at me. I decided that it was a test. If I performed well, I would move up further within the firm's hierarchy.

"Any new business to report?" Jason asked. This was a key part of every partnership meeting. It was our opportunity to shine before Jason and the other partners. Each of us would describe the business he or she had landed that month or might land in the near future. Potential conflicts were supposed to be uncovered by this process, but the real point of the exercise was to give everyone a minute of bragging time. Even if a potential client never actually materialized, we all wanted to deliver good news to Jason.

And then I took the next fateful step. I'm not sure why. Maybe it was because I was part of the greatest law firm in the world, one that bought planes and opened offices in Paris. Maybe it was because of Barbara. Maybe to show Elizabeth. Maybe because I wanted Jason's approval. And maybe because I still knew that I could pull the plug on the scam at any time. But without too much thought, I raised my hand. When recognized, I started to talk.

"Recently, we were contacted by a group that wants us to handle all its lobbying for them. It is dedicated to fighting IRS abuses. They're called Citizens Against Tax Injustice. Membership is quite small now, but they expect to grow rapidly in the near future. It may not pan out to be much, but, then again, it might be a big client for the firm. I'm working to finalize the client relationship."

"Excellent," said Jason, beaming. "Good work. Is there any chance we could do their legal work as well?"

"Absolutely," I continued, drawing out my minute in the limelight. "In fact, they talked to me about helping them manage the organization as well."

Jason looked very happy. "That is just excellent, excellent," he repeated. Several other senior partners also smiled and nodded at me.

But then Walker Dudley coughed. "I think I met with them once and pitched our firm." He stared right at me. "It may have been a while back, before they contacted you, do you know what I mean?"

This was a problem. In law firms, salaries and bonuses are determined by the amount of business you land. If Dudley made the case that he helped me land the client, he would soon ask for some of the credit. It was ruthless and piggy of him, as he knew he had nothing to do with it. This was how he kept his numbers up. He was daring me to cut him out of the action.

Perhaps if it were a real client, I would have shared with him to stay on his good side. But I was concerned that he might look into the client and discover it was still a figment of my imagination. I had to cut him off.

"Really? You met with Warren Ford, the executive director?" I asked.

"I think so," he replied, "at a political fundraiser. He had never heard of us, and I told him about the firm. I especially told him about you. He said he would call you." Dudley continued to watch me closely. He wanted in. I had to cut him off.

"Are you talking about the guy who is medium height with thinning hair?"

"Yes," he said slowly.

I closed the trap. "You're thinking about Herb Jones from the Tax Coalition. He did tell me about meeting you. Unfortunately, the Tax Coalition is not hiring anyone now. Warren Ford is with an entirely different group."

Jason stepped in. I think he could tell that both Dudley and I were lying over the credit, but he didn't care as long as the end result was more business for the firm.

"Richard, congratulations on the new client. Tell them we will do everything we can for them. I will be watching your progress on this one." Then he gave me a big smile.

CHAPTER III
DIVERSION

I drove to work the next day feeling very pleased with myself. I was having fun with my scam. I knew it was a good idea. It would work. And even at that early stage, it had impressed Barbara and gotten me noticed by Jason. Yesterday, I was one of dozens of junior partners. Today, I was one of Jason's favorites.

Traffic was horribly congested. The heat was oppressive, and the air conditioner in my car barely kept up. I tried not to move too much as my car crawled along the George Washington Parkway and into the city.

I was going to be late. Not that it really mattered. I was in the private sector, in a trendy Washington law firm, and no one would say anything if I missed the targeted arrival time. Particularly since I had landed a big new client, the Citizens Against Tax Injustice.

I studied the car in the next lane. It was old and dented, with the windows down. Inside the car were four middle-aged men, with their coats off, in short sleeves with narrow ties. Government bureaucrats, going to work in a car pool. They all looked tired, hot, and unhappy. They too were going to be late, but they would get in trouble or have to fill out some form. I gave them a patronizing smile as I turned off on my exit at the Key Bridge. I was going to Georgetown, while they had to journey further downtown. I saw them in my rearview mirror as they continued their stop-and-go. *Yes*, I thought, *I like my status*. And it would only get better when my scam started to work.

I parked in the firm's underground lot and rode the elevator, dreaming about the scam. I remembered that my calendar was clear, so I would be able to dream about it some more that day. Unfortunately, my job intervened.

Kathryn was standing at the elevator door when I got off at my floor. "The Troll is here," she whispered. My good mood vanished.

"Next week," I corrected her, hoping she was wrong.

"No, he is already in your office," she said.

"Isn't he scheduled in for next week?"

"Yes, but he's here today, too."

"Why?" I asked. Two visits in two weeks from the Troll were too much.

"He told me he got an invitation to Senator Kelly's party tonight."

"You mean that political fundraiser?"

"Yes. He said got a personal letter of invitation."

"Does he know that six thousand people got a personal letter of invitation?"

"No. I think you need to tell him."

I walked to my office, knowing my day was shot. Sitting at my desk, using my phone and reading the papers on my desk, was Douglas Dezube.

Dezube was the executive director of the American Hand Towel Manufacturers Association. This trade association was dedicated to keeping high tariffs on imported hand towels from developing nations. This permitted the domestic hand-towel makers to charge inflated prices for their products. To Dezube, increasing the tariffs again on imported hand towels was the most important issue facing the federal government. The problem was that Dezube wanted the issue to be equally important to everyone he saw in Washington. He was hurt by the knowledge that things like medical care, taxes, and education seemed more critical to Congress. But he was convinced that if he, and I, worked harder, we could turn that around. His office was in Atlanta, close to all the towel plants located in the South. But he was constantly in Washington, urging me to raise the profile of his industry's case.

Dezube could drive me crazy, and frequently did. I knew he was disappointed in my lack of progress on his issue. At times, I think he would have fired me if I had been anyone else. But we were bound to each other by our past history, and he remained loyal to me. After all, I got him his job.

Two years before, the previous executive director of the American Hand Towel Association had suddenly resigned. There were two vice presidents, one of whom was Dezube, and they started a monumental war of succession. From the start, Dezube was outgunned and outmanned. He was going down for the count.

Johnson, Woods & Hart was handling a minor employment case for the association at the time. Jason looked at the fight as an opportunity to get all the lobbying work as well. Jason publicly stated that the firm would remain neutral in the fight, but I later found out that he was helping Dezube's opponent, who was the sure winner. One day, Dezube called Jason for advice. Not surprisingly, Jason didn't take the call, which was then referred to me, as I was in my office at the time and he was insistent that someone talk to him. I had never worked on the account, and was unaware of Jason's plans when I took the call.

"The board of directors will vote me out next week," Dezube lamented. "They don't think I have any clout in Washington. I have to prove I do."

Trying to help, I suggested that he get a letter of support signed by some members of Congress. He was pleased by my strategy, and amazed when I actually got a letter signed by two new congressmen, both of whom owed me a favor. When the board met, Dezube trumped his opposition with the letter. The board voted to make him the executive director. He, in turn, announced that I was to be his lead lobbyist. Jason was delighted by the results. Dezube became my responsibility. At times, I wondered if it was worth it.

Whenever he was in my building, Dezube would stride up and down the halls, calling out to all the lawyers and staff. His voice was loud and his laugh louder. He was a big man with a constant grin and wild eyes. His hair always started the day combed to one side, but by midmorning it would be sticking straight up. The support staff had started calling him "the Troll."

"Doug, great to see you," I said as cheerfully as I could manage. I shook his hand as he hung up the phone. Kathryn stood at the door, waiting to receive coffee orders.

"Where have you been?" he boomed. "While you were driving to work at a leisurely pace, I flew up from Atlanta and took a cab here. I guess we know who works harder."

"Yes, but had I known you were coming, I would have slept on the floor of my office to be here when you arrived," I said. Dezube laughed.

"Or maybe I would have stayed away all day." His laughter grew louder. He looked at Kathryn. "He's always teasing me. Does he treat all his clients this badly?"

"Only the special ones." She smiled and left the room—figuring, I assume, that Dezube didn't need any coffee.

"Excuse me, Doug, while I sit at my desk," I said. I inched around my desk to the chair as he slowly got out of it. I sat down. He started pacing my office.

"Why are you here, by the way?" I asked.

"I came so you could arrange some meetings for me today," he said.

"Who do you want to see?"

"Steve, Melanie, Irma, and Roger," he replied, naming four staff members from various congressional offices.

"Doug, we saw them two weeks ago."

"I know, but we need to bring them up to date on the latest developments in the industry."

"Which are what?"

"Remember when I told you the trade association members would meet on Friday and vote out the resolution calling for increased tariffs? Well, we met and we did."

"That's not news."

"The vote was unanimous. I didn't tell you that."

"You think we need to see people in congressional offices to tell them that?"

"Absolutely. This is a good government issue. I'm doing their staff work, keeping them up to date on the latest information."

"Look, Doug, these are very busy people. We don't want to wear out our welcome. They have lots of responsibility and many issues they follow. We should keep our visits to a minimum. Then when we need their help, they will be happy to oblige."

Dezube continued pacing, his eyes on the floor.

"Doug, will you please sit down?" I asked. He went to a chair in front of my desk, head down the whole time, and sat heavily, still looking away from me. He had heard my speech before, but it never seemed to sink in. He just sat there shaking his head while I tried to think of something we could do that would not be counterproductive.

About that time, Walker Dudley passed by the door. He glanced in, saw Dezube, and came in with his hand outstretched.

"Doug Dezube, it is always such a pleasure to see you," he said. "How are you doing today?"

"Hi, Walker. I'm fine, I guess." Dezube was still averting his gaze from me.

"Great, great," said Dudley, not paying any real attention to the client. "How's Richard treating you? I hope he's giving you great service, do you know what I mean?"

"Well, he won't set up any meetings for me."

This caught Dudley's attention. He was always ready to side with a client over one of his attorneys. He felt it kept us on our toes. He raised his eyebrows at me. "Why aren't you doing that?"

"We saw all the key congressional staff two weeks ago."

"So? I know they love to see Doug here. Just pick up the phone and call them."

Dezube perked up and nodded.

"I'm not so sure it's a good idea."

"Yes, it is, isn't it, Doug?" Dezube nodded harder. "Just call them, set up the meetings, and take Mr. Dezube up to see them, you know what I mean?"

"We really don't have anything to tell them."

"So? I bet they just want to know the latest developments, right, Doug?"

"Right." Dezube nodded. "We've just passed a new trade association resolution."

"See," Dudley agreed. He looked at me. "Why are you keeping this information away from them?"

I was not going to win this battle as long as Dudley and Dezube were playing off each other. I wondered if Dudley was getting back at me for the partners' meeting or if he really didn't know better.

"Okay. I'll call."

Dudley got a smug expression. "Good. Good. You all just keep Doug happy. Do whatever he wants." He turned to Dezube. "If you ever have concerns about any members of my section of the firm, come straight to me." Seeing the look of death on my face, he quickly added, "Not that you would ever have any reason to complain about Richard here."

I decided to strike back. "Walker, do you want to get a briefing on the resolution from Doug?"

But Dudley was already retreating from my room. "No, no. That's detail stuff. I follow the big picture, you know what I mean?" As he left the room, he threw out one last line: "Doug, don't be a troll, hiding in that cave they call Atlanta. Come up here anytime."

The support staff up and down the hall started giggling. Dezube, basking in the attention, smiled.

The day went from bad to worse.

"Steve," I said on the phone to the fifth congressional staff person I called, "my main man Doug Dezube is in town. He's got some new developments to discuss with you. Have you got a minute to see us?" Dezube was still in the chair opposite me, listening to every word.

"Are you are on drugs?"

"Just a few minutes, anytime today."

"He never stays a few minutes. He starts telling me how he's doing my job for me."

"I know it's the last minute . . ." I shrugged at Dezube.

"Tell him I'm leaving with the congressman on a trip to China."

I covered the mouthpiece and said to Dezube, "He's checking his schedule. Do me a favor and ask Kathryn to get me the file." He walked out. I spoke back into the phone, quickly and quietly, "Look, how about if we take you out to lunch?"

"I'm busy."

"You've got to eat. Any restaurant in town. You pick."

"I'm busy."

"Please. Do it as a favor to me."

"Only if I don't have to see him the next four times he comes to town."

That was too high a price. "How about the next two times?" I asked, as Dezube walked back in.

"I'm busy." He hung up.

I looked at Dezube. "He said he's leaving with the congressman for a trip to China. He's real sorry to miss you."

"Well, it looks like you struck out everywhere," he said, shaking his head again.

"I know. But it was the last minute. And you do have the fundraiser for Senator Kelly tonight, so the day isn't a total loss."

"I guess not. But we don't want to waste the day either." I knew what was coming next, and I dreaded it. "Let's work on those draft letters you wrote for me last week."

We spent the next several hours rewriting five letters I had prepared earlier. We reviewed them line by line. Changes were made everywhere. The letters did not get better, but they included Dezube's input.

Later we went to lunch. He discussed the importance of keeping inferior towels made in developing countries out of the US. I discussed voter attitudes in South Dakota.

Senator Kelly's fundraiser started at 5:30. For two hours, the senator would talk to the various contributors who paid $1,000 for the privilege. Drinks would be served and some light food. Dezube was invited because Senator Kelly was the newest member of the Senate Finance Committee. The Finance Committee had jurisdiction over all tariffs. In addition, Senator Kelly had, in fact, recently introduced legislation at the behest one of the biggest hand-towel companies located in his state. It was called the "Hand Towel Equity Act." It raised tariffs for imported towels. The association, and Dezube, were delighted. No one pointed out that Senator Kelly had introduced 238 other bills already that year, and none of them had passed.

By 4:30, Dezube was restless. I was trying to get some other paperwork off my desk as Dezube paced around my office. "I don't want to be late," he said, his hair standing straight up.

"It's a ten-minute drive and a two-hour reception."

"The senator might not stay the whole time."

"It's a better bet that he won't get there right at 5:30."

Dezube continued pacing. "What are you working on?" he asked. Dezube didn't really care. In fact, he resented that I didn't spend full-time on his project. Unfortunately, he paid the firm only a small monthly retainer, requiring me to handle other clients, to his chagrin.

"Nothing as important as the Hand Towel Equity Act." That answer pleased him. But he continued to stride back and forth.

I looked up. "Why don't you go ahead and I'll meet you there."

"Where?"

"The fundraiser."

"Where is it?"

I told him.

"How will I get there?"

"Take a cab."

"Where do I get one?"

"Right outside on that corner." I pointed across the street.

"I don't see a cab."

"They come all the time."

"Where?"

"Right there." I pointed again.

"I don't see one." He peered out the window for a while. "How much longer will you be?"

I tried to hide my annoyance . "Only a few minutes. Look, please don't let me hold you up."

"Well, I just thought we could take a cab over together so we won't get separated."

"I'll find you."

He started pacing again. I tried to ignore him and finish some paperwork.

"Do you think Walker is going to the fundraiser?" he asked suddenly.

"I doubt it."

"Why not?"

"People in our firm get invitations to ten different events each night. We have to split up. It's the only way we can cover everything."

He thought about that for a minute. "Do you think Barbara Lehman is going?"

"No."

"Why not?"

"Did you hear what I just said? We have to cover a number of events."

"I thought you just meant the partners had to split up. It might be different for the associates."

"Doug, we don't get extra credit for sending two people from the firm. It doesn't work that way."

"Maybe it does for Barbara. She sure looks hot."

"I agree with you there," I said. I meant it. I thought about her as Dezube resumed wearing away the surface of my floor. Suddenly he stopped.

"Where's Jason? Let's go see him."

"I don't think he's in town today," I quickly said. I wasn't going to squander my status in Jason's eyes by letting Dezube bother him.

"No, I saw him in the hall earlier today. Let's see if he is still around."

I gave up trying to get anything else done. "No time to do that, Doug. I am ready to go."

"Really?"

"Yeah. Let's go."

"I'm glad I waited. Did you have any idea you'd be done so quickly?"

As we walked out, my phone started ringing. I picked it up at Kathryn's desk.

"Mr. Brewster?" It was a soft voice.

"Dr. Garrity, how are you?" I asked, recognizing the voice of another client.

"Fine, thank you. I was wondering if you needed anything from me."

Dr. William Garrity had invented a vaccine he thought would prevent children from getting chicken pox. The vaccine still needed testing and approval from the Food and Drug Administration. He had tried to navigate the bureaucratic process alone and got lost. He hired Johnson, Woods & Hart to help him complete the process.

"No, Doctor. What you sent me was fine. I may need you to come to Washington to make your case in person."

"I'll come, but only if you think I am needed. I hate to bother busy people."

I heard a thumping down the hall and saw Dezube fighting the elevator door, hitting the rubber strip that kept opening the door. I turned back to the phone.

"Doctor, I know the process is slow. We submitted our material to the agency for its review last week. It will be two or three months before we hear back."

"I know. I am not complaining. I just keep thinking about the children . . . Sorry, I know you are doing the best you can. God bless you."

"Doctor, as soon as I hear anything, I'll call you."

"Thank you, son."

"Thank you, Doctor."

I walked to the elevator. It was 5:10.

———————

Because of heavy traffic and scarce parking, we arrived at the hotel where the fundraiser was held at 5:45. As we walked in, I studied the schedule of events flashing on a television screen. "Too bad we're so late," Dezube said under his breath. I ignored him as I reviewed the list. Three fundraisers were going on that night, each in a different ballroom. It would be easy to milk the lobbyists for campaign funds tonight. I found the right room, and we headed off.

Entering, I saw the standard setup. In the middle of the room was a table filled with dishes of cheese, cold cuts, small biscuits, and fruit. In opposite corners were two full bars. A small crowd gathered around the food and larger crowds around the liquor tables. Along one wall, a receiving line led to the senator.

"Too bad there's such a long line," Dezube said.

"Let's get a drink first," I suggested.

"No, I think the senator should know we're here."

"Don't worry. He got our check. He'll know we were here."

"Do you know I got a personal invitation to this event?"

"Did it look like this?" I pulled out my invitation from my coat pocket. "I got three. Actually, I think this one was addressed to my son Matt."

Dezube looked hurt. I took pity. "Let's go see the senator," I said.

We got in line and made our way to the front of it. Finally, we stood before Senator Kelly.

"Richard Brewster and Doug Dezube, Senator," I said, holding out my hand.

"Of course, Richard. It's good to see you both." The senator beamed as he shook our hands warmly.

"Thank you for the personal invitations," Dezube said.

"Thank you for coming," the senator said.

"Also, thank you for introducing the Hand Towel Equity Act," I added.

"Yes," said Dezube, "that's an important bill."

"Glad to do it," the senator said. "I think we might hold hearings on it in the near future."

"Really?" asked Dezube. "When?"

A staff aide standing behind the senator intervened. He did not want the senator to make a firm commitment right then and there. Instead he introduced the senator to the next person in line. I took Dezube's arm and led him to the bar.

"Nice event," he said.

"The best," I agreed.

"I think it was important I came," he said. I could see him trying to justify in his mind the expense of round-trip airfare and a wasted day for thirty seconds with a senator who ranked twelfth out of twelve in seniority on the Finance Committee. I decided to make him feel better.

"Absolutely. When you get to know a senator on an informal basis like tonight, it pays dividends when you see him on business."

"You think so?"

"They gotta know you in order to listen to you."

"Do you think he'll remember me?"

"No question about it," I said, looking at his hair.

Dezube was smiling again. "Why don't you make an appointment to see him the next time I am in town? I'll bring him up to date on the latest developments in the field. I want him to look at me as a resource."

Later, the crowd thinned. Dezube was in a corner, droning on to a congressional staffer, when I spotted the senator standing alone at the food table, looking at the picked-over plates of food. I moved up next to him. "Looks like a good turnout," I commented.

"Not bad." He faced me and stuck out his hand. "Senator Jonathan Kelly," he said.

I shook his hand. "Richard Brewster."

"Nice to meet you, Richard."

"Nice to be here. Thank you for inviting me tonight."

"Glad to do it."

Leaving the reception, Dezube and I got caught up in a large crowd of people heading into the largest banquet room. Following along, we found ourselves in a reception for Congressman Conlin, chairman of the House Ways and Means Committee, with jurisdiction over taxes, welfare, social security, pensions, trade, and health care. Conlin was a power in the House.

The room was four times bigger than the room holding Kelly's event. A huge chandelier in the center of the ceiling threw light everywhere. A band played on a stage. There were four bars and two tables loaded with salmon, roast beef, imported cheeses, baby lamb chops, fruits, vegetables, and desserts. Waiters walked around with platters of finger food.

But even with all the distractions, everyone's attention focused on the middle of the room where the congressman was greeting people. Congressman Gerald Conlin wasn't tall. He was getting heavy. His clothes were rumpled. His voice was soft. But he dominated the room. The receiving line wound out the door. There were two staff aides whispering in his ear. As the guests in line reached him, the congressman looked each one straight in the eye, and for a brief moment, he gave them his undivided attention. His face would light up in a fresh smile for each guest as he gave them a strong handshake. Then, unapologetically, he moved on to the next person in line. But he left each person he talked to with the distinct impression that if Conlin had his way, he would spend the entire evening just with him or her.

The firm hadn't signed up for this event and we hadn't made a contribution to his campaign, but I was sure we would. I figured that was good enough, especially since no one was checking the guest list. So we got in line and made our way to the front.

"Richard Brewster," I introduced myself as we shook hands, "with the law firm of Johnson, Woods & Hart."

He gave me a warm smile. "You hired Barbara Lehman."

"Yes, sir."

"She's a good one. Smart as hell and sexy too," he said with his eyes sparkling. "Quite a package."

"I couldn't agree more."

Dezube cleared his throat. Turning, I introduced him to the congressman. Dezube immediately started rambling about tariff bills. After a suitable amount of time, Conlin cut him short.

"You know, for over 140 years, this country depended on tariffs for one of its main sources of revenue. I take tariff laws seriously, although I do not want to hurt our international trading position." Before Dezube could say anything further, Conlin turned to the next person in line. But as we moved away, Conlin looked my way again and winked at me.

Dezube walked off in a daze. "This is great. Congressman Conlin supports the Hand Towel Equity Act," he said.

"That's not exactly what he said."

"He said he supports tariff bills."

"He said he takes tariff bills seriously."

"I think he said support."

"I don't think so. Besides, he said he doesn't want to hurt our international trading position."

"Our bill doesn't do that."

"Maybe, but the guy is a pro. He will do what is right after he looks at the issue. He gave himself enough wiggle room to go either way. Please do not overstate his position. Please. We do not want to get crossways with him."

But Dezube focused across the room, not hearing me.

Later, as Dezube was at the bar, I stood at one of the food tables, eating my third baby lamb chop. I figured it was my dinner, as Elizabeth would feed the children long before I got home. Next to me I found one of the congressman's legislative assistants, Russ Ratto. I nudged his arm and, when he looked up, extended my hand.

Russ was an old friend. We went to college together and shared lots of memories, staying in contact when he spent five years in the National Basketball Association until his career was cut short by a knee injury. Congressman Conlin, who was a raving basketball fan, hired him immediately. Russ didn't know the first thing about Washington when he arrived. I taught him all that I knew, as I had been working for Senator Laxalt since leaving college. He learned quickly.

"Hey, nice event, Russ." We shook hands.

"I didn't know you were coming tonight," he said. "Why didn't you tell me?"

"I didn't know about it. We were just in the hotel for another event and got swept up in the atmosphere. I'll make sure the firm sends a contribution tomorrow."

"The old man certainly brings them in the door," he said, pointing to Conlin. "Did you do anything interesting today?"

"I pushed the Hand Towel Equity Act."

"I asked if you did anything interesting. That bill sounds like a real dog."

"Not if you make hand towels in a factory in Georgia," I said, defending my client's interest. We went back to eating.

"Actually, I have a problem," I confessed. "Have you ever heard of a Dr. William Garrity?"

"No."

"He thinks he's found a vaccine that prevents chicken pox. Unfortunately, he can't get the Food and Drug Administration to run tests to approve it."

"Why not?"

"I'm not sure. Maybe it's just bureaucratic inertia. I've submitted all the data to the agency, but I haven't gotten any action yet."

"Do you want me to light a fire down there?"

"Would you mind? He doesn't live in the congressman's district."

"No problem. I'll make a few calls to the agency. Send me some material on it tomorrow." He took out a card and made a note to himself.

"Thanks."

"Hey, Richard Ricardo, who's this?" It was Doug Dezube's booming voice.

"Russ Ratto, meet Doug Dezube. Doug, meet Russ Ratto. Doug is the executive director of the Hand Towel Association. Russ is Congressman Conlin's legislative assistant." I conveyed the key information, hoping Russ would get the picture and not trash the Hand Towel Equity Act again.

"I was just talking to your boss," Dezube said. "He told me he supports the Hand Towel Equity Act. Are you handling that issue for him?"

Ratto took one look at my client and said, very firmly, "No." He turned back to the food on the table.

I raised my hand to catch Dezube's eye. "Great party, right, Doug? A fine end to a good day."

"I just wish we had some appointments."

At that moment, I felt a second presence. At first I could only sense it—I knew someone else of significance had entered the room. I turned to survey the crowd. I wondered if it was a cabinet member or maybe a key senator. But then I spotted him, Mr. Charles E. Nagle.

He was dressed in a hand-tailored suit of expensive British wool. Despite the long day and the heat, his suit looked freshly pressed and his shirt was wrinkle free. The light from the chandelier caught his gold cufflinks and Rolex watch. He was tall, angular, and graying very slightly at the temples.

He walked in with purpose, heading straight towards the congressman. Seeing Nagle, the congressman took two steps forward so that he was away from the receiving line, standing alone. Both men held out two hands and joined in a double handshake. Their smiles were genuine.

As they chatted quietly, the noise level in the room seemed to drop. No one else approached. The men looked intently at each other with their heads bowed, discussing some important matter.

I drifted towards them, the power drawing me like a magnet. As I got within earshot, they concluded the business part of the conversation. They both looked up. Then Charlie asked the congressman, "Do you know what the president does when he has a hard-on in a cabinet meeting?" He whispered the punch line in Conlin's ear. They both laughed loudly.

That was a Nagle signature—a concluding joke. Always very funny. Always about Washington personalities. Usually dirty. They shook hands again, and Nagle exited the room. Conlin returned his attention to the next person in the receiving line. The noise level in the room went back up.

Dezube had watched the whole scene with fascination. "Who was that?"

"Charlie Nagle."

"Wow," he stretched out the word, "he really knows the congressman."

"He knows all the key members of the House and the Senate."

"I wonder if he could have gotten me appointments today?"

"I'm sure he could have."

"Really?" Dezube appeared surprised that I would make this admission. Perhaps he was trying to decide if he should change lobbyists.

"Absolutely, for all his clients. Anyone that can pay his minimum annual fee of $300,000."

Dezube apparently decided I wasn't so bad after all.

"Are you ready to go?" I asked.

"Yes, I have to get to the airport."

"I need to get home, too."

"How do I get there?"

"Where?"

"The airport."

"Catch a cab."

"Where do I get one?"

"Right in front. This is a hotel."

"How are you getting home?"

"Driving. Remember, I drove over here."

"Okay, I just thought we could discuss the day's events . . ." His voice trailed off.

We compromised. I drove him to the airport, but we didn't discuss anything. Instead, we listened to my Rolling Stones tape.

CHAPTER IV
THE SETUP

I began the next day with a workout with my personal trainer, Emilio. I had avoided all the other trappings that usually accompanied the Washington lobbyist—a BMW, a Rolex, tailor-made suits—but I enjoyed lifting weights with a personal trainer. Besides being a physical therapist, Emilio was fun to talk to. He was young, but bright. He wasn't tall, about five-ten, but he had a big chest and strong arms. He was dark and virile. He had curly hair. He caught the eye of many women in the gym.

As he put me through my exercises, we would talk constantly. Most of our conversations were pointless, but at times he could get me to discuss personal concerns and work problems. That was as therapeutic as the weight lifting. He was sympathetic at the right times and enthusiastic when it was called for, usually rewarding my ideas with the phrase "Cool beans."

In an attempt to get him to forget to count the number of repetitions on the leg press machine I was doing, I told him I was starting my own interest group to fight IRS abuses.

"Cool," he said.

"It is designed to help people and perhaps reform the IRS."

"Will it make a buck?"

"Oh, yeah, that too. Are you still counting? I think I'm done."

"Not quite. Three more to go. Are you quitting the law firm?"

"No, this will be done through and with the firm."

"How about your idea of starting a health club?"

"You laugh, but it's a good idea."

"It's a great idea. It could be very profitable."

"I still think about it from time to time."

"Well, I want to work there."

"Work there! You'd manage it for me."

"Cool beans."

———

Later at the office, I called Dr. Garrity to tell him about the involvement of Congressman Conlin's office on his case. He was very happy and grateful. Then I returned a few calls and cleaned my desk of paperwork. I was very efficient, and had been ever since I invented the scam. It had become a reality to me even though all I'd done was make a list, write an ad, and talk about it. As I was finishing my chores, the internal phone buzzed.

"Could you please come to Mr. Johnson's office, if you are not too busy?" Jason's secretary asked politely. She could afford to be polite; everyone always agreed to her requests.

Entering Jason's office, I saw him sitting in one of the easy chairs in the raised section of his office. He waved me in. "Thank you for coming," he said.

"Glad to be here," I answered, settling down into a rich, soft chair. I had never been in here alone with Jason before.

"Congratulations on your new client."

"Which one?"

"The tax interest group. The one you told us about."

I was surprised that he had remembered. I figured he heard so many potential client stories that he forgot them all until they materialized. I should have deflected his interest right then and there. Given myself some wiggle room. Told him I was still working on landing it. Instead, I said, "Thanks. It may become really big for the firm."

"I certainly hope so, for your sake as well as for the firm. Always good to land a big one." He leaned in and looked me directly in the eye. "Do you really think it could be big?"

I was caught for a second, but only for a second. Then I jumped right in. I looked back at him. "Absolutely. It's as big as your imagination."

"Good. Good." He leaned back in his chair. "Say, how are you coming on the public relations project?"

"Well, Walker Dudley hasn't called a meeting of the group yet, nor given out any assignments."

"That's why I put you on the panel. I wanted some action, not a bunch of Southern bullshit."

"Do you want me to go around Walker?"

"Well, let's just say I hope you make suggestions to him and move him along." He smiled conspiratorially at me.

"Fine with me." Obviously Dudley was out of favor that day and I was in. I liked the feeling and resolved to do whatever I needed to do to preserve it.

"Did you see today's *Washington Post*?" he asked.

"Some of it. What story in particular?"

"The Style section." He pointed to a copy on his coffee table. On the front was a picture of Charlie Nagle talking to some Catholic nuns. The headline of the story was *The Mother of All Charity Fundraisers*. Jason pointed to the story. "We do just as many charitable activities here at Johnson, Woods & Hart. Why aren't they covered? Who does Nagle know at the *Post*?"

"I don't know, but when we're through, we'll know that person's boss."

Jason started laughing. "I like your attitude. Listen, charge ahead. Don't wait for any meeting. Just get started."

Returning to my office, I pondered the next steps for Citizens Against Tax Injustice. I felt the need to live up to the promise I had shared with Jason. I thought that maybe I could make it work. That at least I should get serious about it to see if it really was a good idea.

I had the basic concept in my head. I had a proposed announcement. But to make it work, I would need to get large numbers of people involved. I had to get the word out about the organization throughout the US.

In quick succession, I called a few news magazines and newspapers and requested their advertising information. While I waited for the responses to come back in, I had lunch with my friend Russ. It was always good to spend some time back up on Capitol Hill. I had left the Senate staff years ago, but in a way, no staff person ever really leaves.

I had spent eleven years working on the staff of Senator Paul Laxalt. Senator Laxalt was from Nevada and served two terms, from

1975 until 1987. He was a warm person, quick with a smile or a compliment. No matter how tough the legislative battles, he never lost his temper or his graciousness. As a result, he never had enemies in the Senate. From the first day of his initial term until the last day he served, he considered every other senator his friend, and they all considered him one too.

Working for the senator had been a rewarding experience. He encouraged each of us to learn the ways of the Senate. He listened to our advice. He delegated authority. Yet he kept control of the office, knowing that ultimately he alone had been elected by the people of Nevada.

I had come to the senator's office right out of college for a summer internship and stayed on, eventually attending Georgetown Law School at night. I did every menial task he asked, using my enthusiasm and work ethic to cover for my lack of knowledge. And as I gained experience, he promoted me again and again, until I finally became the staff director of one of his congressional subcommittees. From that position, I helped guide legislation through the Senate. We made a good team. He trusted me, and I never violated that trust. Together, we got lots accomplished.

When he announced his retirement, I too left congressional employment. I felt I had been with the best and had an experience that could not be repeated. It was time to move on. And due to the reflected prestige I had from working for the senator, I immediately got a job offer from Johnson, Woods & Hart.

Returning to my office, I found the material I requested had been faxed from the magazines. After carefully reading all the literature, I decided to place my solicitation to join CATI in *American Magazine*. *American Magazine* was a Sunday insert in most US newspapers. The magazine featured inspirational messages, recipes, and the inside story on the personal lives of celebrities. The circulation of *American Magazine* topped seventy million each week. Even more important were the statistics I found about it. Nearly three-quarters of the readers did not read books, news magazines, or even the editorial pages of the paper. The demographics were excellent. I was not searching for intelligent, involved, well-read individuals to join CATI. I was looking for the easily-interested-with-simple-sentences individuals.

However, the advertising rates were shocking. A full-page color ad cost over $240,000. The cheapest rate was $60,000 for a quarter of a page in black and white. I got out a ruler and determined the size of a quarter-page ad. The ad would have to include the text describing CATI and a membership application. I had also hoped to include an irrelevant but patriotic picture, like the American flag or the Statue of Liberty, but there wasn't room. Without any pictures, the ad was boring. But it would have to do.

I was carrying the scam to its logical conclusion. If I wanted to proceed, I would need a check for $60,000. Originally, of course, I had never intended to go this far. But the scam had taken on a life of its own. It was a risk, but I was confident it could work. I knew the system so well. If it was a success, it would place me in the firm's innermost circle of the largest producers—close to Jason himself. As an added bonus, it seemed to turn Barbara on, not that anything would happen there. And it would be fun to do. And I couldn't think of much of a downside.

But first there was the matter of the money for the ad. I wondered if I could get a check for $60,000 from the firm. First, I tried the easy way. I filled out a form. It was an official Johnson, Woods & Hart form for a new-client disbursement. This was designed to cover expenses related to new clients before the firm had gotten paid, things like court-filing fees. To make it seem usual, I sent Kathryn down to the accounting department with it. She quickly returned empty handed.

"No client disbursements in advance for more than $5,000," she told me. I hadn't heard of that rule before. Actually, I was surprised that there were any limits on expenditures at the firm. I tried another tack. I filled out another form, requesting a check to pay for public relations activities. I told myself that CATI, if I proceeded, would generate publicity for the firm.

I was never so right about anything.

I took this form down to the accounting office myself. Again, I was rebuffed, politely but firmly. "Expenditures of this magnitude can only be made by the senior project manager," I was told. That meant Walker Dudley.

I trudged back to my office, contemplating my options. I had three realistic choices. I could forget the whole exercise. I could let Dudley into the scam. Or I could forego the budget and solicit members by posting flyers on telephone poles. I decided to follow a fourth course. I would see if I could fool Dudley.

Dudley was talking on the phone when I arrived in his office. He must have eaten Mexican food that day, as there was salsa on his shirt. When he hung up, I walked in and sat down. He stared at me, clearly still peeved over the public disloyalty I had displayed at the last partners' meeting. He didn't show it when we were with Dezube but when it was just the two of us, his anger was visible. Before that day, I would have been concerned at having angered my section leader. But I was now moving into Jason's company and was unconcerned about what Dudley thought of me.

"Walker, Jason asked me about our public relations effort this morning. Should we schedule a meeting or something?" I asked. I knew this would upset Dudley. At the highest levels at every law firm is always a small group of attorneys constantly competing to be the managing partner. They reminded me of bulls in a field, prancing, snorting, each trying to prove he's the toughest and meanest son of a bitch around in order to lead the herd. In law firms, these activities translate into gathering the most clients, getting the most fees, hiring associates, working eighty hours a week, calling junior partners at home with demands, and arguing with other senior partners. Out of this process, a firm leader emerges who commands the loyalty of the firm until another partner takes his place—by pushing even harder. Personally, I thought the behavior of senior partners at most American law firms made bulls look civilized.

I intended to use this sense of drive to get Dudley's approval for my expenditure. Dudley headed the government relations section of the firm. Dudley considered it the high-prestige section. Lawyers in our section influenced public policy every day. We rubbed elbows with presidents and politicians. We didn't have to follow the law; we would just change it. Dudley believed he should be the firm's spokesman and leader. Jason dismissed him as a blowhard and a slob.

He looked at me coldly, forgetting his anger with me as he focused it on Jason. "We will have a meeting when I have time to call one. I am up to my ass in client work. I don't have time to have a bunch of unprofitable internal meetings like Jason, do you know what I mean?"

I had an answer. "Well, I have an idea or two that could take care of the problem. In fact, I've looked into an advertising campaign. It could really bring attention to the firm. I've been working with an advertising firm, and I came up with a proposed ad. It's ready to go. We can get the campaign started and keep Jason from bothering you." I slid the check-request form across his desk and pointed at the line that required his signature.

"What kind of advertising?"

"A public relations thing. It would focus on our lobbying capabilities."

"Would it mention our civil litigation section?"

"No."

"Good. I hate those bastards."

He looked at the form quickly and started to sign it, then suddenly stopped and looked at it more closely. I saw his eyes widen as he looked at the line that listed the amount requested. "This is expensive."

"Yeah, it sure is," I acknowledged. "Can you approve amounts that big? If not, I can run it by Jason." I reached for the paper.

"No," he said, grabbing it back.

"I've already signed the form in my space. You just need to countersign it."

He looked at me, then down at the paper, then back at me again. I knew what was coming next.

"That new client of yours. What's his name?"

"You mean Dr. Garrity? The guy with the new vaccine?"

"No."

"Who, Dezube?"

"Hell no. The tax guy."

"Citizens Against Tax Injustice? Warren Ford?"

"Yeah. I'm sure I met him last month."

"No. I asked him about you." I stared at Dudley. Fuming, he picked up the check request again and read it very slowly and carefully. He looked up at me. "What's this about advertising in *American Magazine*? Why do we need to plug our firm there?"

"It's for the tax group. It's a public affairs issue. It's great publicity for the firm as well. You can kill two birds with one stone. And you can do it without calling a meeting of the public affairs committee. Eventually, the tax group will pay us back, so it won't cost the firm either. It's a win-win." I was rambling. "It's good public relations and won't cost us a dime in the long run."

"I don't think so," he said. "I think you want the firm to cover the expenses of one client." Of course, that was untrue. I wanted the firm to cover the expenses of a nonexistent client. I had to think fast.

"You know, even though you didn't meet Warren Ford, he knows you by reputation. In fact, he specifically told me that he hired our firm in part to get your help on his case."

"Really?" he asked. Dudley knew I was lying, but it was getting him what he wanted, so he went with it.

"Yes. He wants you to be an integral part of his legal team."

"Well, I want to contribute to his effort, do you know what I mean?"

"He was counting on that."

"Well then, shouldn't I get some of the credit for the fees?"

By now, I was prepared for this request, even as I was shocked by the greed it displayed. But I was trapped. I couldn't do anything without the check request, and he had to sign it.

"How about ten percent? I will do most of the work, so that seems about right."

"How about I get half?" he responded. "Kinda hard to justify a check of this size otherwise, do you know what I mean?"

"It's only a cash flow issue. The fees will cover this disbursement before you know it." I was getting annoyed even as I knew I needed his approval.

"Maybe. But there is still the immediate outlay. You can ask Jason to sign it, but now that I know about it, I will express my concerns to him about your unwillingness to recognize the contributions of your partners. Do you want that?"

I didn't want to start this project with more scrutiny than necessary. And bickering over credit was one way to end up with it. So much for putting one past Dudley. I should have known that when it came to money, he was as sharp as anyone. "How about twenty percent?"

"A third."

"A quarter. Period." I was very angry now about Dudley's greed in taking credit for fees from a client that didn't even exist.

He didn't care. He smiled, signed the paper, and pushed it back to me. He had just forced me to share credit and revenues of what he thought was a big new client. One that he had no intention of working on. I scrutinized him and decided he made a good bull. Especially with the red salsa on his shirt.

Returning to my office, I called the sales representative of *American Magazine* to talk about placing an ad. I told him it might be the first of many orders. In return, he promised to place the ad in a good location. The ad would run three weeks after he received the check.

Next I made CATI a legal entity. I dragged out my legal files. They were very thin, but they did include the forms for creating a charitable corporation in the District of Columbia. I drafted up a corporate charter and wrote the by-laws for the Citizens Against Tax Injustice. I called a messenger, who took the charter down to the city's government center. An hour later, he came back with the officially approved charter. The cover page was stamped with the seal of the District of Columbia.

I strutted down the hall and found the firm's office manager, Bill Meyer. A former Army major, he appeared like a strong administrator. Unfortunately, he spent most of his time trying to seduce the secretaries. His administrative skills were nonexistent. This left all the real management responsibility for running the firm on the shoulders of Jason Johnson—just where Jason wanted it.

I had a request I felt even Bill was capable of handling. I asked for access to one of the firm's unused post office boxes. I got a number. I double-checked and found it had been assigned to another client weeks ago. I asked for another and this time got an unused one.

I headed over to the tax section of the firm. Picking up the necessary forms, I returned to my office. I filled out forms to get a tax identification number for CATI, and to request tax-exempt status. I liked the idea of having the IRS grant special tax status to an organization dedicated to becoming its watchdog. I gave the forms to Kathryn to type.

I returned to my desk. All I had to do now was send in the ad with the check, and my scam would finally be off and running. But I hesitated. This was the moment of truth. Nothing I had done to date was irreversible. But once the ad copy was mailed, along with a check, I could not go back. The scam would become a reality.

Kathryn brought in the typed forms. Without thinking, I asked, "Should I do it?"

She knew exactly what I was talking about. "Is it legal?"

"Everything is legal in Washington if you fill out the right forms."

"Why do you want to do it?"

"It might be fun."

"Will any good come from it?"

"Will any good come from the Hand Towel Equity Act?"

"I'm serious."

"So am I."

"You know what I mean," she persisted.

"Yes. We may actually accomplish something."

"Then why are you asking me?"

Why *was* I asking? She was watching me intently. I had started the conversation with her, but obviously I was really questioning myself. Why did I hesitate? Why did I need a scam? Had I been in Washington too long? Why did I feel the need to manipulate the political system for my own personal enjoyment? Had I become that cynical? Why wasn't I happy focusing on the positive aspects of my profession?

Why didn't I just write a novel?

I glanced around my office. On the walls hung the standard pictures of me with various politicians. On the credenza was a letter to me signed by President Reagan, thanking me for my work in the Senate. Next to it were items collected from my travels, from stone pyramids from Egypt to cork carvings from China. I had a comfortable life that provided for my family. What was this impulse that encouraged me to be so frivolous?

I looked back at Kathryn. She was still watching me closely. "Maybe I'll wait a bit before proceeding . . ."

She looked relieved. "I think that's good. You need to take things more seriously."

Again, I glanced around the room, this time focusing on the television, which was on but muted. It was tuned to a twenty-four-hour news channel. On it appeared the White House press secretary. His young face looked intent. I turned up the sound.

"President Clinton's statement, made while jogging today, did not reflect administration policy on immigration policy. The president was bothered by a blister on his foot when he answered the question."

A diagram of a huge foot appeared on the screen while a medical consultant pointed out the location of the blister.

And then, to complete the scene, my phone rang. It was Dezube. "I think we need hearings on the Hand Towel Equity Act. Has Congressman Conlin scheduled any yet?"

"Not yet."

"I'm coming to Washington next week to help you move the project along."

"I don't think it's necessary."

"I've got some new information that will really force the Congress to proceed."

"Don't be surprised if the hearing schedule is full for the next month. You might want to wait a while before demanding a hearing. And before coming up here again."

"This is a good government issue. Do they know that?"

"I think they know the situation."

"Set up some meetings for me."

"I really think we should wait."

"I'll be in Monday night."

"I have plans for Monday night."

"I'll meet you in my hotel lobby bar at 6:30 to discuss our strategy." He hung up.

I looked pointedly at Kathryn. "And this is the world I need to take seriously? CATI will fit right in."

She shook her head. Ignoring it, I told her to prepare the envelope as I picked up the CATI ad for one final review. I made some changes in the text. I worked quickly, my doubts about the scam behind me. Any city that paid attention to Doug Dezube and had press conferences to look at pictures of the president's foot deserved whatever I did.

Within minutes, I had rewritten the text of the ad:

WARNING! WARNING! YOU ARE NOT SAFE!

Do you know that government agents can seize your house, rob your bank accounts, and throw you in jail? Do you know these agents threaten your financial and personal safety? And do you know that no one is trying to stop them?

The agency is the Internal Revenue Service, and the potential victims are every loyal American. If you have not faced the wrath of the IRS, it is only a matter of time. The IRS has the ability to deny individual citizens their rights as Americans. But together, with millions of your fellow freedom-loving friends and neighbors, we can defeat this out-of-control evil bureaucracy.

Join the CITIZENS AGAINST TAX INJUSTICE (CATI), and with other hardworking Americans, we will fight to protect your life and property. Join today! Just sign the form below and send it in with $20 to join CITIZENS AGAINST TAX INJUSTICE. Once you are a member of CITIZENS AGAINST TAX INJUSTICE, the IRS will fear you. Join today—it may be your last chance . . .

Warren Ford
Executive Director, CATI

REPLY FORM

YES, Warren, I want to do my part to stop the abuses of the IRS. Enclosed is my check or credit card number. Enroll me today in the CITIZENS AGAINST TAX INJUSTICE.

Name   _____

Address   _____

Check if the following applies to you:
_____ I have been the victim of IRS abuses
_____ I value my freedom
_____ I am a loyal American

Send your reply form to :
CITIZENS AGAINST TAX INJUSTICE
C/o Johnson, Woods & Hart
Box 573
Washington, DC 20005

I put the ad and the check in the envelope and mailed it off to *American Magazine.*

It would be three weeks before the ad ran. The time passed slowly. A week later, I was in my office with Dezube, trying to think of someone new for us to visit, when I received a call from Congressman Conlin's aide, Russ Ratto.

"I talked to the head of the Congressional Affairs Department at the Food and Drug Administration about Dr. Garrity's vaccine," he said. "They are writing you a formal letter, but they tipped me off about the content. They are very sympathetic to the doctor's plight, but they just do not have the legal authority to help out."

"What do they need?"

"They need Congress to enact a law giving the FDA authority to review and certify vaccines for chicken pox."

"Would the administration support such a bill?"

"Absolutely. In fact, they will testify in favor of the legislation at any hearing."

"Great. I'll look for someone to introduce a bill."

"Congressman Conlin will join as an original cosponsor."

"Thanks, Russ."

"We can win this one, Richard. It's important."

Dezube had figured out whom I was talking to. He started waving at me. "Hold on," I said into the phone. I looked up at him. "Yes?"

"Ask about our bill?"

"Hey, Russ," I said back into the phone, "Doug Dezube is here. What's the status of the Hand Towel Equity Act?"

"Am I on a speakerphone?"

"No."

"The status is that it's a piece of shit."

"I see." I nodded at Dezube.

"A waste of paper."

"I understand."

Russ poured it on. "A joke."

"Right," I agreed. Dezube was watching me closely. "Are you going to have any hearings on it?"

"One day after hell freezes over."

"Anything else I should know about it?"

"Tell Dezube that we asked the administration for its position on the bill."

"Do you expect a response soon?"

"If they ever stop laughing."

"Okay. That's great. Let me know of any further developments."

"You can count on it." He hung up.

Dezube asked, "What's the status?"

"The committee has requested that the administration express its position on the bill. It will act once it knows what the president thinks."

"Which committee?"

"The House Ways and Means Committee, where the House version of the Hand Towel Equity Act was referred."

"Is that Congressman Conlin's committee?"

"Yes."

"And his committee is asking the president his views on the bill?"

"In essence."

"Wow."

"You need to understand something, Doug. This is a common procedure. Congress routinely asks the administration for its position on legislation. It is done at the staff level . . ." I trailed off as I realized that Dezube wasn't listening to me. He was looking out my window, dreamily. He turned back to me.

"So, when do you think that Congressman Conlin will discuss the bill personally with the president?"

———

The next day I called Dr. Garrity. "Doctor, I have good news and bad news. The bad news is that the administration does not have the authority to review and certify your vaccine. The good news is that the administration will go with us to Congress and ask for the authority."

"That's very kind of them. How long will it take?"

"Several months, Doctor. We need to get legislation introduced. Then there will be hearings held in the committees with jurisdiction over the matter. After the hearings, the bill must be passed by the committees and by the full House and Senate. It takes time. Fortunately, the bill should be simple. Without opposition, the process will go faster. But even the smallest bill takes time to get enacted."

"What are the chances of success?"

"There are no sure things in the lobbying business, but this bill has a very high likelihood of success."

"Mr. Brewster," he said quietly, "I think we will have to drop the matter at this time. Thank you for all your help. We would not have gotten as far as we did without your assistance."

I was stunned. "Doctor, what's the matter? You cannot stop now. We are on the edge of a breakthrough."

"Perhaps. But, you see, I have exhausted my funds. I cannot pay your firm, and I don't expect you to work for free."

"I see, I see," I said, considering how Dudley would like it if one of his team spent time on a nonpaying client. But I liked the doctor. I knew I could help him. I didn't hesitate for long. "Doctor, don't worry about it. We will work something out later. How much do you have left in your budget for legal work?"

"About $1,800, minus what I owe you for your work last month."

The bill was already more than that. "Doctor, just send me $500. Use the rest to fly out here so we can work together on your project. Keep the remainder in case you need to come here again for a hearing. How soon can you be here?"

"I can't come until classes are through for the year." Dr. Garrity was also a professor at the University of Nevada, Reno. "How about in two weeks on Wednesday?"

"Fine. I'll look forward to seeing you then."

"Thank you for everything. I would be lost without you."

I hung up smiling. It only lasted for a minute. I would have to finesse things to make them right with the firm, since working for free was not a popular activity. I buzzed Kathryn through my interoffice phone. "Kathryn, pull the Garrity file, please. Change the billing information sheet to reflect that the total bills for the rest of the year shall not exceed $500."

That would clear up the accounting, but it would also get some unwanted attention. Billing information was immediately transmitted to the firm's central computer. From there, it was available to all the partners on their computer screens.

The reaction was not long in coming. Three hours later, Walker Dudley strolled by my office and stuck his head in. "What happened in the Garrity matter?"

"Nothing. I solved the problem. There is very little follow-up work to do, and he put me on a budget to complete it."

"You really solved the problem?"

"Yes."

"What's wrong with you?" he asked. I didn't answer. "Do you want me to look at the file and see if I can find more work for us to do?" he asked. "I bet I can find some follow-on work, you know what I mean?"

"No, that's okay. I've got it covered. However, you can look at the Dezube file if you want."

Dudley was gone.

As the days went by, the scam was never fully out of my mind, whether I was at work, lifting weights with Emilio, or playing with the kids at home. It seemed like such a great idea when I launched it, but now I had my doubts. And every day there was the danger that someone in the upper ranks of the firm would note that I had authorized an expenditure of $60,000 without any offsetting fees yet. True, Dudley had countersigned, and it would be first in line when the fees came in to claim his credit, but I was under no illusion as to how quickly he would distance himself from me if there was a problem.

The first danger point was the next partners' meeting. I needed to keep Walker Dudley away from it. If one of the other attorneys, looking over the month's expenses, noticed the outlay of $60,000 for public relations and asked about it, either Dudley or I would have to acknowledge our actions. If, on the other hand, neither of us were there, the matter would be passed over until the next meeting. That would buy me time to cover the expense.

The meeting was scheduled to start at 6 p.m. on Thursday. I walked into Dudley's office that day at 5:55.

"Walker, Warren Ford from the Citizens Against Tax Injustice is going to place a call to you and me in a few minutes," I said. "He specifically wants to talk to both of us."

"We have a partners' meeting."

"I know. And I know how you hate to be late and interrupt one of Jason's presentations," I said, trying to figure out what he had eaten for lunch. The stain on his tie was small and purple. *Grape juice?* "Unfortunately, it was the only time that Ford could talk to us."

"What does he want from me?"

"I'm not really sure. Didn't you talk to him at some reception?"

"I think so, but I can't remember what we discussed."

"Well, I think it has to do with the tax code and lobbying the two tax committees."

We waited for several minutes. As Dudley grew restless, I said, "I got my bonus check yesterday. Ten thousand dollars. I think it's great."

The thought of the money put him in a good mood. The Southern accent got thicker. "Yeah, I got twenty-five. It will hit the spot, do you know what I mean?"

"What are you going to do with the money?"

"I don't know. Down payment on a new car, maybe. How about you?"

"I don't know either. I keep talking about opening a health club. Maybe I'll use the money to do that."

He side-eyed me. "You won't tell your wife about the bonus, will you?"

"Absolutely not. No need to pay for her spending habits," I agreed. Actually, I hadn't decided whether to tell Elizabeth about the bonus. If I did, any chance of opening a health club would go up in smoke. And I would say anything to stay on Dudley's good side. He grunted in pleasure.

We waited a few more minutes. "Where is that call?" he asked.

"I am sure it's coming in anytime now," I reassured him.

"Maybe I'll head up to the partners' meeting until he calls. You come get me when you hear from him."

I thought fast. "That's a good idea. You should get up there in case you need to answer questions about the activities of the public relations committee." We both knew that he hadn't done a thing on that project, other than our discussion.

He stared back at me. He didn't seem too happy. He wasn't used to my uppity attitude. "I've got some things to do here," he said. "You go down to your office and buzz me if our client calls."

Smiling to myself, I returned to my office. Subsequently I learned that the $60,000 expenditure had been raised by one of the partners with a sharp eye. Jason, without hesitation, told the partners that the public relations committee was hard at work and that we would start to see results in the very near future.

He went on to explain that the enhanced public image should

help with the firm's newest venture. It was a trading company that would specialize in importing fruit from Central America to the Unites States. No one in the firm knew anything about growing or importing fruit. The management team of the new company came from the partnership. Jason had also convinced a number of his Washington friends to serve on the board of directors of the new firm, including a former secretary of agriculture. Already two partners were down in Costa Rica, staying in a Four Seasons hotel—far away from any agricultural land, but making key contacts.

To start the trading company, called Latin Trade and Investment, Jason drew down one million dollars on the law firm's line of credit at the bank. He then had the Latin Trade and Investment, LTI, give a note back to the firm for the money it borrowed. The firm then had a new asset, a note payable from LTI. Based on this new asset, the firm's books were stronger than ever, Jason explained. Jason was at his best at that meeting, and I regretted missing it when I got all the details. I had lots to learn from Jason Douglas Johnson.

———————

Two days later, working at my desk, I was buzzed by the firm's operator and told that a Bob Dickson, director of government relations at the University of Nevada, Reno, was on the phone. I picked up. "Richard Brewster," I identified myself.

"Bob Dickson here," came the reply. "University of Nevada, Reno. I called to tell you that the president of the university just learned that you offered to help Dr. Garrity in the future without charging him. Is there anything we can do?"

"I can't think of anything now, but thank you for the offer."

"We think it is great for a Washington firm to do this kind of work for free. It restores our faith in lobbyists."

"Thank you. By the way, does the university have anyone representing it in DC?"

"Yes, we do. We use a guy named Charles E. Nagle. Have you ever heard of him?"

"Yes, I have. He's very good."

"He is very expensive, but we can get into any office we need."

"Yes, I've heard that."

"Well, again, thanks for helping Dr. Garrity."

While running the next day with Emilio, I told him that I had decided to start the health club with him. I asked him to start looking for locations and to make a list of equipment we would need to buy. He was ecstatic, and burst ahead of me. By the time I caught up with him, I was gasping for breath. As we stood there blowing and huffing, he thanked me over and over.

Smiling, I said, "I have a favor to ask of you. Remember the trade organization I talked about, the Citizens Against Tax Injustice?" We had discussed it during one of our sessions.

"Yes."

"It's an actual organization now. In fact, I'm running an ad about it in *American Magazine* a week from Sunday."

"Cool beans. Where did you get the money to run an ad?"

"I kind of borrowed it from the firm. But once the dues roll in, I'll repay the firm, and everyone will be happy."

He looked disappointed with me. "I hope you didn't do anything wrong." His mother was a former nun. Emilio was a very religious person.

"I didn't really do anything wrong," I reassured him. "Besides, you can't get into trouble unless you get caught, and I won't get caught."

He didn't believe me, and I could see that he was still disappointed. I hated myself for showing my cynical side to someone so young and sincere. "Do me a favor and look for my ad in *American Magazine* when it comes out. I want your honest impression of it. Tell me if it makes you want to join CATI."

"I do want to join it if you are organizing it to help people. In fact, I will join it today."

"Don't worry about it. You can have a free membership if we're partners in a health club."

"Cool beans." Then he was off as fast as he could go. I ran after him, hoping that I hadn't dropped too far in his eyes.

Finally, the big day arrived. It was a hot, sticky Sunday. Unable to sleep, I tossed and turned until I thought I heard the paper slap in the driveway. As the rest of the family slept, I looked out my bedroom window and confirmed that the paper had arrived. I also noticed that the grass was too long to ignore. Cutting it in the heat was going to be miserable.

I was blasted by the heat as I wandered down the driveway to pick up the *Washington Post.* The plastic covering the paper partially melted in my hand as I picked it up. The paper was already yellowing in the bright sunlight. I carried it back to the house and quietly found *American Magazine* in the middle of the advertising inserts.

I flipped through the pages quickly. The first time through, I didn't find my ad. I started back a second time. I felt very hot, and my throat was dry. I had to find the ad. I didn't want to wait another week.

The second time through, I found it. The story on the opposite page was about how to talk to your daughters about safe sex. There was a picture of a girl, about eighteen years old, with a tight T-shirt stretched over her large breasts. The look on her face seemed to indicate that she didn't need any parental advice about sex. No one who read *American Magazine* would miss that picture, or the story. Directly across the page, about nipple height, was the ad for CATI. Next to it was an ad for vitamins. Another good sign, it seemed to me. Everyone liked vitamins. By some marvelous stroke of fate, I had earned a prime spot in the magazine.

I decided to make breakfast for my family. A real homemade breakfast, with scrambled eggs, cinnamon toast, juice, bacon, and cereal. I would trash the kitchen and leave a big mess. Then I would tackle the grass. The prospect of mowing for three hours did not seem so bad any longer. I would need the time to plan my next steps.

CHAPTER V
RESPONSE

On Monday, I couldn't wait to get to work. My mind was so preoccupied about Citizens Against Tax Injustice that I couldn't recall which route I took to work or even if I had waited in traffic. I kept telling myself not to count on receiving any responses to the ad that day, but deep down inside, I hoped I would.

The mail arrived at Johnson, Woods & Hart twice a day, once at 9:15 and again at 4:30. As soon as I arrived at the office, I called the mailroom.

"Yes," mumbled a strange voice.

"Do you have any mail in box 573?"

"Let me check." The phone thumped down, then was picked up again a minute later. "Nothing."

"How about in my mailbox?"

"Who are you?"

"Richard Brewster."

"Let me check." Again the phone rattled on a desk or a countertop. I waited impatiently until the voice returned. "One letter."

"Open it, please."

"It's from the District of Columbia Bar association. It says you need to take some classes to keep your bar certification up to date. Do you want to see it?"

"No, forget it."

"There's also a fax here for you."

"What does it say?" I asked with my hopes growing.

"Something about the Hand Towel Equity Act. It's a newsletter.

There's a picture of a goofy-looking guy holding up a towel. Do you want me to read it to you?"

"No. Thank you. Please put it back in my box. Someone will get it later."

At 4:30, I visited the mailroom personally. There was nothing new either in my personal box or box 573. I walked back to my office, trying to control the feelings of panic. By Tuesday evening, after another fruitless day, I could no longer control my fears. To get my mind off the situation, I met Emilio at a local health club, but I was so distracted that I did everything wrong. Finally he stopped me.

"What's the matter?"

"There has been no response to my ad," I confessed.

"When did the ad run?"

"Sunday. Didn't you see it?"

"No."

"Did you look?"

"Yes, I read *American Magazine,* just like you asked me to."

"You didn't see the ad?"

"No. Where was it?"

"Next to the story about safe sex."

"Next to the picture of the girl with the big tits?"

"Yes, next to the big tits. You really didn't see it?"

"I saw the tits."

"Did you see the ad?" I asked, my voice rising.

"No."

Great, I thought. *Was every potential male member of CATI distracted by the big tits? Was every potential female member offended by them?* I was in total panic now.

Later that night, after the children were in bed, I decided to share my fears with my wife. I found Elizabeth in bed, trying to choose a book to read. She had two splayed before her and was reading the back covers of both.

"Which would you read?" she asked, handing them to me.

"They both look boring," I said. They did.

"They do? I just finished a great book. I hate it. It's depressing to have a bad book follow a good one. Choosing is the key. Which one would you choose?"

"Neither."

"Which one do you think I would like?" she pressed. I took both books and read the back covers.

"Neither," I finally declared again. "Do you want me to suggest something? How about a Washington novel?"

"Get real," she said. "No Washington novel is remotely realistic. I wish someone would write one. In the meantime, I want to read one of those two. Can you help me pick one?"

"Try this one," I said, handing her the top book. She looked at it and apparently agreed, because she started reading.

After a pause, I said, "Elizabeth, I may have a problem."

"Yes. Yes," she mumbled without looking up.

"I mean it. Elizabeth, I may have a big problem," I repeated, with my voice rising. She looked at me. I had her attention.

"Yes," she said slowly. "Is this about buying a Mustang convertible? Did you do it?"

"No. I haven't received a single response to my ad," I confessed.

"What ad?"

"The ad for my tax group."

"When did it run?"

"Sunday."

"It's early."

"What if I don't get any responses at all?"

"What would happen?"

"Well, I'd have to pay the firm back $60,000."

"Anything else?"

"Isn't that enough?"

"Just do what I do. Ignore the bill."

"You ignore bills?"

"Some of them."

"Our bills?"

"Only some of them."

"Do you pay some of them?"

"I put them on our credit cards."

"Aren't we tapped out on our credit cards?"

"They keep sending me new ones."

"Elizabeth, how deeply are we in debt?"

"I have no idea."

"What?" I shouted. Owing the firm was bad enough.

"Shhhhhh!" she said. "Don't wake the children."

"What do you mean, you don't know how deeply we are in debt?" I repeated, slightly less loud.

"I mean I am not really sure."

"What do you mean, you aren't sure?" I was louder again. Much too loud. Weeks of tension were exploding.

Of course, that woke up one of the kids. Elizabeth, with a look of relief, jumped up to deal with the situation. As she rushed out of the room, she said, "Good job. Thanks."

By the time she got things quieted down, my anger had disappeared, leaving me only full of terror. Elizabeth fell asleep as soon as she got into bed, but I spent the night tossing and turning. First I worried about the Citizens Against Tax Injustice. Then I stewed about our financial situation. Finally, around 4:30, I fell asleep.

I dreamt I woke up late for work. I ran out of the house and waited at the corner for a pause in traffic. As the long line of cars ended, I pulled out into the road, only I was running, and not in a car at all. I was wearing only my running shorts and a T-shirt. I was unshaven, unshowered, running up a hill. It was very hot, and the road was soft and sticky under my bare feet. The hill kept growing. I kept climbing and climbing, but the road kept stretching out ahead of me. The scenery on both sides disappeared, leaving only the hill. Finally, I reached the top. I looked over and saw that I was high in the air, at the start of a roller coaster ride. I began to slip over the edge . . .

Suddenly Amy, the baby, started to cry. I looked at the clock; it was 5:37. Elizabeth remained asleep. I climbed out of bed slowly, rubbing my eyes. They stung from the lack of sleep and the humidity.

I retrieved the baby from her crib and carried her downstairs. I fed her and flipped on the television. When she finished, she laid her head on my chest and went back to sleep. So did I.

When I awoke again, it was much later. The television was still on, tuned to the *Today Show*. As my eyes focused, I saw Senator Kelly being interviewed by Katie Couric.

". . . and this is a serious problem," the senator said. "That is why I introduced legislation to prohibit these types of activities." He looked serious.

Katie watched him closely. She leaned forward and asked him,

"Senator, how do you respond to your critics who say you introduced the bill only for publicity?"

The senator sat up straight and looked at the camera. "I've heard that criticism. But the people of my state elected me to solve problems, not just disappear in Washington. Solving problems requires legislation, so when I see a need, I act. If it causes publicity, well, so be it."

Katie cut in, "How do you respond to that, Mr. Ladd?"

On the television screen appeared a heavyset man, overdressed and nervous. He was located in a remote studio with a picture of the city of Chicago behind him. At the bottom of the screen appeared the words *Dave Ladd, President, Ladd Industries.*

Here it comes, I thought. *I can hear him now: "With all due respect to the senator, we totally disagree with the need for legislation . . ."*

"With all due respect to the senator, we totally disagree with the need for legislation," said Mr. Ladd.

Good, my instincts are working today. Now tell them about your industry study that says there is no problem.

"Our industry has just completed a study that convincingly demonstrates we pose no health hazard to the American public," Ladd went on. I had no idea what he was talking about. I wondered where the networks got these industry spokesmen. On the other hand, Senator Kelly sounded better when you had no idea what he was talking about.

Fearing another day of rejection, I wanted to stay on the couch with Amy. But I knew I had to go. With a feeling of foreboding, I asked Amy, "Could it get any worse than getting no responses?" She giggled and drooled on me.

Arriving at the office, I saw Kathryn standing at her desk, studying something on the surface. Lying there were seven responses to the ad. Two of them were properly filled out, but without checks. Two weren't even filled out. One had *Go to hell IRS bastards!* written across the form. Only two were filled out with checks attached. The Citizens Against Tax Injustice had its first two members and a working budget of $40.

"Is that all we got?" I asked.

She nodded and then pointed behind me. I turned and saw Dr. Garrity coming down the hall. Today was his day in Washington. It had slipped my mind until I saw him. I had to focus on the doctor's problems instead of mine. Swallowing my panic, I greeted the doctor with simulated affection.

For the next hour, we discussed legislative strategies. He was an attentive listener. He looked at me with half disbelief and half joy that he could actually change the policies of the US government. By the end of our meeting, I had managed to put my fears about CATI on hold, and was ready to face the Congress on his behalf. Armed with a schedule of appointments and packages of material, we left the building and hailed a cab.

At that moment, the firm's car pulled out of the garage. The back window lowered, and Jason looked out at us. He asked us where we were going. I told him we were on the way to the US Capitol. He told us to ride with him.

I introduced Dr. Garrity to Jason. Jason asked about our mission and listened to the answers. He scanned our schedule and suggested that we also see Congresswoman Dunn, the chairwoman of the House health subcommittee.

"That would be great," I explained, "but she has no time to see us today. I tried to set something up."

"Let me try," said Jason, with a smile. "She owes me a favor or two." He picked up the car phone and called the congressional switchboard. In thirty seconds, he was through to the congresswoman's scheduling secretary. Within another thirty seconds, we had an appointment.

I was grateful and impressed and made no effort to hide my admiration for him. I said to the doctor, pointing at Jason, "That's why he's the managing partner and I'm not."

Jason smiled. "It helps when you have known her for twenty years."

When we arrived on Capitol Hill, Dr. Garrity got out of the car first. Before I left, I turned to Jason. "Thanks."

"Don't mention it."

"Yeah, but this is a charity client. You used a big chit for him."

"So? That's what they are there for." He turned back to the driver and gave him some instructions.

Getting legislation enacted is never simple. You need a minimum of 218 members of the House of Representatives to pass a bill that is identical to a version passed by at least 51 senators, and then get it signed into law by the president of the United States. There are no shortcuts permitted by the Constitution. Instead, there are ten thousand ways to derail the process. The vast majority of bills introduced in the House or the Senate each year never make it into law. Dr. Garrity and I were embarking on one of the world's most frustrating and fascinating tasks. To succeed, we would need a good legislative strategy, a worthwhile cause, hard work, and lots of luck. If we succeeded, we would create a bit of magic.

Dr. Garrity lived and worked in Nevada, so we started by visiting the offices of the two senators from that state. The senior senator listened to us thoughtfully. His legislative assistant, Sheila Reynoldson, joined us for the discussion. I had known Sheila for years. She was one of my favorite staff members in the Senate for three reasons. First, she was competent. Second, she almost always returned my calls. Third, she was willing to meet with my clients and wouldn't laugh at their requests. Of course, I had never presented her with the supreme test; she had never met Dezube.

We asked the senator to introduce a bill allowing the Food and Drug Administration to test and approve a vaccine for chicken pox. It was a straightforward request, and no one could object to its purpose. The senator readily agreed, and told Sheila to work out the details with us. Dr. Garrity, Sheila, and I left the senator and returned to Sheila's workstation.

The Senate staff far exceeds the space available to hold them. As a result, the Senate offices have been subdivided with temporary wall partitions into miniscule work areas. Each station usually contains a small desk, a large computer, a phone with nine or ten lines, two chairs, and stacks and stacks of papers. Everyone looks harried and cramped. Looking at her space, I was reminded of the famous psychological studies where overcrowded rats became violent. Maybe this explains the quality of some legislation that comes from Congress.

Dr. Garrity and Sheila sat, while I remained standing as we continued our discussions. We agreed on the concepts we wanted included in the bill. After we left, Sheila would reduce our ideas to writing. Then, she would send the ideas over to the Senate Legislative Counsel's office, where the attorneys would draft the necessary legislative language and prepare a draft version of the bill. Then it would be returned to the senator's office for a final review and eventual introduction.

This process would take several days. In the meantime, Sheila would prepare a fact sheet about the bill. She would also draft a speech the senator would use when he introduced the bill on the Senate floor. My job would be to provide her with all the information she needed and to line up other senators to support the bill. We had worked together before, and I was confident we would make a good team on Dr. Garrity's bill.

Dr. Garrity left the meeting happy and impressed. He looked at me as if I possessed special talents. Our next meeting was with the other Nevada senator. His office was located in a different building. We could have simply walked between the two buildings out on the street, but instead, I led the doctor down into the basement. Underneath the United States Capitol and its surrounding buildings is a huge labyrinth of underground passages. In them are cafeterias, post offices, stationary stores, phone banks, document rooms, and carpentry shops. The passages also lead under the streets from building to building.

I led the doctor through a very confusing maze of tunnels. He was impressed by all the activity. He was also completely lost. Had I left him there, it might have taken him days to get out. When he gave up on trying to figure out where he was, I put him on an elevator. We went up to the third floor and got out. Across from us was the other Nevada senator's office. The doctor was convinced that I was part wizard. It was all part of the show. Someday, I was confident, he would invite me to a lecture on the chemistry of his vaccine, and I would be equally disoriented.

The rest of the morning, we visited a number of Senate offices. In each office, I had arranged for us to meet the relevant staff person with jurisdiction over health matters. All the meetings went very smoothly. I estimated that we would get the strong support of at least seven of the senators whose staff we met. It was difficult to oppose the doctor's request, and he made a sympathetic case.

As we sat down to a quick lunch in one of the Senate cafeterias, the doctor was radiant. Things had gone so well that I could see he was getting unrealistic expectations. I decided it was time to give him the cold-water talk. There were two purposes to the speech. First, it would help him handle the setbacks that would inevitably occur. Second, it would reinforce his opinion of my abilities if we were able to succeed despite the difficulties.

"Doctor, we had a great morning. You made a good impression on everyone. You represent a worthwhile cause. The handouts we prepared and left at each office were short and to the point. We have the support of the administration. We are on a roll.

"But something will go wrong. I don't know when it will happen or what will occur, but something will go astray. It always does. You have to prepare yourself for that eventuality.

"Remember, I picked the offices we visited today. I know all the staff people we saw. The deck was stacked to find people who would agree with us. I could have picked seven other offices where we wouldn't have even gotten a meeting."

"Why would anyone oppose us?" the doctor asked.

"They might not oppose us. They might oppose any bill the administration supports. They might oppose any bill the senator from Nevada introduces. They might run out of time this year to deal with the bill. They might amend the bill by adding a requirement that only a doctor can dispense the vaccine, or even add two hundred pages of immigration legislation that has nothing to do with your vaccine. Just because they don't object to your original idea, don't assume that someone in the process won't change it so much it becomes unrecognizable and unsupportable.

"But I will stay on top of the bill. I will do everything in my power to see that nothing bad happens. We will work together to overcome the problems as they develop. Don't be overconfident, but don't be discouraged. Some legislation gets through every year. The system is designed to defeat bad legislation and pass good legislation. It doesn't always work, but it works more often than you would believe."

The doctor took the speech well. Some clients resist the idea that anyone would oppose them. Others get discouraged. The purpose of the cold-water speech is to give some clients some basis of reality. Of course, this is difficult to do when you consider that Congress often has no grip on reality whatsoever.

During the afternoon, we worked in the House of Representatives. As in the Senate, we started by visiting the members from Nevada. They agreed to introduce the legislation in the House. Then we worked to round up support from other key House members. Finally, at the appointed hour, we visited Congresswoman Dunn, the chairwoman of the House health subcommittee. Her subcommittee would have jurisdiction over the legislation once it was introduced. She was the most important House member for our effort. If she opposed the bill, it would be very difficult to get it passed. If she supported the bill, we had a good chance of success.

To call the congresswoman tough as nails was an understatement. No nail on earth was as strong as Dunn. The Congress of the United States still has many vestiges of sexism, so to climb to the rank of a chairmanship, the congresswoman had to be twice as bright, twice as hardworking, and twice as tough as the ordinary congressman. Jason had arranged for us to meet with her at the end of a long day, after she had spent over two hours in heated debate on the House floor.

Nearing seventy, the congresswoman was sitting at her desk when we were ushered into her office. There was a stack of papers lying there taller than she was, and she had a determined look on her face as if she intended to read them all before the end of the day. She got up stiffly and greeted us. Then she looked over my shoulder at the door and waited expectantly for a minute. We were silent. Finally she asked, "Where's Jason?"

"He couldn't be with us, but he said he would call you later," I said, making a mental note to make sure that he did.

"What can I do for you?" she asked curtly as we all sat down.

We laid out our problem. She listened, first attentively, then with a pained look on her face. As we finished our explanation, she closed and rubbed her eyes.

"Let me get this straight," she said. "You're telling me that the Food and Drug Administration doesn't have authority to review and approve a vaccine for chicken pox?"

"Right. That's what I understand."

"Those asses," she said forcefully. "Is there anyone in the Clinton administration who is remotely competent?"

"Well, I think . . ." started Dr. Garrity, but I frowned and waved him into silence. It would be a mistake to try to answer a rhetorical question.

I realized that we were going to get a congressional lecture. I was ready to listen.

"I can't believe they can't find some obscure authority that gives them the ability to approve your vaccine. Hell, they seem to find authority to bomb goddamn Nicaragua if they want to. But if someone wants to save a few hundred thousand children in this country from getting a childhood disease, they can't be bothered to be creative. No, instead they dump the problem on Congress. You tell the president that if I carry this bill for him, his administration better support it. You got that?"

"Yes," we both answered. I wondered how I was going to deliver the message to the president.

"Who is introducing the bill?" she asked. Having vented her anger at the administration, she now turned to the practical considerations of getting the bill passed. We told her who would introduce the bill and who we had lined up for support, including Congressman Conlin.

"Good, good," she said approvingly. "Now, you do this for me. After the bill is introduced, you get the sponsors to write me a letter asking me to hold hearings on it. Then you get with my staff and get a date on my calendar for a hearing. Tell them I want a simple hearing, with no dramatics. You bring in one Hollywood star to plead for this bill, and I'll cut your balls off. Do you understand?"

"Yes," I answered swiftly.

"Doctor, you testify, and then we'll hear from the administrator of the Food and Drug Administration. You tell him if he doesn't favor this bill, he'd better have a very good reason or I'll cut his travel budget back so much he'll have to miss all his conferences in Florida next January. Does that cover everything?"

"Absolutely," I said.

"Thank you for coming in."

We stood to shake her hand, but she was already walking back to her desk. She wasn't rude; she simply didn't have enough time in the day to get everything done. She had to get back to her reading.

As we emerged from the building, I was elated, and the doctor was dazed. He was already running late for his plane back to Reno, so I walked him out to the street to hail a cab.

"Doctor, I have been in this business for many years, and I have never had a more successful day," I told him truthfully.

"Really?" he asked, still not fully understanding the day's events.

"Really. You did great. We know what to do next. I'll be in touch with you in the few days, when the bill is introduced in the House and the Senate. Here's a cab. Take it back to your hotel and get your bag and get to the airport."

"Thank you, thank you, thank you," he kept repeating as he got in and headed off.

I felt very satisfied. Such days made my job interesting and rewarding. I was confident of our eventual success.

I grabbed the next cab back to my office. It was 6:41 when I reentered the building. Most of the support staff, and many of the attorneys, were already gone. The hall was quiet as I headed down to my office. On Kathryn's desk were my phone messages. Two marked *Urgent* were from Dezube. Standing over Kathryn's desk, I picked up her phone and dialed Dezube's number. As the phone rang in his office, I glanced over her desk, looking for more responses to the CATI ad. All I saw were some papers to be filed and a picture of her new boyfriend. I think his name was Craig. He was in tennis shorts and looked very stupid.

A recording came on in Dezube's office, telling me to leave a message after the beep. In my lowest tone I said, "Doug, this is Congressman Smith. I am here in Richard Brewster's office right now. I have a question about the Hand Towel Equity Act. If you were there to answer it, I would have endorsed your bill during my press conference tomorrow. But since you are not there, I guess I'll have to oppose the bill. Call Brewster for the details." I hung up. I figured that should get Dezube's hair straight up before he had his first cup of coffee. It was passive aggressive, I knew, and I would pay for it later, but I just couldn't stop myself from tweaking Dezube for being such a pain in the ass, especially after such a good day.

Smiling, I walked into my office. There on my desk was a stack of CATI responses several inches high. On the top was a note from Kathryn: *There are 188 responses, 106 with checks. I deposited all the money received today. There is $2,160 in the bank.*

A wave of relief passed over me. For once that summer, I was not hot. Then I remembered that we were still $57,840 in the hole.

B y the end of the following week, I had received 3,700 paid-up memberships. There was over $74,000 in the bank. The Citizens Against Tax Injustice was a living, breathing lobbying group in Washington. However, the responses were arriving in smaller quantities with each mail delivery, and it looked as if they would soon end.

While the amount of money I had in hand was a good start, I had yet to tally the expenses. So I tackled that chore. I got out a piece of paper and wrote *Budget* across the top. Underneath, I wrote *Revenues–$74,000.* Then I started subtracting the expenses. First, of course, was the $60,000 for the ad. Then I subtracted $5,000 to pay the firm for its out-of-pocket expenses. This included the cost of the computer person that added all the names and addresses to a new CATI database. This left a balance of $9,000. I knew I would have to write every member of CATI, welcoming them and sending them a membership card. I buzzed Kathryn and asked her what it would cost to print and mail 3,700 letters. She checked and told me it would cost $3,800. When I subtracted that amount from the total, I was left with $5,200. With that sum I would have to run the organization for an entire year, send out newsletters, solicit new members, and pay the firm some fees. What a worthless scam! I was disgusted.

I had another concern. What should I do with CATI now that I had created it? What should I tell all the new members about our goals? What were we going to do? I needed for CATI to accomplish something—anything.

I knew I should focus on the second problem first, but instead

I worried about the money. Unless CATI brought in some fees to Johnson, Woods & Hart, it really wasn't much good. How could I look Jason in the face unless my client generated significant revenues? I enjoyed my ascending position in the firm, which was based, in large part, on the promise that I would become a major producer of fees. I wasn't about to let that go.

And what about Elizabeth? I hated to tell her that yet another idea of mine had fizzled.

And what about Barbara? Several times over the past weeks she had whispered in my ear, "How is our private scheme going?" I had assured her that it was fine. I didn't want to bring her in on it until it was an up-and-running operation. Barbara didn't strike me as a woman interested in building something up from nothing. Instead, she seemed to be the type of woman who would properly reward any man that presented her with a full-blown success.

I had obviously made two errors of judgment with my first ad. First, I hadn't charged enough for each member to join. Second, I hadn't generated enough members to make the organization pay for itself. I needed to correct both problems immediately.

I called the salesman for *American Magazine.* I asked what it would cost to run a bigger ad, one that had enough room to include a picture or a drawing. The price was $72,000. I placed an order and told him I would send the ad copy and a check before the end of the day. I decided not to pay the firm back for the first ad yet, and not to get the out-of-pocket expenses reimbursed. Instead, I was gambling that the payoff would be worth it.

I drafted the letter for new members.

Dear American,

Congratulations! You are now a member of good standing in CITIZENS AGAINST TAX INJUSTICE (CATI). You have taken the important first step in reclaiming the freedoms and liberty you deserve as an AMERICAN.

As a member of CATI, you will receive a newsletter detailing our efforts against the IRS bureaucracy. You will also receive special CITIZEN ALERTS, which will warn you about potential threats to your home and property from the IRS. Finally, you will become part of a national network of patriots that can mobilize against illegal acts of the Internal Revenue Service.

We are interested in your struggles with the IRS. We will include them in the newsletters and share them with the other members. Send us a letter today outlining your troubles with the IRS. We will share them with your fellow members.

Today we begin to throw off the tyranny of the Internal Revenue Service!

Yours in Freedom,
Warren Ford

I called Kathryn in, handed her the draft, and told her to send it down to the computer center with instructions to mail it out to each new CATI member. I would now have to wait for the letters and the second ad to work. I couldn't think of anything else to do. I did, however, fantasize about lying in a bed naked with Barbara, waiting for Jason to serve us chilled wine.

Kathryn buzzed me, pulling me out of my dreams, to tell me that the letters would go out that afternoon. I focused on the rest of my life. It was Friday, July 1. Monday was the Fourth of July, giving everyone a three-day weekend. Like most every other day that summer, it was blisteringly hot. Congress had already adjourned for the holiday. The president was out of town on a retreat with the cultural elite. Most offices in Washington, both in the government and the private sector, were emptying out early to take advantage of the holiday and to avoid the heat.

It was still midmorning. I cleared my desk of real client work. Dr. Garrity's bill had been introduced earlier that week. It was called the FDA Improvements Act. Hearings were scheduled before Congresswoman Dunn's health subcommittee. The bill was receiving support from the administration and a number of senators and members of Congress. I drafted a status memo for the doctor, taking full credit for all the success.

I also wrote a status memo to Dezube on the Hand Towel Equity Act. It was fairing much worse. Consumer groups opposed the bill since the tariffs would increase the price of hand towels. Human rights groups opposed the impact on developing-world job markets. Retailers also opposed the bill. The State Department expressed concern that the bill would hurt allies of the United States. The Treasury Department reported that the bill would cost more to administer than the tariffs would raise in revenue. In short, every agency or organization that reviewed the bill hated it.

I wrote an honest report, stating that the chances of success were very small. I knew none of this would faze Dezube. "They just don't understand," he told me on the phone a few days before. "We just need to explain it better. Besides, doesn't some Congressman Smith support the bill?" he pointed out. "Where does he come from, by the way? We need to see him on my next trip." Dezube ignored the fact that the more we explained the bill to people, the more they opposed it. I was sure that the memo would result in many more visits from Dezube over the next months.

I then got caught up on my responsibilities for the firm. Walker Dudley had actually held two meetings of the public relations team. They had both been jokes. Mostly we listened while Dudley told legislative war stories. We had all heard the stories before but did notice that Dudley's role became larger with each retelling. We weren't really worried that our team was doing nothing. We knew from experience that eventually some incident would get the firm press recognition. We just needed patience. Then we would announce that the public relations effort was a success.

However, I decided to write a memo to Jason, detailing our hard work, the better to remain in his good graces and, hopefully, to finesse the fact that I had charged $60,000 to the effort. I needed Jason to think we were doing something so he didn't ask Dudley about the expenditure.

Just then, my phone rang. It was Emilio.

"Richard, is this a bad time to call you?"

"No. What's on your mind?"

"I have been looking for locations for our health club. I found three sites in our target area. Can you see them with me next week?"

"Sure. Call me next Tuesday to arrange a time."

"I will. I have also made a list of the sports equipment we will need. I'll start calling suppliers soon."

"Great, Emilio. You're really moving on this project. I'm impressed."

"I want you to know how grateful I am to you and Elizabeth for giving me this chance. I am going to make this health club a big success."

"I have no doubt about that. You are a good partner. But do me a favor. If you see Elizabeth, don't tell her what we're doing."

"Why?"

"Well, I am paying for this out of a bonus she doesn't know about. I want to present it to her when it is up and running. Otherwise, I might have to use the money to pay other bills."

"Okay. I get the picture. You can count on me."

As I hung up, Barbara Lehman stuck her head in the door. "Got any lunch plans?"

I was pleasantly surprised. It was her first invitation to me.

"No, let's get a bite."

"Let's go to the Potomac Pub. The beer will help us start off a three-day weekend properly."

"Sounds good."

As I got up from my desk, I noticed that she looked sheepish. "What's the catch?" I asked.

"I invited Brad Charness and Mark Waterman to join us," she admitted. They were two attorneys from the firm's tax section. They were nice but boring. I was crushed.

"Why did you do that?"

"I ran into Waterman in the coffee room. He started rambling on about some tax project of his. I think he was trying to impress me. I thought I could get out of listening to him if I invited him to lunch. He never leaves the building, so I thought I was safe. But he accepted and is bringing Brad. That's why you've got to come. I don't want to be alone with them."

"I'm not bailing you out of this one," I said. "I just decided to catch up on some paperwork."

"Come on," she said, giving me her most winning smile. "I wanted to have lunch with you anyway. It might be fun. I'll buy. And if they get too boring, I'll spill your beer on them."

―――――――――――

The Potomac Pub looked just the way it should. From the street entrance, we went down half a flight of steps. Inside, wood panels covered all the walls. The place was dark, and coming in out of the summer sun, it took a few minutes for our eyes to adjust. It was one big room full of small tables and rickety chairs. Across one wall was a huge wooden bar, behind which were three shelves full of beer steins and other mugs. Usually the floor was sticky. The food was mediocre at best and always over-spiced. They served beer in warm mugs. Somehow, though, it was impossible to get a table on most days. Huge crowds flooded the place.

But with the beginning of a long weekend, the Potomac had a few empty tables. We were promptly seated. Barbara ordered a large beer, winking at me. I was debating between an ice tea and a small beer when Brad and Mark ordered mineral water. Barbara rolled her eyes. I ordered a large beer.

"Nice of you to join us," Barbara said to the two tax attorneys.

"Yeah, what's the occasion?" I asked. "I didn't think you guys ever left the office during business hours."

"We're celebrating," said Mark proudly. "We've just finished writing an article."

"I always celebrate a big success with mineral water," said Barbara. She winked at me again.

"Which magazine?" I asked.

"It's called *Tax Notes Today*," explained Brad.

"What's it about?" asked Barbara, rolling her eyes to make it clear that she had no interest whatsoever as she looked around for the waiter and our drinks.

"The Internal Revenue Service just released a new revenue ruling which changes the way you deduct homeowners mortgage interest in complex tax-free property swaps," explained Mark.

"Sounds like a real bestseller," said Barbara. But it got my interest.

"Explain this to me," I asked. "Does this ruling reduce the amount taxpayers can deduct for their mortgage interest on their taxes?"

"In very rare instances," said Brad. "But only if there is a tax-free swap of property involved."

"How many taxpayers will this affect in an average year?"

"Not more than a hundred. You see, there has to be a tax swap of property that has equal valuation—"

I cut him off. I was uninterested in qualifying statements. "You are sure that someone, somewhere in the country, will lose some part of his or her tax deduction because of this ruling."

"Yes."

"Guaranteed?"

"Guaranteed." Brad was obviously happy to have an audience and answered my questions enthusiastically.

"What's the number of this ruling?"

"Revenue Ruling 34-897."

"What was your article about?"

"How the ruling was long overdue. How it clarifies the law."

"Thank God the law got cleared up," said Barbara. "I couldn't sleep at night worrying about it." She peered around the room. "Where is that waitress?"

"Here she comes," I said, spotting her. "It probably took her extra time to find the mineral water." The drinks were delivered and our lunch orders taken.

"You know, this place is a gold mine," said Barbara reflectively, taking a long drink. "Whoever thought up this idea must be making a mint, and having some fun running it, too."

"Speaking of fun, are you going to the firm picnic on Monday?" asked Mark.

"Absolutely," I said. "My kids love it, and the food is always great."

"I am looking forward to my first firmwide event," said Barbara. "I understand that Jason knows how to put on a spread."

The rest of us nodded.

"Are you bringing any friends or clients?" Brad asked the table.

"Yes, Doug Dezube," I said.

"No way," choked Barbara.

"Is that the client you guys call 'the Mole'?" asked Mark.

"Troll, troll," corrected Barbara. Turning to me, she asked, "You didn't really invite him, did you?"

Of course I didn't invite Dezube, but I thought I'd tweak her for inviting Brad and Mark to lunch. "I thought you liked Dezube."

"He gives me the creeps. He leers at me."

"Everyone leers at you," Mark said. Barbara looked pleased.

"Well, I invited a client, too," said Brad.

"I'm sure that will be exciting," Barbara said.

"It's Hugo, the Human Destructo," said Brad, ignoring her tone.

"Who is that?" I asked.

"A professional wrestler."

"What are you doing for him?" asked Barbara. "Writing a law review article?"

"Hugo is having serious troubles with the Internal Revenue Service," replied Brad. "He owes a substantial sum of money." He turned and looked directly at Barbara. "Are you interested in the details?"

"No way," she quickly assured him. "I'm a lobbyist. I don't need facts. It only confuses things. If you say our client is innocent, that is good enough for me."

"Provided he pays our bills," I added.

"Right. Provided he pays our bills," Barbara said, closing the subject. Then she turned back to me. "I can't believe you invited the Troll. I hope he bugs Jason all afternoon about his stupid Hand Towel Equity Act and you get fired."

"He won't bug him, because Jason will be too busy following you around," I said. Actually Jason would never do that, but I knew she would like hearing it.

After the food arrived, our discussion turned to matters about the firm. "I understand that the communications section is threatening to leave the firm again," Brad announced.

"Good, the hell with them," said Mark.

"I agree," I said. "All they ever do is cause trouble. They oppose all Jason's ideas to grow the firm. And who wants to listen to Ed Topp? He makes you tax guys seem interesting." Topp was the head of the communications section.

"You know," said Brad, "some of their objections make sense. I am not sure we can afford all this growth."

"Bullshit," said Barbara. "We want to be the biggest firm in the country, and we need growth to do it."

"How does growth hurt you?" I asked. "We get the same money we would get at any large firm. The only people who aren't making a fair market salary are the big dogs like Jason. If he wants to pay for the new offices and the telecommunications systems and all the trappings, that's his choice."

"Don't you think we should stop growing and consolidate the firm?" asked Brad.

"Yes, as soon as we are the biggest firm in the country. And as soon as we knock Charlie Nagle off the pages of the *Washington Post*. I only want to work at the premier firm in Washington, and I don't want you tax weenies to hold us back," Barbara said. "Richard, are you ready for another beer?"

Later, walking back to the office, I took off my coat jacket. Maybe it was the 100-degree heat, maybe it was the three beers, maybe it was Barbara, but I was hot and sticky. "Slow down," I whispered to Barbara. We both held back while Brad and Mark walked ahead.

"I started the scam," I told her.

"And?" She leaned into me.

"It's beginning to take off. It's brought in over $70,000 already." Needless to say, I didn't tell her that the expenses were far in excess of that amount.

"Really?" She stopped and looked at me. We were both wearing sunglasses, but I could see her eyes. They looked into mine. "Tell me about it."

"Well, we already have about four thousand members, and we are going out for more today. If that pans out, my scam will be a real hit."

"Your scam or our scam?"

"Well, my scam for now, but maybe our scam in the future."

She put her hand on my arm and started stroking it. "Can we have dinner sometime so you can explain it all to me?"

"Sure. I'd like that."

"I'd like that too," she said.

———

Back at my desk, I tried to cool down. The rest of me was hot, but my arm where Barbara had stroked me was scorching. I was determined to earn that dinner. I wrote out the second ad.

CITIZENS AGAINST TAX INJUSTICE

AMERICANS UNITE! The Internal Revenue Service is already making plans to TAKE AWAY YOUR HOUSE!!! Join CITIZENS AGAINST TAX INJUSTICE today or you could be the next to lose your home—or your life!!!

Recently, the bureaucrats at the IRS published a new ruling that could change the way you deduct the home mortgage interest from your taxes. Revenue Ruling 34-897 is just the beginning. First they rob you of the deduction, and then they rob you of your house.

The IRS says that only a few taxpayers will be affected each year. DON'T BELIEVE IT!!! It could be your house—or your liberty—they want next.

In the last few months, over 37,000 loyal Americans have joined CITIZENS AGAINST TAX INJUSTICE. What do they know that you don't?

What protection do they have that you don't??

JOIN TODAY. It may be your last chance. Join today and send in your check for $35. It is a small price to pay for your liberty.

I finished by adding the return form and mailing address. Finally, I included a drawing of the United States Capitol. I wrote out instructions to the people at *American Magazine*, directing them to superimpose the ad over the picture.

I buzzed Kathryn and asked her to take the ad to the mailroom and send it out. She read it quickly and looked up. "There is a mistake here. It says we have thirty seven thousand members. We only have thirty seven hundred."

"Details, details," I muttered, hoping she would drop the subject. She didn't.

"Was this intentional?"

"Not exactly, but what's a zero?"

"You can't send it out this way."

"Look, the ad comes out in three weeks. We may have thirty seven thousand members by then."

"No, we won't. This is misleading."

"All right. I'll change it." I made the correction on my computer and printed out the new version. "There. Can you take it down to the mailroom now and make sure it goes out?"

"Actually, do you mind taking it down? I just went by there, and they're doing a big job. They'll make me wait, but they will send it right out for a partner."

"Okay. No problem. Go ahead and leave for the weekend."

"Thanks. I'm going to the baseball game in Baltimore with Chip tonight."

"Chip. What happened to Craig?"

"I dumped him. I never met a bigger loser. Do you know he's been married three times? He has two children and never pays child support. He drinks and is violent."

"Yeah, sounds like a loser."

"I seem to have a knack for finding them."

"Well, run along with Chip." As she left the office, I took the original version down to the mailroom—the one that listed 37,000 members.

CHAPTER VI
HEARINGS AND HAPPENINGS

The Fourth of July was a beautiful day. For once that summer, the heat stayed low, the humidity was down, and the sky was blue. "Jason luck," Elizabeth and I said to each other when we got up that morning. No one on earth was luckier than Jason Douglas Johnson. Only Jason's wife would have a baby three weeks early on December 31, giving Jason another full tax exemption. Only Jason would lose a client just before it was indicted for mail fraud. Only Jason could find banks in Nebraska that continued to increase the firm's line of credit, even as our debts continued to mount. Jason scheduled a picnic in the middle of a summer heat wave, and we all put the date on our calendars knowing it would be a great day.

Johnson, Woods & Hart took up the top three floors of our building in Georgetown. Half of the top floor was a large patio with a terrific view down the Potomac River. Each Fourth of July, the National Park Service sponsors a festival, which concludes with fireworks over the Washington Monument. From the firm's building, the view of the show was magnificent. Every year the firm had a picnic to share in the national festivities, at least to a limited extent. While hundreds of thousands tourists crowded around the streets of Washington, waiting for the fireworks, the members of the firm were dined and entertained in our private cocoon.

The Fourth of July party was the only time all year that all members of the firm, from Jason Johnson down to the messengers, and all their families, were invited to the same function. It was a command performance for smart, ambitious young partners like me. We were to appear and be seen.

As we walked onto the roof, the number of different tables, each full of food, surprised even me. I thought I was immune to Jason's excesses, but even I was dazzled by the quantity and the variety. "My God," said Elizabeth.

"It's obscene," I agreed.

A band played in one corner. In another, a clown tied balloons for the children. There were three full bars and two more that just served wine and beer. At one table was typical picnic food, including hot dogs, hamburgers, potato salad, slaw, beans, and potato chips; at another, food designed to celebrate the firm's offices in Arizona, California, and Colorado: Mexican food, barbequed meats, and California citrus. Then one table was devoted to cheeses. Another to Chinese food. There was a salad bar, a table of just fruits, one where they were making sundaes, and one full of pasta dishes. A cook prepared little crab cakes and quiches at another table. The spread continued all over the patio.

We had no idea where to begin. As we stood there, getting our bearings, Jason came up.

When in his element, Jason was the undisputed master. He could command two hundred well-paid, egomaniac lawyers with his quiet, disciplined manners and calm voice. But he had little patience for the chaos that resulted from the presence of dozens of excited children. He gritted his teeth and tried to get through the day with a minimum of interaction. At these functions, he walked around simply asking everyone, "Did you get enough to eat?"

"Hello, Jason," I said. "Do you remember my wife, Elizabeth, and my children? This is Matthew, this is David, and this is Amy. Boys, can you say hello to Mr. Johnson?"

"Hi," said Matthew.

"Is there going to be a magician here?" asked David, quickly getting down to business.

"Yes," said Jason, looking serious. "He'll start in a little while."

"This is a beautiful picnic," said Elizabeth.

"Yes," I agreed, "you host quite a party, Jason."

"We host the party," Jason said. "It's your firm as much as mine." A wave of happiness swept over me.

"Is your wife here?" Elizabeth asked.

"Right over there," said Jason, pointing towards his latest life partner. "Enjoy yourself and be sure to get enough to eat." He smiled at us and drifted away.

We moved through the crowd, greeting various members of the firm and their families. Over in one corner, several children surrounded a huge man.

"Who is that?" asked Elizabeth.

"It must be the professional wrestler client of Brad's," I answered. "I wonder if the kids know who he is."

Both my sons noticed the activity. Their faces lit up and they both cried out, "Hugo the Human Destructo!" and ran over to him. When I caught up with them I heard Matthew asking Hugo to throw a table through a window. Hugo politely declined and gave each son an autographed photo. I shook Hugo's hand and welcomed him to the firm's picnic.

"I'm sorry about your problems with the Internal Revenue Service," I volunteered, "but you have the best tax attorneys available."

He looked sheepish as he mumbled his thanks. "I just want to stay out of jail," he said. "I'll do anything, absolutely anything, to avoid it."

I retrieved my sons and got them plates of food. Then I sat them down at a table with other children and went to get my own dinner. As I was standing in line to get a plate of ribs, Walker Dudley came up behind me. In social situations like this, Dudley fell back on his rural Southern roots. His accent got thicker, and he laughed and drank and ate a lot. His colorful shirt obscured any evidence of food spills. On his chest was a button with the letters *BOTH* on it.

"What's the button?" I asked.

He pointed at each initial and read, "Bottom of the heap."

"Okay, that follows. What does it stand for?"

"It's a campaign button for the reelection of President Clinton. Remember when you Republicans called him 'the bottom of the heap,' just before he whipped your guy and sent him packing? Well, this is now a badge of honor. All of us who supported the president from the beginning received these buttons. Reelection starts the day after the last vote is counted. I'm showing it off."

"Thinking about reelection is all you're going to do, because we are headed for a big win next time."

"With whom? Don't take on the big leagues with minor league

players," he said, smiling. This was a constant refrain between us. We didn't exactly get along, but we both knew it was better to have one of the firm's partners on each campaign so we were covered no matter who won. Having our candidate win the election was important to each of us personally, but not nearly as important as protecting the interests of the firm. We could rib each other on this subject with good humor.

Getting serious, I asked, "Are you really going to work on the campaign again?"

"Absolutely. In fact, I am on the Special Trade Advisors Committee."

"What does that committee do?"

"We help formulate the president's trade policies. We are also available to speak on behalf of the president's trade policies to the public."

"That should be interesting. There is a new round of trade talks coming up with the Chinese. Are you involved with that?"

"I'm up to my ass in it, do you know what I mean?"

I was going to ask him more about it, but Dudley was staring off across the roof, watching Barbara Lehman. Barbara wore a green sundress that set off her red hair, which glowed in the sunlight. She was surrounded by three young associates, all competing for her attention. She, however, was scanning the patio until she saw me. She smiled and winked at me, then turned back to her companions.

"God, that woman wants me," Dudley said, "do you know what I mean?"

"What are you talking about?" I asked.

"Barbara. You didn't see it, but she just sent me some body language. I haven't scored with her yet, but it's only a matter of time."

I knew that wink was meant for me. Didn't I have the scam? Or maybe he was right. He was a senior partner, and maybe she hadn't been around long enough to realize that he was full of shit. I decided then to schedule my dinner with her soon.

We had reached the head of the line, and Dudley turned his attention to the food. We loaded our plates, and I went to find my wife, who was holding the baby at the sushi table. Together we went back to sit with the boys. There, Elizabeth and I took turns holding Amy as we ate.

As it grew dark, the children got restless. We decided to leave early to avoid the holiday traffic that would flood the streets after the fireworks. So as the display started, we left and began our drive home. I told the boys to look back so they could see the fireworks over the city. For a while, they watched in silence. Then David said, "It looks like bombs exploding."

"Yeah, Dad, the bombs are hitting the picnic," agreed Matthew.

"That's just an optical illusion," I reassured them. "As we drive further away, the fireworks look like they are exploding over the picnic, but they aren't." I looked at Elizabeth, and whispered, "But maybe tonight there will be fireworks at home."

"Get a grip" was her response.

Matthew kept watching the lights. "No, Dad, the bombs are hitting the picnic."

I laughed. "Really, Matthew, there aren't any bombs hitting the firm. I promise."

Matthew didn't look convinced.

＝＝＝＝

Ten days later, the House Subcommittee on Health held its hearing on the Food and Drug Administration Improvements Act. The chairwoman of the subcommittee was Congresswoman Dunn, and Dr. Garrity was scheduled to be the featured nongovernmental witness.

There are two types of hearings in Congress—working hearings and show hearings. Working hearings are designed to elicit information from knowledgeable witnesses to improve legislation. Show hearings are aimed at getting on the network news.

This was to be a working hearing. The subcommittee would take testimony on a number of bills that day. The witness list was prepared with an eye towards gaining maximum information from a minimum number of witnesses. Statements would be short, and questions would be to the point. There was no need to play to the audience or the television cameras because the audience was small and there were no cameras. It would be a fast, business-like hearing.

Dr. Garrity had flown in. We had prepared his testimony in advance and spent the day before practicing his delivery in my office. We had also practiced answering sample questions. The doctor was very nervous but knowledgeable, and I hoped that his command of the facts would overshadow any delivery shortfalls.

Our bill was the first to be considered during the hearing. Congresswoman Dunn started the day's proceedings promptly at the announced time. She sat in the center of the members' table, which was on a platform at the front of the room. Behind her sat the staff of the subcommittee. On her right were the other subcommittee Democrats. On her left were the Republicans. She sat high in her chair and banged the gavel to commence.

"This hearing will come to order," she said as the room quieted. "Today we will review a number of bills before this committee. We will start with the Food and Drug Administration Improvements Act. This act is designed to give the FDA the authority to review and approve vaccines for some childhood diseases, including chicken pox." She was reading from a prepared text. Then she looked up and over to her fellow members on the subcommittee. She continued, but not following any text. Her voice was slower and more reflective.

"Frankly, I was surprised that the FDA did not have authority over this matter. I think it is unfortunate that the agency must wait until this legislation passes before it can test and approve a vaccine that could help hundreds of thousands of children avoid a disease. I wish that agencies that deal with human health were on the ball enough to alert this Congress, and this committee in particular, when there are gaps in the law that prevent them from carrying out their duties."

She looked back at her text. "Today we will hear from Dr. Neil Sims, an acting assistant administrator of the Food and Drug Administration, and Dr. William Garrity, a scientist at the University of Nevada at Reno, who has possibly developed a vaccine to prevent chicken pox. Dr. Garrity is accompanied by his counsel, Mr. Richard Brewster, a partner in the firm Johnson, Woods & Hart."

She looked up again. "Gentlemen, welcome." Then she looked at the other members of the subcommittee. "Before we begin, does anyone else have an opening statement?" The rest of the members demurred, and she turned her attention back to us.

Dr. Sims was first. All of us were situated at a table in front of the chairwoman, with microphones and name tags in front of us. At the end of the table sat the official recorder, who took down every word that was said. Later, a transcript of the hearing would be published.

Dr. Sims had five minutes to present the administration's position. He was a young man with a full beard and deep, expressive eyes. As he started to testify, I detected an Australian accent.

"Good morning, Madam Chairwoman. I am Dr. Neil Sims, acting assistant administrator for the Food and Drug Administration. I appreciate the opportunity to appear today, to present the views of the Clinton administration on the Food and Drug Improvements Act."

I held my breath. One could never predict how the administration would testify. Even if they liked the idea behind a bill, they might quibble over some detail, and we would have real trouble getting it passed.

"The administration has a history of support for children's programs. President Clinton is also personally committed to eradicating childhood diseases whenever possible. No child in the United States should suffer from a disease if it is preventable. Therefore, the administration strongly supports the Food and Drug Administration Improvements Act . . ."

I let out my breath, poked Dr. Garrity, and whispered, "Yes!" Hearing no response, I looked into the doctor's face, which was frozen, staring at the chairwoman. "Doctor, are you all right?" I asked. He nodded, but his eyes remained riveted to the chairwoman. I began to worry about my star witness.

Dr. Sims continued with his testimony. "However, we encourage the committee to give the FDA more resources to administer the law if it passes. Last year, our workload increased by eight percent, but our budget was held steady. Important tasks cannot be completed on a timely basis. We suggest that the law be amended to include an allocation of more money and people. In this way, we can fully perform these important new responsibilities.

"Thank you for your time. I'm happy to answer any questions you may have."

Congresswoman Dunn leaned forward and glared down at Dr. Sims. "Do you mean to tell me, Doctor, that the FDA will not enforce this law unless we give you more money?"

Dr. Sims squirmed in his seat. It was obvious to me that it was not his idea to ask for any money. Probably some unknown budget officer added this paragraph to the testimony, and now Dr. Sims was going to feel the wrath of the congresswoman.

"Absolutely not, Madam Chairwoman. We will fully comply with the direction of the Congress. We are merely suggesting that we need additional resources to carry out all our responsibilities."

"Let me see here," said the congresswoman, reaching around and taking a piece of paper from one of her staff assistants sitting behind her. "I understand that last year your agency spent over $45 million for travel, including one senior management retreat to Hawaii in January. Do you think you could cut that back by, say, ten percent and find the money to save millions of American children from getting a serious disease?"

A gleam appeared in Dr. Sims's eye, and I saw the hint of a smile. "I totally agree, Madam Chairwoman. In fact, I think we can survive a cut in our travel budget of twenty percent."

The congresswoman looked surprised. Government employees were not expected to offer up budget cuts under any circumstances. Obviously, Dr. Sims was new to his job. He wouldn't last very long.

"In fact, I suggest that you review our construction budget to find additional savings," he volunteered. *This guy clearly has a death wish*, I thought. He didn't take his government job too seriously. I liked him. He would be perfect for my sister. His answers also disarmed the congresswoman. She had been prepared to grill him about the spending habits of the FDA, but here was a witness offering more examples of waste than even she knew about. She was so surprised that she let him off the hook.

"Thank you, Doctor. Are there any other questions from the members of the subcommittee?" She looked both ways. No one moved. Then she turned back and looked directly at Dr. Garrity. "The next witness is Dr. William Garrity. Dr. Garrity is a biomedical researcher at the University of Nevada, Reno. He may have discovered a vaccine that prevents chicken pox in young children. Thank you for being here today, Doctor. Please proceed."

Dr. Garrity sat there and stared at the chairwoman. The room was silent, and the members, staff, and audience waited for the doctor to begin. The seconds passed.

"Go ahead, Doctor," I whispered. "Just stick to your text, like we practiced."

Dr. Garrity didn't move.

"We are looking forward to hearing from you, Doctor," the

congresswoman said encouragingly. Then she gave him her sweetest smile.

He continued to stare. "Doctor, get on with it," I hissed.

"Go ahead," said Dr. Sims. "You can do it."

The chairwoman looked at me. "Counsel, is there a problem?"

"Just one moment, Madam Chairwoman," I said. I covered the microphone and whispered to Garrity. "Doctor, you have spent years developing the vaccine. This is your only chance to get the government approvals you must have. The congresswoman won't bite your head off. Defer any questions to me. I live to be yelled at if necessary. But she won't yell. We are on the right side of this issue. Just take a deep breath and read your script."

"Do you want me to stick my foot into my mouth again?" asked Dr. Sims. Despite the tension, I had to stifle a giggle.

Suddenly, Dr. Garrity looked up. His eyes focused, and he started reading his testimony: "Madam Chairwoman and members of the committee, thank you for the opportunity to appear before you today . . ."

The entire testimony was read as one incredibly long run-on sentence. I don't believe I saw the doctor breathe. Yet I was afraid that if I stopped him, or asked him to slow down, he would freeze up again. Instead, I let the fiasco continue. The members of the subcommittee stared in disbelief, but they did listen. At last, he completed his remarks and looked up at them. The room was silent again.

The chairwoman recovered first. "Thank you, Doctor. I have one question only. Does your vaccine use the new gene splicing technology?"

The doctor froze up again. I turned to him and repeated the question. "No," he mumbled. I turned around and said into the microphone, "Madam Chairwoman, the doctor tells me that although he has done extensive work with gene splicing and that it is a promising technology, he did not use it in the creation of this vaccine."

"The doctor told you all that, Counselor?" the congresswoman asked innocently. "Thank you." She looked at the other members of the committee. "Are there any other questions for the doctor?"

"Yes," came the answer from one of the junior members of the committee. He had been talking to his aide but now turned back to the hearing. He asked, "Does this vaccine use the new gene splicing technology?"

Dr. Garrity looked confused. He turned to me and whispered, "They just asked me that question!"

I whispered back, "I know, Doctor, and we'll answer it again."

"I hope you are not changing your answer, Counselor," said Congresswoman Dunn with a slight smile.

"Not at all, Madam Chairwoman." I turned to the questioner. "Congressman, that is a good question. The vaccine does not involve gene splicing technology."

"Any further questions?" asked the chairwoman. "If not, the witnesses may be excused. The committee will recess for five minutes to allow the next panel to take its place." She banged down her gavel. The room erupted into noise as everyone stood and started moving. At that moment, Jason walked in. He approached the chairwoman, and they embraced warmly. Seeing Garrity and me standing by the witness table, he waved us over and reintroduced the doctor to the congresswoman.

"How did he do?" Jason asked.

"Excellent," said the congresswoman. "We were particularly impressed by his answers to the questions."

"Great, great," said Jason. Turning to us, he asked, "Isn't this the best chairwoman in the Congress?"

The doctor mumbled something unintelligible.

I asked, "Jason, what brings you up here?"

"I always like to check on our clients when they are testifying before a congressional committee," he said. That was total bullshit, and I knew it. Every day the firm had people before Congress, and Jason never came. There had to be another angle.

"Over here," said a voice. I turned and saw a photographer from the *Washington Post*. The congresswoman and Jason started talking to each other again. They positioned Dr. Garrity between them. Fully realizing what was happening, I backed away and got out of the picture. The flashes started. Jason and the congresswoman then gave an interview to a reporter about the importance of the bill and about Garrity's work. At one point, I heard Jason explain that he was sure that the vaccine was made, in part, with the new gene splicing technology. The doctor just stood there nodding.

Standing about six feet away, also taking in the show, was Dr. Sims.

I moved over to him and shook his hand.

"Good job, Doctor. I know that you had to ask for more money, but I liked how you finessed the issue."

"Oh, thank you. I'll probably get into trouble over my answers, so I think I'll go have lunch before I go back to the office.. Do you want to join me?"

"I'd like to, but I'd better stay with my client. I'll call you sometime, if that's all right. Are you in the section that will review the chicken pox vaccine?"

"No. I'm in the seafood safety section. I'm a marine biologist."

"Why did they send you up to testify on a children's vaccine?"

"They said I needed the experience."

"I see. After today, I probably won't see you up here testifying again, Doctor."

"Probably not. So I will have a cold beer with my lunch. Join me if you change your mind. Nice meeting you."

He ambled out of the hearing room. I turned back and watched the ongoing press briefing. Jason was going on and on about the new vaccine. He invited three science reporters to have lunch with the doctor and him to get more quotes. Jason had clearly sized up the doctor and realized that Garrity would offer no competition with the press. He stood dazzled between the congresswoman and Jason as the flashes continued blazing. I was forgotten. I turned and ran out of the room after Dr. Sims.

CHAPTER VII
BIG MO

The response to the second ad was much better than the first. Two weeks after the ad ran, over 26,000 people joined the Citizens Against Tax Injustice. Unfortunately, a large number did not send along checks with their applications. I decided to keep everyone on the rolls of the organization, in hopes that I could find another way to convince the nonpaying members to eventually send along some money.

The second ad had taught me an important lesson. It was mildly effective to threaten someone in general. It was far more effective to raise a specific threat—in this case, the threat to their homes. Obviously Revenue Ruling 34-897 was going to be one of the keys to the success of CATI. I would use it as my sword against the IRS and other evils of the world. I had even taught my children how bad the ruling was. Now when they wanted to insult each other they called out, "You are Revenue Ruling 34-897!"

No one seemed to notice that I had increased the membership dues. Now that CATI was protecting their homes from Revenue Ruling 34-897, even $35 for a membership seemed cheap. Kathryn pointed out to me that over two hundred people had signed up at $20 and signed up again at $35. Of course, thousands of others had not sent in a dime. The American public!

I did hit a jackpot of an idea with my request for members to write in with their own horror stories. I received a flood of letters detailing stories of abuse at the hands of the IRS. Some were clearly fabricated. But there were enough to reassure me that I had hit on something big.

Unfortunately, an analysis of the financial situation still left a lot to be desired. After paying all the actual expenses, there was only $70,000 in the organization's bank account. Actually, there should have been even less, but I had decided not to pay the firm back the original $60,000 I borrowed to pay for the first ad.

The day after the health subcommittee hearing, the *Washington Post* ran a series of articles about problems at the FDA. One feature story spoke about the hearing and the need for legislation to allow the FDA to review and approve children's vaccines. There were two pictures of Jason, Congresswoman Dunn, and Dr. Garrity. The doctor was described as a champion of children. Jason was described as the mastermind of legislative strategy on behalf of worthy causes for nonprofit clients. Congresswoman Dunn was described as the conscience of the House. Even Sims was described as the voice of reason at the FDA, putting service to children ahead of travel and construction. He didn't get fired. He was promoted. All in all, I figured that it was worth $60,000 in publicity for the firm. In fact, I figured that Jason owed me. He wanted his name in the paper, and I had delivered.

But although the financial situation hadn't improved yet, I felt I had a good base of action. There were members from every state, and every congressional district. The members seemed committed from the tone of their letters. They hated the IRS in particular, and the government in general. They came from all ages, income groups, and political parties. The members were a broad cross section of America. I just wished they had generated more money.

I was tired of waiting for the financial rewards. And so, then and there, I took another step to a place of no return. To justify my efforts, I decided to pay myself. I couldn't use the funds in the bank, as I would need them for future real expenses. So I just made up a different source. I directed Kathryn to prepare a bill for the firm's services to CATI for $50,000 and to report it to the firm's accounting department. Of course, there was no actual money to pay the bill, but I fully intended to pay it out of future membership dues.

The response was immediate. Within two hours, I received a call from Jason to congratulate me on sending out such a big bill. He promised me that it would be remembered at bonus time.

"Of course, I need to collect the money, Jason," I said, in an attempt to gain some future wiggle room. "Sometimes it's hard to get every dollar in the door."

Jason would have none of that. "I have every confidence in you," he assured me. "I consider it money in the bank." He then went on to ask if CATI was completely current in its account or if it owed the firm more money. I quickly assured him that CATI didn't owe us any additional money.

"Too bad," he said. "It would have been nice to count on a bigger payment from them."

"You can count on more payments, Jason, but after we do some more work."

"That will take some time, won't it?"

"Of course. What are you driving at?"

"Nothing. It's just that if the communications lawyers leave the firm, we may have a slight cash flow problem for a month or two. Nothing serious and nothing long term."

"But, Jason, Brad told me that you told the attorneys in the tax section that if the communications section left, it would help our cash flow."

"In the long run it will," he reassured me, "but I want to get over the next few months. How are your other clients? Have they all paid?"

"All except Dr. Garrity. Remember, he is our famous charitable case."

"Don't spend any time on him. Focus on the paying clients. Let's make it a great month and collect everything we are owed."

"You told the *Washington Post* you wouldn't rest until the doctor gets his bill through Congress."

"Who believes the *Washington Post*? Keep up the good work." He hung up before I could reply.

I received more calls throughout the day from other senior partners in the firm. First, Ed Topp, the head of the communications section, called me. He told me that he had always followed my progress in the firm with interest. He was pleased that I was becoming such a big producer. He encouraged me to visit with him at any time to discuss the firm's future. I asked him if he intended to leave the firm along with his whole section. He denied it. "I threaten every once in a while just to get attention. I am committed to this firm. Any disagreements I have regarding growth or with Jason are no reflection on my basic loyalty. We are all in this together. Let's discuss the subject anytime."

Twenty minutes later, John Horn, the head of the firm's litigation section, called me from the firm's new plane. He was on his way to Boston where he was meeting a client.

"Brewster, congratulations on the big bill. I've always known you would be a star in the firm. Keep up the good work."

"Thank you, John. I'm impressed that you know and pleased that you called."

"I follow the firm's business quite closely. Have you heard from Jason yet?"

"Yes, about an hour ago. Also Ed Topp called me."

"That ass. What did he want?"

"Well, he told me he wasn't leaving the firm."

"Don't believe him. He will leave and wants you to go with him. He's talking to all the big producers. He is not committed to the firm like the rest of us. He is a constant thorn in Jason's side."

"He said that he's been watching my progress for a long time."

"That bullshitter. I doubt he knew your name until one of his boys pointed out that you sent out a big bill. Stick with Jason. Anytime you want to discuss this matter with me, just come up to my office." He hung up.

The congratulatory calls continued all day. I even got a call from the head of the firm's office in South Dakota, a two-man office that handled grain cases. Obviously, all the bulls in the firm were watching the firm's finances. I had prepared the bill to justify the time spent on the scam, with the full intent of getting paid later. But in the meantime, I had created expectations throughout the firm I was not sure I could meet. It was nice to receive all the attention from the senior partners, but what would they do to me if I failed to deliver?

The only section head who ignored me was Walker Dudley, my own leader. Late in the day, he stuck his head in my door and said, "That was our tax client we billed today, wasn't it?"

"The firm billed the Citizens Against Tax Injustice today."

"Yeah, right, our new client. I sure like getting the first bill out the door, you know what I mean? Just be sure to collect every dime before bonus time." And he was off. I was sure he couldn't believe his good fortune. Here was a big client he'd gotten a piece of that had all the potential to be a huge moneymaker. And he hadn't done any work for them. I was steamed, and acted without thinking, putting both me and the firm deeper in the hole.

I called Jason. His secretary—in another sign of my rising status in the firm—put me right through to him. "Jason, about our call earlier today," I rushed out. "I called Warren Ford from the Citizens Against Tax Injustice and asked him to forward fund our next month's bill. He agreed to pay us another $25,000. The total bill should now read $75,000."

"That's great, just great, just great work," Jason said enthusiastically.

"But, Jason, there is just one problem," I went on quickly. "You know that Walker Dudley is on the account with me even though I landed it. Well, now I understand that Warren thinks Walker is not doing a good job. I have no idea what happened between the two of them, but there's bad blood. I think if we keep Walker as one of the account managers, we may lose the client. And, Jason, it looks like a big one."

Jason heard what I said. More importantly, he understood the deeper meaning. He didn't miss a beat. "You just let me handle that. Tell the client you are the exclusive partner in charge of his account. I'll deal with Walker when the time is right. Will that keep him happy?"

"I am sure it will."

He asked the real question. "Will it keep you happy?"

"Yes. By the way, Warren Ford would like to meet you." I finished the job of cutting Walker off. If it became known that Jason was personally involved with my client, no one would mess with me. "Could you spare a few minutes the next time he's in town?"

"Sure. Have I already met him? Is he the tall man with a beard?"

"No. He is a short Black man with a mustache."

"Then I haven't met him. I'll be happy to do so for such a big client. Let me know the next time he is in town."

"Thanks, Jason."

"Thank you, Richard. One last thing. The bank holding our line of credit may want to know how likely it is that we will get paid by your client. Can I tell the bank the money will definitely come in?"

"If you had met Warren Ford, you would know that his word is his bond. As long as he is a living, breathing person, he will guarantee our payment."

"That's just what I expected you to say. I am glad the firm can count on you."

"Anytime, Jason."

———

With firm politics out of the way, I returned to work on CATI. I decided to create a four-page newsletter that I would send out to all the members periodically. I would put a story on the first page, reprint letters on pages two and three, and devise a fundraising appeal for the last page. The newsletter would be printed on glossy paper and include lots of pictures—expensive to prepare, but I was sure it would be worth it.

With the general outline clear in my mind, I began to work on the first issue. For page one, I drafted the cover story. It was about Revenue Ruling 34-897. Having effectively scared thousands of people to join CATI, it was still my best issue. I would continue to ride it.

I had Kathryn get me a copy of the law-review article that Mark Waterman and Brad Charness had written about the ruling. It was very dry, and I had a difficult time understanding all the tax jargon. However, I understood that each year there were a limited number of cases where taxpayers swapped their houses in complicated land deals. When this happened, the taxpayer had to make a determination to see if the deal was tax-free. To make this determination, there had to be a review of the value of the properties involved. Often the properties had changed in value due to inflation or other factors. Since there was no sale of the properties in the open market, it was often difficult to determine their value. Thus the IRS, in response to a few inquiries, had issued Revenue Ruling 34-897, which created a way to value the properties. It was very complicated and obscure. Who had the money to swap multiple properties? I was sure that attorneys and accountants handled every case. There was no way Revenue Ruling 34-897 would affect a single member of CATI.

Yet the ruling—or, more accurately, my description that the ruling would lead to the eventual end of the tax deduction of mortgages— had caused tens of thousands of Americans to join CATI. Their letters reinforced this impression.

I always expected the IRS to do something slimy like this, wrote one man. *I just never expected that they would start with Revenue Ruling 34-897. Thank you for identifying the danger.* There were many more along the same lines. Who was I to deny the will of the members of CATI? If they were against Revenue Ruling 34-897, so was I. Or, at least, so was Warren Ford, the executive director. I was just the lobbyist for the organization.

I started writing the lead article. Across the top of the page, I wrote, *Stop Revenue Ruling 34-897!!!!!* Underneath I wrote,

The excesses of the Internal Revenue Service must be stopped!!! At risk is your home. Next may be your liberty. The IRS has released Revenue Ruling 34-897. The evil bureaucrats claim it is a technical ruling only. Don't believe it. It is the first step towards taking away the mortgage deduction! The next step is to take away your house. The bureaucrats at the IRS will not be happy as long as any American taxpayer strives to own his own home! Their greed is unstoppable.

The Internal Revenue Service says Revenue Ruling 34-897 will only affect a few taxpayers a year. Don't believe it! They can't really know how many people will be hurt. No one knows!! Do you own a home? You may be next!!

The IRS won't ask Congress to remove the mortgage deduction from the tax code. There are still a few courageous Americans in the Congress who are not afraid to stand up to the bureaucrats. They are few in number and they are dwindling, but the IRS won't take them on directly. Instead the IRS sneaks around Congress with Revenue Ruling 34-897. What will they do next?

It is not too late to stop them. STOP REVENUE RULING 34-897!!! Write your senators. Write your representatives. Tell them it is time to stand up to the bureaucrats at the IRS. Tell them to repeal Revenue Ruling 34-897. Their congressional addresses are on page 4 of this newsletter. Write them today. Before it is too late!!!!!

That should get them fired up, I thought. *Let's just see how powerful CATI really is.*

Next I started reading through the mail. After about twenty minutes, I found a perfect letter:

Dear Warren Ford,

I am a medical technician at a hospital in Philadelphia. Recently a Quaker hospital company located in Camden, New Jersey, purchased us. The hospital serves the poorest communities in the Philadelphia area. There are lots of uninsured patients that we treat every day. The hospital barely makes its payroll every two weeks.

When the new owners came in, they discovered the old owners had not kept current on their employees' Social Security tax payments. The Internal Revenue Service seized the hospital's bank accounts and grabbed the payments due to the hospital from Medicaid and Medicare. There is no money left to make the next payroll. The new owners are trying to find other sources of funding, but it is unclear it they will succeed. If they don't, the hospital will close. People will not get the medical treatment they need. Hundreds of employees will be out of work. Is this what the IRS wants?

Please help in any way you can. I hope the CITIZENS AGAINST TAX INJUSTICE will stop this kind of arbitrary action by the IRS.

I put the letter on page two. I found another letter about an IRS agent who had seized the wrong bank account. That went on page three. Then on page four, I put the addresses of senators and representatives. I also asked for money. I asked members to send in their contributions to defeat Revenue Ruling 34-897. I told them we would create a special task force to stop the ruling. I told them I hoped I could count on them.

I finished by writing, *Yours in Freedom*, and signed Warren Ford's name on the last page. I wrote out instructions on how the newsletter should be laid out and put them on Kathryn's desk. It was well past quitting time, and the office was empty. Tomorrow, she would take the text to the printers and give them instructions. In two days, the first newsletter would be printed, addressed, and mailed. All together the newsletter would cost $52,000, leaving only $18,000 in the bank.

———

The next morning, I was in my office reading more letters from CATI members when there was a knock on my door. I looked up and saw Emilio.

"Did you forget me?" he asked.

"Oh my God, I did. I'm sorry, Emilio."

"I waited at the club for twenty minutes, then figured that you had more important things to do."

"I'm sorry. I totally forgot. I was wrapped up in my new trade association." I waved my hand over the mounds of letters on my desk. Emilio stopped looking hurt and approached my desk. He perused the letters and picked one up to read. "Are all these letters about your tax group?" he asked.

"Yes," I said with pride.

"How many do you have?"

"Over twenty-six thousand at the last count, with more coming in every day."

"You must be doing something very important."

"Maybe. It seems to be a good idea which has taken off."

"What is Revenue Ruling 34-897?" he asked, reading the citation off a letter.

"It's an obscure IRS ruling that deals with the valuation of property."

"It sure has people upset."

"It's a beautiful thing, isn't it?" I asked. He looked puzzled. "We needed an issue to get everyone interested," I explained. "People only join organizations if it offers them something they want or protects them from something they fear. Revenue Ruling 34-897 has everyone scared."

"Will it hurt anyone?"

"The ruling? Probably not, but if the people fear it, it is our job to kill it."

He looked down at the floor. "Is the group making money?"

"Some. Not enough. But every time the public gets stirred up, they pay more." He continued to avoid my eyes. I hated to disappoint him. "Look, Emilio, it's a bad ruling and needs to be eliminated."

"Even if it doesn't hurt anybody?"

"Even if it doesn't hurt anybody."

"Who is Warren Ford?" he asked, changing the subject.

"The executive director."

"Is he around here? Have I met him?"

I decided to level with him. He was my confidant. "He's right here."

"Where?"

"Right here." I pointed to myself. "Emilio, he doesn't exist. He is the means to an end. He helps me create a successful organization that can do some good. Not just fighting Revenue Ruling 34-897, but real things. Trust me, Emilio, this will all work out fine. Besides, CATI will help me afford to open a health club."

"I was afraid that you had dropped the idea."

"Not at all, not at all. Where are we on that?"

"I had hoped we could look at a townhouse I found after we worked out today. It was going to be a surprise. It's a great location for a club."

We spent the next hour looking at the location he had picked out. It wasn't very large but would probably do the job. We would start small. Emilio, as the trainer, would stay on the premises all day while I did the legal work and the accounting in the beginning. As we grew, we would add staff.

At first, we would only have minimal equipment and locker rooms and provide only running and weight-lifting services. As the membership grew, we would move to a bigger location, and add more services. We had it all worked out. The initial investment would be $10,000, all future investments to come from the profits. It was a conservative plan.

Emilio had thrown himself into the project with enthusiasm. He spent days looking for the location, he told me. He had carefully drawn up a list of equipment we needed, always trying to keep the costs down. He knew all I had was my $10,000 bonus check. I knew he didn't have two nickels. But with a little wisdom, careful planning, and hard work, the health club would be a success.

He introduced me to the rental agent. We again walked all through the rooms as Emilio explained where he would put everything. It was an old townhouse but clean and well built. It looked perfect for our purposes. Emilio told me he had filled out the necessary application forms. If approved, we could take possession of the house in a few weeks.

We left and found a sandwich shop for lunch. As I sat down, I noticed him bowing his head in prayer. When he was done, I told him, "I like the house. It looks fine for our needs. I am confident we will need more space in time, but that's a good starting place. Let's stay conservative."

He nodded, grinning. "Cool beans."

"What's next?"

"We should order the equipment."

"Good. Let's look at the equipment list again."

He handed it to me, telling me, "I called a dozen companies to get the best prices. I think this place in Texas is the best."

"You have certainly done your part, Emilio."

"I want this to be the best health club in Washington. I want to show you I am the best partner you ever had. No one ever took a chance on me before. I'll never forget it."

"I know. I believe you."

"I want to do everything I can to show you how much I appreciate your trust."

"Just make the club a success, and that's thanks enough."

"Cool beans."

When we got back to the office, I gave Emilio two checks. The first was $1,500 for the first month's rent of the townhouse. The second was $8,500 for the equipment. I was broke but the proud owner of a health club. Maybe I'd become a famous health club king. If I ever got tired of lobbying for the CATI and the Hand Towel Equity Act, at least I could hand out towels at my health club.

could run, and I could hide, but eventually I would have to see Doug Dezube again. Later that week, he arrived from Atlanta. He had a business meeting in Denver that night but decided to spend the morning with me. Lucky me.

Things had gone from bad to worse for the Hand Towel Equity Act. The administration came out solidly against the bill, and the little support it had in Congress evaporated. Meanwhile, the opposition continued to mount. The nation's retailers had decided they would make an example of the bill. They were tired of paying the increased tariffs on products sold in their stores. Sales leaders started flying to Washington to meet with key senators and members of Congress. They had one message: kill the Hand Towel Equity Act.

Then it got worse. Most of the countries that made hand towels for export to the United States were very poor. Their ambassadors protested against the act to the State Department and the White House. Even the United Nations passed a resolution calling for worldwide free trade in hand towels. The American ambassador to the United Nations voted in favor of the resolution.

Just when I thought the prospects for the Hand Towel Equity Act could not sink any lower, the prime minister of Bangladesh visited the United States. After meeting with President Clinton, the prime minister met with the press. There he announced to the world that the US and Bangladesh would cooperate on a new program to help the development of his country. Included in the program was the promise to allow the continued free import of hand towels made in Bangladesh into the United States. "We are a very poor country," the prime minister said on the television. "We need to develop exports to improve our economy. Your president shares our concerns."

In ten minutes, Dezube was on the phone. "Poverty is no excuse for thievery!" he yelled. "The government of Bangladesh is subsidizing the production of those hand towels! This violates all trade principles. I'm coming to Washington, and you better have a plan to stop this bullshit."

So there I was, sitting across from a highly agitated client with his hair standing straight up in the air. Dezube was a man who would get upset when a cab driver overcharged him twenty cents. At this point, he felt the entire world was against him. For once, he was right. He started pacing rapidly across the room.

"Who can we meet?"

"I'm working on that right now, Doug."

"Who let the president agree to the free import of hand towels? He's done some stupid things before, but this is the dumbest. He is a one-termer, no doubt about it. He has no political savvy, and he has the worst staff of any president in the twentieth century."

"Including all the crooks in the Harding administration?" I couldn't help goading him.

"Yes!" he thundered. "They were all a bunch of thieves, but at least they knew what they were doing. These sons of bitches are a disaster. Don't they remember who their friends are?"

"You and your association supported the Republicans last election," I pointed out. "They lost."

"You're goddamn right we supported the Republicans. And they wouldn't have created this mess. Who are we going to see?"

"I'm working on that now. Go get a cup of coffee." *As if you need coffee*, I thought. As he stamped down the hall, I quickly started calling congressional staff to arrange some meetings. I had struck out on every call I made the previous day, and I wasn't doing much better now. The first three calls were dry holes. I was getting desperate, and Dezube would be back any minute, so I pulled out all the stops and called my friend Russ Ratto.

"Russ, I need a favor," I started out. "Can I bring Doug Dezube up to see you?"

"Not today, Richard. I am very busy, and the meeting would be waste of time."

"I realize the meeting would be a waste of time, but would you do it for me?" I pleaded.

"Not today."

I heard Dezube coming down the hall and panicked. Without thinking, I spoke quickly into the phone. "Russ, remember that trip to Salt Lake, when you ended up in the wrong hotel room with the wrong bimbo and I covered for you with your wife? Well, now you can repay me. I want you to go to lunch with Doug Dezube and me, and I want you to be nice to him. George Washington is closer to life than his Hand Towel Equity Act. He needs some sympathy and someone to talk to besides me."

The line was silent for a minute. He didn't think I'd ever mention Salt Lake. But I was in a corner. Finally, he said, "If I go to lunch with you, you'll never mention Salt Lake again. Never."

"Never, never, never," I agreed.

"My choice of restaurant?"

"Anywhere you want to go. I'll fly you to Paris if you want."

"The Potomac Pub."

"Russ, you know we can't get in there on such short notice. Pick anywhere else."

"The pub or forget it."

"All right. Meet us there at noon."

I knew that I couldn't get a reservation. I had no Salt Lake incident I could hold over the owner. But I also knew that every day the pub saved a few tables for walk-in traffic. They were usually gone by 11:15. I called Kathryn into my office and asked her to take two of her friends and go have an early lunch at the Potomac. She had to be there by 11 and be done by noon. We would squeeze into the table before anyone noticed. I gave her a firm credit card. Another expense on the old firm.

I could hear Dezube raving outside my office. Apparently, the more he thought about his situation, the madder he got at the White House staff. He had decided to start an effort to fire the president's chief of staff. Having cornered two young summer associates, he was attempting to browbeat them into picketing the White House. I let him go on for a minute so the budding attorneys could get the full flavor of client relations. Then I called him down to my office.

"I've got great news. Russ Ratto, the legislative assistant to

Congressman Conlin, wants to have lunch with you to discuss your bill. He insisted we meet."

"I met the man. He seems young. Is he powerful?"

"Are you kidding? In Congress they call him Tropicana because he has so much juice. He is the main man, the boss with the hot sauce . . ." Dezube did not look amused. I slowed down and said seriously, "He is the key staff member for the chairman of the House Ways and Means Committee. The Hand Towel Equity Act is currently before that committee. With his help, we may get the bill on the House floor. Without his help, we don't stand a chance."

"Can he help us get the White House chief of staff fired?"

"No, but that's not what you really want. What you really want is to get your bill passed. Keep your focus on the important things."

"Where are we in the Senate?"

"Well, Senator Kelly has already introduced the bill in the Senate. I assume he will push hard for any bill he introduced." That was a lie and I knew it. The senator had just introduced his 485th bill. Not one was going anywhere. In fact, the senator's attention span on any legislation seemed to last about forty-eight hours.

———

The Potomac Pub was as busy as ever. We retrieved our table, and as we waited until Russ Ratto joined us, I noticed Barbara Lehman and Walker Dudley standing in a very long line to get a table. With a knot in my gut, I waved them over and asked them to join us. I had two reasons for that. First, I wanted their help with Dezube. Second, I couldn't stand the thought of the two of them eating alone together. I needed to make my move with Barbara before something happened between them. I did not want her showing up at work with stains on her clothes.

I could see the debate going on in their minds. Was it worse to wait another forty minutes for a table or to join Dezube and me for lunch? Dudley looked particularly unhappy about the choice, as I am sure he didn't want to share Barbara with anyone else. But when I told them Ratto would be joining us, Barbara insisted that they sit down. Barbara had worked with Russ, and they were close friends.

As they got seated, Ratto arrived. He hadn't even gotten the entire way into his seat when Dezube launched into him. "Is your boss going to demand the resignation of the White House chief of staff, or is he going to wimp out on us?"

"What are you talking about?" asked Ratto, already looking around to leave.

"Russ, Doug is convinced that the White House staff is badly advising the president about the Hand Towel Equity Act," I said. "Do you think that the president has really focused on the issue? Is there hope that there may be another review of the bill?"

"I think it's the First Lady," snapped Dezube. "Someone should tell that bitch to keep out of international affairs."

Dudley responded. "I don't think the First Lady is your problem. I think she would be quite supportive of your position if she knew about it, you know what I mean?"

"Then why haven't you talked to her yet? Aren't you one of the firm's big Democrats? When can we see her?"

Dudley's mouth snapped shut.

Barbara chimed in. "It seems to me that the real key is the Congress. I don't think firing the White House staff, or dumping on the First Lady, is the answer."

"Well, where is the Congress?" Dezube turned on Barbara. "Don't they know this is an important issue? I am doing their work for them."

I bounced back in. "Congress is working on the bill. Don't we have a senator on it?"

"Yeah, Senator Kelly," Dezube agreed. "He is doing a great job. I just wish the rest of Congress was half as good."

"Amen," the rest of us said simultaneously. Russ rolled his eyes. Barbara suppressed a laugh. Dezube was quiet. It was time to distract him before he went off again. Apparently, Barbara had the same idea.

"Did you read the paper today?" she asked, looking at me with a smile. "There was a story about a woman who claimed she was raped by her husband. She waited until he was asleep and cut off his penis with a knife."

The four men at the table flinched. *God*, I thought, *only Barbara would bring that up*. But it seemed to work, as Dezube's eyes widened.

Russ joined in. "I saw that story. The wife left the house with his member then threw it out of her car. Later she called the police and told them where to find it."

"What happened next?" asked Dezube with genuine interest.

Dudley answered, "They sewed it back on in a nine-hour operation. Everything appears to work, except how do you test it, you know what I mean?"

"Are you pulling my leg?" asked Dezube.

"Absolutely not," I assured him. "It was in the paper today."

"Do you know the man?"

"The paper didn't list the name, but I heard it was Charlie Nagle," I said. We all laughed. "No way it was Jason. It would take a chainsaw to get his penis off. And a truck to haul it away." As I said those last remarks, Dudley stopped laughing and frowned at me. I knew he hated any mention of Jason's prowess.

Dezube turned serious. He glanced at all of us and started slowly. "I know that the hand towel industry is less than one-tenth of one percent of the gross national product. I know that it could disappear tomorrow and no one would notice. I even know that the production of hand towels is much more important to the economy of Bangladesh than to the economy of the United States. But it is a US industry, and it does employ American workers. Those people have the right to know that someone cares about their livelihood.

"Maybe it is a small issue in Washington. Maybe it is far more important for the US government to police the world and run the economy. In fact, it is. But to the people I represent, these are their jobs and their economic security. We may not win, but shouldn't we try for them?"

The table was silent. Everyone, especially me, was amazed by Dezube's speech. It was rational, and it made sense. It was disconcerting.

Russ reacted first. "You know, I could ask Congressman Conlin to write a letter to the president. We could lay out the best case as to why we need the Hand Towel Equity Act. We could ask the president to review his policies, and perhaps, to change them."

Not to be outdone, Dudley added, "I'm on the president's private-sector task force on trade. There are some key negotiations with China coming up. I'll see that hand towels are on the list of items to discuss."

I joined in. "After we get a response from the administration to Congressman Conlin's letter, I'll lay out a legislative strategy with Senator Kelly to push the bill through the Senate later this year."

Barbara closed the subject. "And I won't mention the severed penis again."

———————

Leaving the Potomac, Dezube headed to the airport. I asked Russ what he was doing that afternoon. "I'm heading back to the office. By the way, one of the bills on the floor this afternoon is your chicken pox vaccine bill. They scheduled to bring it up today. Do you want to ride to the Capitol with me?"

I had planned to watch the debate on TV, but I welcomed the opportunity to spend another minute with Russ. I hoped he wasn't angry at me for mentioning Salt Lake. We shared a cab up to the Capitol. On the way, I thanked him over and over for joining us for lunch. "I know I owe you," I said, "but I have a tip for you that will make us even. Get your boss to publicly oppose Revenue Ruling 34-897."

"We already got two letters about that," he replied. "I called the IRS and found out that it is a complicated, procedural ruling. There is no impact on most taxpayers. I figure some interest group just made a mistake on the number. Some of those groups are pretty screwed up."

"Not this time. The number is right. I know it looks like an obscure ruling, but actually it could affect the mortgage deduction on income taxes. Get Congressman Conlin to oppose the ruling. Make him look like a hero."

Russ didn't look convinced. "There are bigger problems at the IRS than that."

"Like what?"

"Well, believe it or not, the IRS just sent us draft legislation asking for authority to get and keep every taxpayer's credit reports. It is a dumb idea, and we told them we would never think of even introducing such a measure. It would never pass. We talked them into shelving the idea. Thank God the press never found out about it. It would start a real political firestorm. I'm glad we stopped that one before anyone found out."

"Wow. That's nuts. It is a good thing you killed it. Again, thanks for joining us for lunch."

"You know, Dezube isn't such a bad guy."

"He only got rational when he thought about having his penis cut off. Otherwise he is off the wall."

"He is your client."

"Believe me, I know."

After we parted, I worked my way up to the gallery of the House. On the floor, the members of Congress were voting on another matter. Members were rushing onto the floor, voting, and then standing around talking to each other. The chamber grew noisier and noisier. Finally the vote ended, and the acting Speaker banged down his gavel and called for order.

The Food and Drug Administration Improvements Act was up next. I looked down and saw Congresswoman Dunn in the middle of the House Chamber. As chairwoman of the health subcommittee, she would manage the bill on the House floor. She had moved the bill through her committee in record time, demonstrating her commitment to the issue. Now she was taking advantage of a slow day in the House to get the bill passed.

Requesting recognition, Congresswoman Dunn laid out the case for the bill quickly and accurately. She discussed the need for the legislation and why the bill would do the job. She outlined various sections of the bill. Then she wrapped up her remarks by discussing the chicken pox vaccine.

"My committee heard testimony from a doctor who may have developed a vaccine to prevent chicken pox in children. This vaccine needs to be tested to see if it works and if there are any adverse side effects. The FDA needs this legislation to perform this important job. The doctor was certainly not a professional witness, but he was sincere in presenting his case. We need to pass this bill to help the millions of American children who would otherwise get chicken pox."

As I sat in the House gallery, I couldn't prevent my smile. This was what the legislative process was all about. There was a real need for government action. We had presented our case. Congress had reacted by passing sensible, limited legislation. No one had taken advantage of the system to score partisan points. A problem would be solved.

And I felt good about my role in the process. This was a case when a lobbyist had played a major role in making the government work. Without my help, Dr. Garrity would have run out of patience and money. He probably would have stopped working on his vaccine out of frustration. But I knew the process and the players and put my knowledge to work for his benefit. And, of course, Jason had been instrumental in getting Congresswoman Dunn to help. I had to hand it to Jason; he was good. I was glad he was on my side.

Other members of Congress stood and expressed their support for the FDA Improvements Act. The debate was over quickly, and the House voted on the bill. It was so noncontroversial that the bill passed without opposition. The bill would now go over to the Senate. We were halfway home.

I left the House gallery and waited outside the chamber. After a few minutes, Congresswoman Dunn emerged with a folder full of papers tucked under her arm. She was followed by two staff aides trying to keep up with her in the busy hall. I stepped in front of her and thanked her for her work on the bill.

"Thank you," she said. "Now tell that doctor to hurry up and complete the testing on the vaccine."

"I will. I'll call him this afternoon."

"If he has any trouble with the FDA, you tell him to see me."

"I can't imagine any agency would oppose us, especially now that you are on our side," I flattered her.

She was too sharp to miss what I was doing. She looked over her glasses and smiled at me. Then she said, "Tell Jason I appreciated his phone call."

"Jason called you?"

"This morning, to thank me for pushing this bill. Tell him I appreciated hearing from him."

As she moved off, I stood motionless in the hall. Jason never ceased to amaze me. I did not tell him the bill was due up on the House floor. He had kept track of my activities and lent a hand when he felt it was needed. It was good to be part of Johnson, Woods & Hart.

Regaining my composure, I headed across the Capitol to the Senate side of the building. It was full of tourists, staff, and lobbyists, all watching the legislative process. Despite the air conditioners, the building was hot due to the masses of people. I made my way down the halls and into the underground passages to the Senate office buildings. There I visited with Sheila Reynoldsen, who was handling the Senate version of the bill. She reported to me that the bill was making slow but steady progress in the Senate. She expected the bill on the Senate floor in the near future.

Returning to my office, I called Dr. Garrity to give him the good news. "Doctor, I have good news for you," I started. "The House passed your bill today. It passed unanimously."

"What about the Senate?"

"The Senate is working on the bill, too. It should pass there soon."

"Thank you, thank you. I am blessed to be working with you," he said as I smiled to myself.

Shedding my coat, I emerged from my office to get my phone messages. Kathryn stood waiting with the telltale pink slips in her hand and an impatient expression. "I need to leave a bit early today. I have a date with Jonathan, and I need to get ready."

"What happened to Chip?"

"He is a totally self-centered jerk."

"Okay. So, you are moving on. You'll find the right one soon enough. Which messages are the most important?"

"There is one from a real estate agent, about your health club site. Also there is an emergency partners' meeting in ten minutes. You received this fax from the Oklahoma office about the meeting," she said, handing me the paper.

"Did Jason call the meeting?"

"No."

"Did the communications lawyers call for it?"

"I don't know, but I understand that Jason isn't happy about it."

"Okay. I'll put something on your desk that I want to go out to the entire CATI mailing list tomorrow. You can go now. Say hello to Chip for me."

"Jonathan."

"Jonathan."

After she left, I read the fax from one of the partners in the Oklahoma office, Ed Scuffer. The Oklahoma office was very small, but Ed was angry that he wasn't held in more regard. He was constantly talking at partner meetings about the high cost of salaries in Washington. No one ever bothered to tell him that he was overpriced by any standard—Washington or Oklahoma.

His current fax consisted of a new compensation formula that he claimed would be more equitable. There were about thirty-two variables in the formula. Together they made no sense, except I was sure that it would increase Ed's salary and reduce Jason's. I couldn't wait to hear him describe the plan at the meeting.

But before going upstairs, I called the real estate agent back.

"Mr. Brewster, would you mind cosigning the lease for Mr. Ramirez?"

"Why, is there a problem?"

"Not really. You see, Mr. Ramirez is quite young, and young people often have credit problems. I pulled Mr. Ramirez's credit report and, let's say, he is a typical young person."

"So, there is a problem."

"No, not really. But we need you to cosign the lease."

"I'll think about it."

"Please let us know by tomorrow."

I stared at the phone for a minute before hanging up. I would have to ask Emilio about it tomorrow. It didn't bother me too much. I would have preferred a health club partner without credit problems. But then again, I would have preferred a wife who didn't have credit problems. In fact, was it any guarantee that adding my credit history to the lease would help? For that matter, I would have preferred a law firm that wasn't so deeply in debt. But my lot in life seemed to be to live over my head in bills.

As if on cue, the phone rang again. It was the First National Bank of Lincoln, Nebraska. A soft voice asked to speak with a "Mr. Brewer."

"There isn't one here. Are you actually looking for a Mr. Brewster?"

"Yes. I think that may be the name. Is that you?"

"Yes. How can I help you?"

"Our bank is one of the consortium that holds the debt for your firm. Yesterday, Jason Johnson requested us to loan the firm another $50,000 based on the money you are owed by a new client—a tax group, I think."

"Yes. What can I do for you now?"

"Well, we made a mistake. We loaned the money before we checked with you to see if you think the monies will be paid. Your firm has already drawn down the funds. If you don't confirm that the debt is good, we will have to ask Mr. Johnson to see that the money is repaid. So I am asking you, for the record, is the debt owed by the Citizens Against Tax Injustice good?"

I swallowed hard. I couldn't force Jason to repay the money. Besides, I was sure the funds would eventually come in. And Jason didn't borrow against all the funds. The bill was for $75,000. Maybe the firm financial condition wasn't so bad. I spoke confidently into the phone. "Yes, it is all good. The executive director, Warren Ford, has guaranteed that the bill will be paid."

"You are sure."

"I am as sure as if we owed the money to ourselves."

"Thank you. We were just checking. Mr. Johnson said you were one of the most reliable members of the firm. We will now release the remaining $25,000. Have a good day."

So the First Bank of Lincoln, Nebraska, had covered its ass and put me on the hook for $75,000. I needed to make the scam start paying. Fast.

I picked up a piece of paper and wrote, *Citizens Against Tax Injustice—Alert!!* across the top. Underneath I quickly added,

Today I learned that the Internal Revenue Service has proposed to get access to the credit report of every living American. Yes!! Even you!!

Congress may deny that it received the proposal. Don't believe it! The IRS may say the idea is dead. Don't believe it! Bad ideas like these never go away. They only disappear until loyal Americans aren't watching. Then they reappear and become law. Write your senators and congressional representatives today. Also send in your contribution to help CATI fight this major threat to your financial health. With your help, we can defeat this move by the IRS.

Yours in Freedom,
Warren Ford

By now I was late to the partners' meeting. I briefly considered not going but decided it would be a shame to miss the show. More importantly, I owed Jason for calling the congresswoman, even if he had already spent the money I hadn't collected from CATI.

The meeting was in full swing when I entered and found a seat next to John Horn, the head of the litigation section. John was a large man with a deep voice. He also had the trait that makes many trial lawyers successful: he believed, with all his heart and soul, whatever his client's position was. Even if it was diametrically opposed to the position of three weeks ago. Within the firm, he believed in Jason. As a result, he believed that Ed Scuffer, and anybody else who stood in Jason's way, was a total ass.

Scuffer was wrapping up his presentation. "And so, I believe that this formula will provide for everyone fairly. There are no uncertainties. At the same time, there are enough factors to make sure everyone gets credit for their contribution to the firm."

John made signals like he was masturbating. The entire end of the room erupted in laughter.

After Scuffer finished, the room was silent. I waited for Jason's usual defenders to pipe up and crush the Oklahoma upstart, but apparently everyone was making the same decision, and no one spoke. I glanced over at Jason. He was surveying the room with his eyebrows raised. I decided to repay Jason for his earlier help. I had already forgotten the call from the bank.

"May I respond?" I asked. Jason nodded. "Ed, your formula is certainly helpful, but isn't it a strange time of year to be changing the compensation formula of the partners?" I looked back over at Jason, who was smiling.

"It might help if we have to cut partner salaries due to any financial troubles," came Scuffer's reply.

"What troubles, Ed? Are you having trouble in Oklahoma?"

I knew the Oklahoma office was losing money. Jason had instructed Bill Meyer, the office manager, to show me the office-by-office figures of every office outside Washington, very privately and discreetly. He had also instructed the office manager to show the same figures to every Washington partner, very privately and discreetly. It served to reinforce our belief that we were carrying the rest of the firm, as every office was losing money. Of course, we had no idea how the DC office was doing.

"I believe that the Oklahoma office will show a profit by the end of the year," Scuffer said defensively.

"Well, wouldn't that be the time to make your case—when you can show it works for the firm as well as it does for you? You wouldn't want to start using a formula that would give, say, you a raise when your office is costing the rest of us money, would you now, Ed?"

"This doesn't help me one bit."

"Well, who does it help? Who really benefits from this formula, Ed?"

"I don't know. That's the whole point."

"Well, if we don't know who it helps, then no one has a vested interest in using it. Why don't we keep things the way they are until the end of the year? Then we can make changes."

There was a long silence. No one came to Ed's defense. It was a rout. Again, Washington had showed the yokels in the field who ran the show. Jason quickly wrapped up the meeting and adjourned.

It was too late to go back to work, so we stood around for a few minutes, talking in small groups. John Horn turned to me and said, "Nice work."

"Thanks."

"Scuffer is a total ass, do you know that?"

"I do. He certainly thinks he deserves a raise."

"He is lucky we're carrying his worthless ass."

"Now, John, you know he's worried about the firm losing money," I said sarcastically. Then I turned serious. "Did you see the figures from the Oklahoma office?"

"They won't be profitable in ten years, the dumb shit. If he was so interested in saving money, he wouldn't stay at the Four Seasons every time he comes into town with a special car to drive him everywhere."

As we were talking, Jason approached. "Nice work."

"Thanks. I was glad to do it. Also, you should know that a bank from Nebraska called me about the CATI bill."

Jason looked concerned. He quickly glanced into Horn's eyes, and they both turned to me. "What did you say?"

"I told them the debt was good. They seemed satisfied."

Both Jason and Horn smiled.

"Thanks," Jason said. "We needed that money to make the payroll this month. I would have hated to hear people like Scuffer if we had cut anyone's salary."

"Well, I was glad to report that the money was as good as in."

Horn said, "Brewster, you have a great future in this firm." Jason just smiled.

"Thanks. And, Jason, thank you for calling Congresswoman Dunn on behalf of Dr. Garrity today. His bill passed on the floor."

"I didn't. I called her about something else. She brought up the legislation, so I just played along. Did I help?"

"Yes, you did."

And he had helped.

So he hadn't kept close tabs on my clients or me, but it didn't matter. It was just another example of "Jason luck."

CHAPTER VIII
RED, HOT, AND BLUE

We were hot. Very hot. The Citizens Against Tax Injustice was making a name for itself. New members joined every day. We had finally run a full-page color ad in *American Magazine* including pictures of Abraham Lincoln, George Washington, and Thomas Jefferson. Our monthly newsletter was printed on the highest quality paper and included pictures and color graphs. Our mailing list was computerized and broken down by state, city, congressional district, political party, age, sex, and race. We had all the trappings of the best trade association in town. We were as hot as the weather that year, and that was record breaking.

I still spent every dime that came in on expenses. I had failed to turn over any fees to the firm. I made up bills, reported them to the accounting department, and pretended to send them out, but I had not collected any money in excess of our expenses. According to the firm's accounts receivable list, Warren Ford and CATI owed Johnson, Woods & Hart over $175,000. I kept hoping that the next big fundraising appeal would finally bring in enough money to pay the bills.

But, really, no one seemed to mind. As long as the banks kept extending us credit based on the bills, it didn't seem important to Jason when we got the money in the door. As for the banks, this was the 1990s, and no one doubted that Washington law firms, with big lobbying sections, were good for every dime they were loaned.

On paper, I was having a great year. I was becoming one of the largest billing partners at Johnson, Woods & Hart. It did not go unnoticed. When one of the founding members left suddenly, complaining about the firm's lack of financial sanity, Jason suggested that I take his office. I moved up from the fourth floor to the seventh floor—right around the corner from Jason's office. I was now in the power hall. My new office was three times bigger than the old one. It had a fireplace, as well as a door leading out onto the patio where we held the Fourth of July party. I didn't have enough furniture to fill the room, so I took some large potted plants from the hallways to hide the bare spots. The firm's personal decorator, employed by a chic furniture store, started calling me to arrange a time for her to drop by and offer me suggestions.

One afternoon, as I sat absorbed in my work, I heard a knock on my open door. Looking up, I saw Barbara Lehman leaning against the doorsill, smiling at me. "Nice office. Why haven't you invited me up here yet?"

I stumbled as I jumped up from my chair. "I was waiting to get some more furniture."

"I think the location alone is impressive." She crossed over to me. "And the size. Size matters to me, you know, Richard."

"I didn't know that, but now I do."

She leaned into me, whispering, "Is your office bigger than Walker's because of your scam?"

"Yes."

"It must be profitable." She looked me in the eyes.

"It has the potential to be very profitable." I held her gaze.

"It must be very exciting."

"It is."

"When are we going to have our dinner?"

"How about next Thursday?"

"I think that works for me. I'll check and let you know."

"Great."

At that moment, Kathryn walked in. Barbara and I tried to look casual. I don't think it worked. Kathryn had a handful of pink slips of calls for me to return. She took one look at us and started backing out of the room.

"Come in, Kathryn. Richard and I were just finishing up."

"Yes. Let me have my slips."

Kathryn handed them to me and left quietly. Barbara followed her. As she reached the door, she turned and said, "There is only one thing bad about this office."

"What's that?"

"The open door to the patio lets the hot air in."

"Yes. It is hot in here, Barbara."

———————

It is through the currency of influence that effectiveness and power are measured in Washington. And by that measure, CATI was becoming a force to reckon within the capital. Within a week of releasing my citizens' alert about the IRS attempt to get credit records, thousands of phone calls and letters were flowing into congressional offices. Most senators and members of Congress were opposed to the idea on principle. They quickly communicated their concerns to the administration. The Treasury Department, in turn, announced its firm opposition to the idea and directed the IRS to drop the issue. The IRS complied, and the proposal was buried forever.

CATI had scored a major success in record time. It helped that there was no political support for the idea and that the administration had reacted so quickly to kill it. But it was a victory nonetheless, and CATI took full credit for the win with its members. A follow-up citizens' alert went out after the events transpired.

A MAJOR VICTORY !!!

The CITIZENS AGAINST TAX INJUSTICE has once again preserved your liberty. The Internal Revenue Service had proposed seizing the credit reports of law-abiding taxpayers like you. With this information, no one would be safe from their prying eyes and hands. With this very personal, private information, the IRS would undermine the financial security of innocent taxpayers everywhere. Not even in IRAN or NORTH KOREA does the government have access to such private financial data!! But the CITIZENS AGAINST TAX INJUSTICE discovered this outrage before it could be put into effect. With the help of thousands of vigilant Americans, like you, CATI stopped the IRS dead in its tracks. Because of you, and CATI, Americans can sleep safely in their houses tonight.

I wish I could tell you that the IRS bureaucratic monster was defeated forever. It is not. The IRS will look for other ways to jeopardize your life and your money. We must keep up the fight. Together, the CITIZENS AGAINST TAX INJUSTICE, and you, will keep America free.

Yours in Freedom,
Warren Ford

———————

A few days later I called Russ Ratto to see how he was progressing on the letter from Congressman Conlin to the president on the Hand Towel Equity Act. I could tell from his voice when he got on the line that he was having a bad day.

"What's the matter?" I asked.

"I just had a rough session with the congressman. He's trying to track down who leaked the information about the IRS and the credit reports to the outside. He caught hell from the administration, which blamed Congress for the leak."

"I can't believe that," I said, truly astonished. "Everyone knows the administration is full of leaks. They can't keep a secret for more than three minutes. The congressman didn't really blame you, did he?"

"Well, he did. See, the IRS only briefed about four offices about their idea before it all exploded. So the list of suspects is pretty small. My boss doesn't think the administration is the problem this time. He raked me over the coals. Fortunately, I could assure him that I wasn't the source of the leak. Thank God I didn't tell anyone about it that I couldn't trust."

"Hang in there, Russ. I am sure the congressman knows you were not the problem. He was probably just frustrated and lashed out."

"I hope so. We're going into a tough reelection campaign, and the boss does not need a dispute with the president."

"It'll all blow over in a few days."

"That goddamn Warren Ford. I think I'll call him and ask him where he got his information."

"Don't try. The guy is impossible to reach. Then he doesn't answer questions when you do get him on the phone."

"How do you know that?" he asked quickly.

"Well, I thought I told you," I said, knowing I had not told him anything about CATI. "Warren Ford hired our firm to lobby for him."

"He did. Well, then you ask him where he got his information."

"I will, but I doubt he'll tell me either. He plays things pretty close to his vest."

"Richard," he said slowly. I knew what was coming next. "Did you tell him about our conversation?"

I decided to be honest with him. "Russ, I swear to you that I never discussed it with anyone. He must have found out about the same time I did. He just wrote the newsletter and sent it out."

"Irresponsible jackass."

"I know. What can you do with a butthead like that?"

"I'd cut off his penis."

"Doesn't that sound a bit drastic? Besides, they'd just sew it back on. You can't keep those people down. By the way, did you take me up on my tip and get the congressman positioned against Revenue Ruling 34-897?"

"Not yet. The mail on it is increasing, but I still don't think it will be a big deal."

"Well, we'll see. On another matter, have you done anything further regarding the Hand Towel Equity Act?"

"Yes. I got the congressman to send a letter to the president about it. The letter laid out all your arguments. It requested that the administration review its position on the bill."

"Was there a response?"

"Yeah, and it's bad. The administration said that it would veto the Hand Towel Equity Act. In fact, it would veto any bill that contains the provisions of the Hand Towel Equity Act, even if it likes the rest of the bill. No matter what."

"Wow! Not much wiggle room there."

"Apparently President Clinton has become personal friends with the prime minister of Bangladesh. He is taking a hard line on this matter. I'll send you a copy of the letter we got from the administration. I am sure Dezube will want to see it as soon as possible."

"I have to send it down to Dezube as soon as I get it. But what's the hurry on your end? Take your time getting it to me. Or do you want him coming up here to tell us how to do our jobs?"

"Good point. I'll send it over to you when I get around to it."

After we hung up, I sat at my desk and thought about Revenue

Ruling 34-897. Russ had a good understanding about the details of tax legislation, but he was wrong on the big picture of this one. As a potential political bomb, it might be a dud, but it would probably explode.

And it was time to light the fuse. The administration had quickly disavowed the credit report scheme, defusing the anger of my members before they could really get going. Political movements have a special dynamic. To truly succeed, the anger of the people had to feed off the press and congressional pressure. That hadn't happened. The idea about the credit reports was so outrageous that almost anyone with minimal political skills could understand the problems and react. But Revenue Ruling 34-897 was such an obscure part of the tax code that the administration might miss the significance of it and mishandle the situation when it came to light. At least, that was what I was hoping for.

Fortunately, Congress was scheduled to adjourn at the end of the week for the monthlong annual August recess. Already members of the House and Senate were starting to leave on "critical" fact-finding missions to Europe and the Far East. Within a week, Washington would be a ghost town. Then the letters from CATI would begin to flow in. It would be a new issue, one that the staff would not understand. They would not be able to consult with their bosses to get political directions. Thus they would sit on the letters. I would then take advantage of the silence to stir up my members even more. By the time Congress returned in September, Revenue Ruling 34-897 would be a political firestorm. That was my game plan.

I had already written about the ruling in the newsletter and in one of the ads. I now pulled out a piece of paper and wrote a citizen's alert comparing the ruling to the *Communist Manifesto* and Satan worship. I described how it was a threat to the whole American way of life. I pulled out all the stops.

Finally, I prepared a tear-away on the bottom of the page with a preprinted message to Congress. Lazy members of CATI could just cut off the bottom, sign the printed form, and mail it in. Of course, I told the members that it was more effective to write their own letters, but the printed ones were better than nothing. After all, I told them, it was crucial to flood the Congress with letters of opposition to Revenue Ruling 34-897. I called Kathryn in and described how I wanted everything to look and sent her off to the computer center to start the production.

I chuckled to myself as she left. It would certainly make for the most interesting August in years.

Later, as I was sitting in my chair, staring out the window, thinking of all the trouble I was causing, Jason stuck his head in my door. "You look comfortable in here."

I turned quickly. Seeing his relaxed posture, I admitted, "I am."

"I like the way you put plants everywhere."

"Well, they cover up the bare spots."

"We'll have to get you more furniture."

"As soon as it arrives, I'll cut up the plants and burn them in my fireplace."

"No, we save our fires for unpassed legislation."

"There's not much of that around here."

"Except maybe the Hand Towel Equity Act." He smiled at me in a way that I had never seen before. It was genuine, not forced. I had arrived; Jason was growing comfortable around me. I felt a surge of warmth. "Good work on the tax client," he said. "By the way, I talked to Walker, and I don't think there will be any misunderstanding about whose client it is. And it certainly seems to be a big one."

"Over $225,000 in billings so far this year."

"Right. And we don't want to jeopardize that golden goose, do we?"

"Absolutely not."

"Well, it's not an issue anymore. You reassure the client that you alone are the account manager. Is that what you want?"

"It's not me, Jason. It's Warren Ford."

"Well, will this make Warren Ford happy?"

"Yes. I am sure it will."

"Good. Keep up the good work. We won't forget you at bonus time this year." And he was off. There was no mention of collections. I was being rewarded on the basis of billings alone. Phony billings. I wondered how much of the firm's future was resting on the CATI house of cards. And I wondered how many other similar houses of cards were hidden in the books of Johnson, Woods & Hart.

About an hour later, Walker Dudley came by my office and

looked in. He entered and sat down, his expression dark, his brow furrowed. He had spent the previous week in China as part of a trade delegation along with representatives of the administration. While he was gone, I had moved up to my new office. This annoyed him for many reasons. First, he wanted the office. Second, he objected that any of his people would move off the fourth floor, even if it was okay for him to do it. Third, I had moved without asking him for permission or advice. In short, he had been left out of the loop.

On the other hand, I was no longer one of his exclusive boys. I was clearly one of the firm's new golden partners. Jason was taking an interest in me. I was bringing big potential fees into the firm, and no one could ignore that. Finally, I seemed to have the exclusive ear of Warren Ford, one of the firm's premier clients. Walker was terrified that Warren would complain about him again and get him into more trouble with Jason. So he was confused about me and it angered him. He looked at me silently, until finally I said, "How was China?"

He answered slowly, "It was fine. The administration laid down a hard line on trade issues. The Chinese didn't respond formally. The Americans looked great. Politically, it is always good for an American president to look firm on trade issues."

"So, we kicked their butts?"

He got more enthusiastic as he discussed his political work. "Officially, it was inconclusive. Each side presented its side and left. The next official talks are scheduled for after the midterm elections. So, officially, we have a draw."

"What about unofficially?"

"Unofficially, the Chinese rejected our position. They responded after the trade mission left. A few private-sector representatives stayed on to conduct other business, you know what I mean? Then after two days, they called us in and gave us a letter categorically rejecting the American position."

"So the talks were a flop?"

"Yes, but no one will know until after the midterm elections."

"Did someone communicate the information to the administration?"

"We will, but there is no hurry. No one likes to deliver bad news, you know what I mean? Didn't you ever delay informing clients of bad news?"

"Never."

"You should try it sometime."

"I'll think about it."

He stood to leave. I could see that he was studying the room again, trying to decide how he felt about me and my new position. He turned back and said, "Nice office. I'm glad one of my lobbyists is on the power floor. Put in a good word for me with Jason around the men's room, you know what I mean?"

"Don't worry. I'll do it, but you probably don't need it."

"Don't be too sure."

"By the way, can I see a copy of the letter from the Chinese?"

"Sure."

About an hour later I found the letter in my mailbox. I put it on my desk along with all the other paper piled there. I was glad to see that Walker was responsive. I was having a good day and hoped it would get better. For this was the Thursday night I scheduled to have dinner with Barbara.

I hadn't allowed myself to think too much about it that day. I knew if I did, it would distract me from everything else. But as the day drew to a close, I couldn't help but dream of an exciting evening. Finally, the time arrived. I asked Barbara to come up to my office, to remind her of my favored position in the firm and to see me again in my new digs. She readily agreed to come up.

Then reality intruded.

"Your wife is on the phone," Kathryn announced on the intercom.

I tried to sound casual as I picked up the phone. "Hey."

"What are your plans for tonight?" Elizabeth asked.

"Why?"

"Well, I need you home as soon as possible."

"Is there something wrong?"

"David is sick. He threw up. And I need to take the other two over to the pool. The baby has a heat rash."

"Everyone has a heat rash these days. It's the hottest year on record. Can't you give her a bath?"

"I can, but what are you doing?"

"I have a dinner tonight."

"You didn't tell me anything about it. Who is it with?"

I had to think fast. I usually told Elizabeth about my evening activities so she could plan accordingly, but today I had forgotten to set the stage. I didn't want to lie to her. So now I was paying the price.

"Let me check my calendar," I said, buying time. "I think it's one of my clients."

"Didn't you just entertain Dezube?"

"Yeah, it's not him." She knew my client list too well. I had dragged her off to enough dinners with them. "It's with Walker Dudley."

"You can see him anytime. Besides, I thought you hated eating with him."

"True enough, but he really insisted. He is a senior partner. I think it would be good for me to spend some time with him."

"Do you want to go out with him?"

"Of course not. I actually would rather go to the pool with the kids."

"Then tell him. I gave you an excuse. I really need you here. I am sick of the firm events. You never had so many when you were in government service."

"I make a lot more money these days, too. How much money do you want me to give back so I can have a less demanding job?"

"Very funny. Look, please, the baby has been crying all day. David is sick, and I don't want Matthew to get anything from him. Do you want me to call Walker and ask him to let you off the hook tonight?" I was getting a headache. I could see that I wasn't going to win this one. I swiveled around in my chair and faced the wall. The pictures weren't hung yet. The blank wall matched my mood. "Okay. I'll get out of my dinner. I don't want to go, anyway. I am sure it would be boring. I'll be home soon." As I hung up, I turned back and saw Barbara standing there. She didn't look happy..

I tried to be casual. "Hey there."

"Hi. I guess I was interrupting. I probably wasn't supposed to hear how much you were dreading your dinner."

"It was Elizabeth."

"I gathered."

"She needs me home. It's an emergency. One of the children is very sick. I think we may need to take David to the hospital."

She didn't buy it. "What is the emergency? Heat rash?"

"No, that's Amy," I answered before thinking. She smiled.

"Look, Barbara," I rushed ahead. "I didn't plan this too well. I should have told her I was having dinner with an important client. Or something."

"That's okay. I understand. Anyway, I just ran into Walker Dudley and he asked me out for dinner. I said I had other plans. Apparently, I was wrong."

"Walker. You can't eat with him."

"Why not?"

"He's a pig. He'll get food all over you."

"He's a well-respected member of the Washington establishment."

"He's a big fraud. You know that."

"He's our section leader."

"Yeah, but I have this office."

"Good point. It is nice. I do like all the plants. Kinda makes it look like a jungle. Kinda wild."

"Dudley's not the future of this firm."

"Maybe not. But we are just having dinner."

"Bullshit," I said. She turned to leave. "Barbara, give me a rain check. I want to discuss the scam with you." She slowed down. "The numbers involved are huge. I didn't get this office because I'm cute."

She laughed. "That's got to be true. Okay, you get your rain check. But I am still having dinner with Walker." She started leaving again.

"You can't, Barbara."

She continued out the door. "Why can't I?"

And I said it without thinking: "Because he's married."

She was out the door. She stopped and glanced back. "So are you."

CHAPTER IX
THUNDERSTORMS

In Washington, it never lightly rains in the summer. It is either hot and sticky under a dull gray sky, or there is a thunderstorm. The thunderstorms start when the sky grows darker and darker. One or two drops fall, evaporating as soon as they hit the dry, dusty earth. This is followed by a momentary stillness—so still that the world seems to move in slow motion. If you are outside, you can smell the dirt. Suddenly, a lightning bolt shatters the peace. Usually you don't see the first flash. Instead, the entire sky blinks white. The thunder is sharp and loud. Then the rain starts—huge drops, so big they hurt if they hit you. Finally, the wind whips up. It mixes the other elements of the storm into one terrifying soup of wind, water, branches, and debris.

One Saturday night in August, there was a particularly fierce thunderstorm. The power in our home was out for hours. When it was restored even as the rain continued, the electric clocks in our bedroom flashed on and off, showing the incorrect time. Their green glow added to the surreal nature of the storm. Eventually, the thunder woke the children, and Elizabeth and I spent hours calming them as they huddled in our bed.

Early Sunday morning, I decided to let Elizabeth sleep. The children woke at their usual early time, so I got them dressed, piled them into the car, and took them out for breakfast. As we drove out of our development, the streets were full of tree limbs and puddles. The damage caused by the storm was extensive.

We drove to the local coffee shop. In the parking lot, I held the car door open for the boys and got Amy out of the car seat. Then, struggling, I got everyone into the shop in a fairly organized fashion.

Even though it was early in the morning, the store was crowded. Most of the patrons were sleepy workers getting coffee before heading out to their weekend jobs. They shot wary looks at me and my crew, begging me silently to keep my children quiet until they had their coffee and were safely out of the store. But over in one corner, sitting at a table, was an older man dressed neatly in a pair of slacks, a long-sleeve white shirt, a tie, and a sweater vest. It was already a hot day, but he looked cool and refreshed as he sat there. He smiled at us.

"What a beautiful family you have," he said.

"Thank you."

"What are their names?"

"This is David, and this is Matthew," I said, pointing to each boy, "and this is Amy."

"Those are very nice names. And, sir, what is your name?"

"Richard."

"Richard what?"

"Richard Brewster."

"Well, Richard Brewster, you have a beautiful family."

"Thank you."

By then we had made our way up to the front of the line and ordered our donuts and juice. As we waited for our order, the man came up and started talking to my sons. "Matthew, David, do you want to hear about the greatest power on earth? I want to share my vision with you."

I snapped my head around and noticed the strange look in his eyes. There was a vacant smile on his face. His glance was fixed on my two boys. "I want to tell you boys something special."

I grabbed our food and ushered my family towards the door. "Come along, boys, it's time to go," I said loudly.

"Why, Dad? You said we could eat here," Matthew argued.

"We just need to go," I said as I kept moving for the exit.

"Share some time with me, and I'll share my vision with you," the man said.

"Dad, you promised we could eat here," Matthew said.

"We need to get these back to your mother."

"You said Mom needs to sleep."

"I want to talk to you and your children," the man said. His voice remained quiet, but he started following us. I hustled the boys out of the store as they protested and argued with me in the parking lot and the car.

Protection of family is one of life's most basic instincts, I thought. God help the person who ever tried to hurt my family, I vowed. I drove home quickly through the streets filled with storm debris.

━━━━━━

The next day, I sat in my office and thought about the thunderstorm as a metaphor for my efforts with the Citizens Against Tax Injustice. The first drops of mail on Revenue Ruling 34-897 had already fallen. They had made little or no impact. Now was the quiet time, with Congress in recess. Hopefully the storm was coming.

I took an elevator down to the tax section of the firm and found Brad and Mark. "Have you received any requests for your article on Revenue Ruling 34-897?" I asked them innocently.

"It's been unbelievable," said Brad. "We have received more requests for copies of that article than anything else we've ever written. People keep calling and asking us for information."

"Really? That's great. Are you getting any new clients from your efforts?"

"Not a one. The requests for assistance are from congressional and governmental offices. We can't charge them any money."

"That's too bad."

"You work for this guy Warren Ford, don't you? He seems to be stirring up the pot. Does he understand that this is a very technical issue?"

"I think he understands exactly what he's doing."

"Does he need our help to analyze the ruling? If you're the source of his information, he is in a lot of trouble."

"No, I don't think he needs any more facts. You don't want to confuse him, now, do you?"

"It sure would be great to work for him. Have I seen him around here? Someone said he was tall and Black. I thought I saw him in the lobby yesterday and I was tempted to introduce myself."

"No, that's not right. Warren Ford is a big White man. He is really big. He needs to lose a few pounds. He doesn't come around here much. I would be very surprised if you saw him."

"I guess you're right. I haven't seen anyone that looks like that."

"Well, I am glad you're getting recognition for your writing."

"Thanks. Who would have thought that this ruling would be so interesting?"

"It may be just the beginning. You never know."

———

By the time Congress reconvened after Labor Day, everyone was talking about Revenue Ruling 34-897. During the congressional recess, thousands of letters had poured into every Senate and House office. In meetings all around the country, angry members of CATI confronted members of Congress and senators. The members of Congress were yelled at and questioned about the ruling. Not a single one had a clue about what Revenue Ruling 34-897 did. However, being excellent politicians, they all promised to look into the matter and to respond appropriately. They called their Washington offices and asked for more information. Their staffs had no idea about what the ruling did, so they called the IRS and demanded the information. And the IRS, never anticipating such an interest in an obscure ruling, had prepared nothing and simply sent out copies of Revenue Ruling 34-897.

When the congressional staff received the material from the IRS, they tried to read it. The ruling was written in extremely technical language, with cross-references to other statutes and rulings. No one without a strong background in tax law could really figure out what was going on. For those few offices that had staff assistants with tax backgrounds, the ruling was properly analyzed and explained. But in the vast majority of offices, there was no one with sufficient knowledge to understand it. Under pressure to explain the ruling, the staff members called the IRS and demanded that the agency explain the ruling in plain English.

The Internal Revenue Service is a monumental government bureaucracy. It employs tens of thousands of employees and costs billions of dollars to run. Like all bureaucracies, it doesn't appreciate outside oversight. It prefers to be left alone to carry out its mission. When scrutiny occurs, the bureaucracy will not cooperate, in the hope that the prying eyes will eventually go away.

Even worse, during that particular August, there was no political leadership at the top of the IRS. The director had recently resigned for health reasons. The deputy director was away on vacation. The number three person was in Canada, completing negotiations on a new tax treaty. No one could force the agency to assist Congress in getting to the bottom of its enquiries. The bureaucracy was leaderless and unsupervised.

Thus, when the requests for more information came in from Congress, the agency refused to help. They simply continued to send out copies of the ruling. When congressional staff members called to find out anything they could, they were sent on an endless round of phone tag, directed to call office after office after office, until even the most diligent staff member gave up in frustration. And yet, their bosses were calling for answers every day.

Fortunately, one outside group, the Citizens Against Tax Injustice, was prepared. Warren Ford, the executive director himself, had prepared a fact sheet about the ruling. There was not one untrue statement on it. But there was a lot of missing information, such as how many people the ruling would impact each year.

Congressional staff members gobbled up the information gratefully. Diligent staff tried to confirm the information with the IRS but were stymied by the bureaucracy. Other staff members tried to call Warren Ford with questions, but they were unable to locate him. Fortunately, CATI had a lobbying firm—Johnson, Woods & Hart—with a rising partner, Richard Brewster, as the lead attorney for the organization.

Russ Ratto continued to brood over our firm's participation in CATI. One afternoon he called me. "What the hell are you doing?"

"What do you mean?"

"Warren Ford is a kook!"

"No, he's not."

"Bullshit! Who else would claim that an obscure revenue ruling that deals with real estate valuation on tax-free swaps, for God's sake, is a threat to homeownership?"

"Maybe it is. I don't know for sure. I haven't looked into the matter too closely."

"Well, let me assure you, it isn't. This guy must be a real nutcase."

"Well, probably he is, but Jason made us take the client. Apparently he thinks it will be a big one for the firm."

"That goddamn Jason."

"Look, isn't it better that *I* work with Warren Ford rather than some of the really irresponsible lobbyists in Washington?"

"What makes you think that I think you are not a really irresponsible lobbyist? Haven't you been mentioning that ruling to me for weeks? How long have you been involved with Ford?"

"Not too long, but I did hear about the issue before we landed the client. See, that's why I gave you a heads-up. I wanted your boss to be ahead of the issue."

"Well, I admit that you called the politics on this one right. It is a firestorm. I never could have predicted it."

"I'll take that as a thank-you."

"Just keep Warren Ford under control. You better handle him better than you handle Doug Dezube. Tell Ford that if he gets out of line, I'll cut off his penis."

Fortunately for me, no one else in Congress understood the ruling as well as Ratto. I took a huge number of staff calls and advised everyone that Congress should oppose Revenue Ruling 34-897. It was too difficult to explain, and there didn't seem to be any downside to opposing it. And the grateful staff all wrote memos reflecting my advice.

Congress finally reconvened the day after Labor Day. In the House, after reciting the Pledge of Allegiance, members are allowed to speak for one minute on any subject they choose. On that particular day, the Republican whip, the number two person in the Republican leadership, waited patiently for his turn to speak. His speeches were always listened to carefully as he used the speeches to announce the Republican positions on upcoming issues.

"Mr. Speaker," he began. He was tough, articulate, and very partisan. His nickname was "the Crowbar" because he always pulled out the last vote. "Today I want to discuss a very serious threat to the taxpayers of this country."

I was in my office with the television on and the volume on low. When I heard the next sentence, I quickly turned up the sound.

"Revenue Ruling 34-897 is yet another example of how the Clinton administration is trying to raise taxes. I thought that every member of this House supported the sanctity of the American home and the homeowner's mortgage deduction. I thought the administration supported the values embodied in the family and the home. But

I have learned that the Clinton administration, through the IRS, intends to challenge those values and to deny some taxpayers the home deduction they currently have.

"Mr. Speaker, I ask, what is next? I have been told that this ruling may affect only a few taxpayers. But no one can tell me how many Americans will be hurt. More importantly, is it all right that only a few taxpayers are unfairly robbed of their hard-earned income due to this ruling? How many taxpayers have to be hurt before it becomes wrong?

"No one can tell me what the Internal Revenue Service will do next. No one at the IRS can tell me, with any certainty, that the home mortgage deduction won't eventually be denied for every taxpayer. No! Mr. Speaker, I say now is the time for the administration to admit that this ruling was a terrible mistake.

"I would call upon the president to withdraw this ruling. I am not sure we can trust any man who would allow such a ruling to go into effect. To guarantee the protection of every American taxpayer, I say that we should, and we will, pass legislation that will defeat this ruling forever!!"

By the end of the day, bills had been introduced in both the House and Senate, directing the Internal Revenue Service to withdraw Revenue Ruling 34-897. Several members of the House claimed credit for drafting and introducing the legislation. The situation was the same in the Senate. However, the loudest, most vocal supporter of the bill, the man who hated Revenue Ruling 34-897 the most, was Senator Kelly.

"I've worked on many important issues during my tenure in the Senate," he said, "but none is more important than this threat on innocent taxpayers."

It was a slow news day at the White House. No major policy announcements were released as the entire political leadership in the city was getting back from vacation. The daily news briefing in the White House pressroom centered on questions about lost luggage and sunburn. But in the middle of the jocularity, someone asked, "What is the administration's position on Revenue Ruling 34-897, which the Republican whip called a threat to the home mortgage deduction?"

The deputy press secretary, who was running the briefing and still chuckling over a previous joke, looked unconcerned. She had no idea what the question referred to. But the Republican whip was mentioned, and she knew if the Republican whip was against it, the administration was probably doing something right.

Half in jest, she said, "If the Republican whip wants to protect the tax breaks of his wealthy friends, he can do it. We stand by the actions of the administration, which is dedicated to tax fairness and justice." Then she moved on to the next question.

I wish I could take credit for arranging all the actions of that day. I cannot. I certainly did not see or talk to the deputy press secretary at the White House, nor to the Republican whip. I did not request any senator or member of the House to introduce the legislation to repeal the ruling. I certainly did not meet with Senator Kelly, even to introduce myself for yet another time.

However, in a bigger sense, I caused the events of that day. After spending almost twenty years in Washington, I understood how the place worked. I started the process rolling through the actions of CATI. Once started, it followed the inevitable course I had predicted. The thunderstorm had begun in earnest.

It was one payoff of the scam. I hadn't made a dime off it yet, but I knew I was a master of the world, working the levers of the most powerful government in history. And all for my own enjoyment. Not bad. And then to make it even better, I prepared a bill to CATI for another $125,000. I was now up to $450,000. Not one penny had been added to the firm's coffers, but I was now officially one of the biggest billers.

Finally, riding on an ego high, I took the elevator down to Barbara's office. She was working over a sheaf of papers on her desk, and looked none too happy about it.

"Did you hear about our bill?" I asked.

"I heard from my old officemate Russ Ratto. He thinks you've gone over the deep end with the tax matter. Is that your scam?"

"Yes, it is. And we got a speech about it on the House floor, a statement from the White House, and several bills introduced about it. Impressed?"

"Not really." She was still angry about our cancelled dinner and had been cool to me for days.

"According to the firm's books, the scam has also billed $450,000."

She looked up. "Now I'm impressed. Have you collected all that money?"

"Not all of it. But that doesn't seem to matter to Jason. He's borrowing against the accounts receivable. So the firm has the money to spend."

"No wonder you have the big office."

"I am busy tonight, but I still want to tell you all the details. If you're interested."

"I guess I am. Next time we plan something, however, let's avoid sick children. You don't want me to spend another evening with Walker Dudley, do you?"

"No. Not at all. I want to protect you from him. He is yesterday's news." And I left. With my hands resting firmly on the levers of power in Washington.

CHAPTER X
EIGHT SECONDS

I have been told that in professional rodeos there is an event where cowboys ride an unbroken horse, or a wild bull. The animal does everything it can to throw the competitors to the ground. The ride is so wild that cowboys only have to ride the animal for eight seconds to win. I have also been told that, for the riders, those eight seconds are the most thrilling of their lives.

The legislation to overturn Revenue Ruling 34-897 was moving. Within five days, 67 senators and 285 members of the House had cosponsored bills designed to overturn the ruling. Every day, there were speeches on the floor of the House denouncing the IRS. Town hall meetings were held across the country to discuss the best way to ensure passage of the bills.

The Citizens Against Tax Injustice had put out two more citizens' alerts, keeping the membership informed about the progress of the effort. It had run ads in a number of local newspapers, explaining the threat of Revenue Ruling 34-897. Each ad brought in new CATI members. Each ad ignited more outraged citizens to call for action from their congressional representatives. And the new ads again used up all the incoming money.

Only the Clinton administration seemed unconcerned about the furor. The White House stood behind its original statement—it was an attempt by the Republicans to protect their rich patrons. The administration asserted that the ruling would not hurt the vast majority of taxpayers, and definitely would not hurt any middle-class taxpayers. The administration was right. But it failed to make its case often enough. Believing the matter to be inconsequential, the administration did not put any effort into explaining exactly what the ruling did and did not do. Its half-hearted statements were drowned out by the surrounding noise.

And it wasn't just a partisan matter. Democrats from all over the country had jumped on the bandwagon and supported the legislation. The White House was right in considering the matter inconsequential, but, as a minor issue, there was little penalty for Democrats to oppose the administration on it. Many Democrats who had loyally supported the president on a number of unpopular votes were looking for an issue to prove their independence. They decided to make a stand on Revenue Ruling 34-897.

No one was more vocal than Senator Kelly. Although he had not been the first to introduce the bill to kill the ruling, he certainly made the most noise about it. He called a press conference to announce that he would suspend his activities on all other legislative matters until the bill was signed into law. No one in the press pointed out that none of his other legislative initiatives were going anywhere anyway. He was always good for a quote, so the reporters loved him.

However, one cynical journalist asked the senator exactly what he would do to move the bill through the process. Senator Kelly thought about the question for a full minute because he had no idea what to do. He assumed that holding a press conference was enough. Then, inspired, he announced that he would hold a hearing and call the architect of the effort, Mr. Warren Ford, to testify.

The next day I was called up to his office by his panicked staff. I introduced myself to Rob Fitzgibbons, his legislative assistant who was in charge of tax bills. Rob looked to be about my age, which told me I was dealing with a longtime Hill staffer. He wore a polyester suit that looked like a bad tailor in Thailand had made it. I had hoped for a savvy professional, but I could see I was going to be working with a congressional nerd.

"The senator wants to run this meeting himself," Rob told me excitedly, as if this information would thrill me. Actually, it was the worst possible news. I wanted to work quietly with the senator's staff to plan a hearing that would reflect well on both of us. Instead, I was going immediately into a command performance. I could tell that Rob was excited by the opportunity to work closely with the senator on a high-visibility issue. I gathered that Rob didn't have much quality time with the senator, probably because tax matters bored Kelly. Rob saw this as his moment to shine.

As we walked back to the senator's office, Rob quietly whispered, "If he says he wants a first-class hearing, he means he wants at least three television cameras."

"I take it that the substance of the hearing is of less importance?" I asked. Rob looked disappointed with my cynicism.

We entered the senator's office. Senator Kelly sat behind his desk, reading a local newspaper from his state. He put the paper down and stood to greet me. We shook hands warmly.

"Richard Brewster," I announced.

"It's a pleasure to meet you," he said in his rich, deep voice. His suit was made from expensive Italian wool, cut to flatter his muscular figure. He was tall, with sandy hair, every strand of which was in place. Looking tanned and rested, he came around his desk, and we all sat in overstuffed chairs.

"I'm glad you could see me on such short notice," the senator said with false modesty. Then he waited for me to properly kiss his ass. I did.

"I am glad to be here, Senator. I'm very pleased that you have decided to hold a hearing on Revenue Ruling 34-897. You have the reputation of really working an issue once you get started. I am sure that the bill will pass now that you're involved."

"I feel strongly about this issue, right, Rob?"

"Absolutely." Rob beamed.

"I am concerned that not all of my colleagues understand the issue like I do. That is why I want to hold a real first-class hearing. Do you understand what I'm saying?" the senator explained.

"I certainly do. You want to see that the issue is fully addressed by experts in the field," I said.

"Well, yes, I do," he said slowly, "but I want a real first-class hearing."

"A hearing to fully demonstrate the problems inherent in this ruling," I went on.

"Well, of course," he continued, "but I am particularly concerned that we have a first-class hearing. Rob, do you understand?" He looked at his aide. Rob looked at me nervously.

After a moment, I bailed him out. "Of course, you can't have a first-class hearing unless you have a lot of media attention."

"Exactly!" the senator said, smiling broadly. Rob seemed relieved as he settled back into his chair. "Let's get this Warren Ford to testify," the senator went on. "He has certainly made a name for himself on this issue."

"I don't think it's a good idea," I said. I'd had twenty-four hours to prepare for this exchange, and I was ready for it. "Warren Ford is the worst witness I have ever seen. He would bore his mother. If you want the television cameras to leave, just get him up there."

"I don't care if he is boring," the senator said. "I'll make a statement and ask the questions."

"But he will answer them in the most convoluted of ways."

"Really boring, huh?" the senator asked, disappointed.

"The worst," I confirmed sadly. "Look, he's my client. I'd like nothing better than to be able to have him testify. But I have too much respect for you to be anything but totally honest. Keep him off the stand. He'll destroy any credibility we might gain on this issue. You can believe me, as a witness, Warren Ford is a total zero. I have a much better idea for you, someone who will guarantee your hearing receives the media coverage it deserves . . ." And I laid out a strategy.

The hearing was scheduled for the following week. In the interim, the media continued to follow the issue. It was a good old-fashioned fight between the Congress and the administration—a fight that would sell papers and improve ratings. The fact that there was very little to the story made it even easier for the press to follow. Since no one understood the ruling, there was no need to waste news space or time explaining it. Instead, the news stories focused on the human angle. They interviewed average Americans, all of whom said the ruling was bad for the country.

The following Saturday, I was barbequing dinner with the boys. Elizabeth was in the kitchen making a salad. She had the television on and was watching one of the political talk shows that everyone in Washington watches and no one in the rest of the country pays any attention to. Suddenly, she called me to come in and watch. As I entered, I saw that the program was showing a clip of an interview with some man on the street identified as a regional director of the Citizens Against Tax Injustice. I had never seen him before, but he was doing a good job, so I didn't get upset. He was taking about Revenue Ruling 34-897.

"Isn't that your group?" Elizabeth asked. I nodded my confirmation as we both watched the dialogue that followed:

Moderator: "Issue three. The president is taxing our patience. This week the administration again showed its tin ear when it comes to hearing the voice of the American people. The IRS—that's the Internal Revenue Service—has issued a ruling that could cause some taxpayers to lose their home mortgage deduction. Predictably, the American people are outraged. Capitol Hill has been flooded with letters and phone calls from angry taxpayers demanding an end to the ruling. Legislation has been introduced in both houses of Congress to overturn this latest bureaucratic outrage. Yet the administration has refused to recall this ruling, or to do anything other than call it a Republican plot to protect rich taxpayers. Why is the administration missing the ball on this one? I ask you, Pat?"

Pat: "John, this proves again that the administration talks like populists but acts like elitists. There is a groundswell of taxpayer outrage against this ruling, and the administration is ignoring it. President Clinton, and his advisors, just can't stand the thought that there is some tax money out there that they aren't collecting. They are hanging tough on this ruling, and it is a mistake."

Moderator: "Well stated, Pat. Eleanor?"

Eleanor: "John, I would expect you and Pat to protect the fat cats involved in these sophisticated tax deals, but don't expect the administration to defend them. The people who are protesting don't want to pay taxes at all, and I think the president is exactly right in not caving in to them."

Pat: "Eleanor, that is just plain nonsense. The people against this rule know they have to pay taxes. They just don't want to be blindsided on the home mortgage deduction."

Eleanor: "Pat, how many of the people who are protesting this rule would be affected by it?"

Pat: "That's not the point. The point is that the administration isn't listening to average Americans. Joe Taxpayer is concerned about this."

Moderator: "Tony, what are the political repercussions of this lack of attention to this matter by the administration?"

Tony: "Negligible." (Everyone laughs.)

Moderator: "You think the president can continue to ignore the protests of taxpayers without paying a penalty?"

Tony: "This issue, by itself, is not important. However, if the administration continues to ignore public opinion on relatively minor issues like this, they will eventually get into big trouble on some important issue."

Moderator: "Ah-ha, so you think this is not an important issue on its own, but does tend to indicate that the administration's antenna to the American people is broken?"

Tony: "Whose antenna?" (Everyone laughs)

Moderator: "Morton?"

Morton: "Tony has it exactly right. On its own, this is a minor issue. But it shows that the administration has lost its touch with the American people. It needs to find it again, before a bigger mess comes down the line."

Moderator: "Well stated, Morton. The administration has been given a warning call. It must heed it. Exit question. On a scale of one to ten, one being no damage whatsoever and ten being total impending doom, how would you rate the damage caused by the president's refusal to withdraw Revenue Ruling 34-897? Pat?"

Pat: "Four."

Moderator: "Really? Eleanor?"

Eleanor: "One."

Tony: "Three and a half."

Morton: "Three and a half."

Moderator: "The answer is six. Next we will discuss the Supreme Court's latest opinion."

The screen faded into a commercial about airplane jets.

Elizabeth stood staring at the television, her mouth and eyes open. Deep down, I knew she thought I hadn't done any real work since I left the government. She knew I left the house each day and returned each night, but beyond that, my career was a mystery to her. My attempts to explain what I did usually were met with disbelief. She thought it was a full-time circus at Johnson, Woods & Hart. She didn't complain as long as I got paid; of course, when I told her about the firm's financial problems, she looked at me like it was time to get a real job. But now she had evidence that what I did mattered. I wasn't sure she was impressed, but she did have to acknowledge it.

Her amazement intensified the next morning when she saw the *Washington Post*. The Sunday *Post*, delivered to almost a million households in the Washington area, had an op-ed piece entitled "The President's Misguided Ruling." The column began by stating that tax collectors had been hated since the time of the Babylonians, but this time they were really threatening innocent people. It called the president to task for not telling the IRS to withdraw the ruling. It particularly praised that lone individual, Warren Ford, who stood up for tax justice. The point of the article was not to explain the ruling but to trash the administration, fitting in with the general views of the author. It did trash the president, and it did it beautifully.

By Monday, there were more stories in all the major dailies about the ruling, the administration's mistake in not withdrawing it, and about the hearing to be held by Senator Kelly. Washington correspondents travel in packs, and the pack was clearly on the story now. Reporters diligently undertook their research, which amounted to reading each other's stories and repeating the findings. The stories, in turn, generated more letters and phone calls to Senate and House offices.

When I arrived at work that day, I had a phone call from the editor of the Style section of the *Washington Post* and the People section of *USA Today*, among other press enquiries. They all wanted to do features on Warren Ford. I called to tell them, with great regret, that Warren Ford was unavailable for a story at this time. They were not happy but were mollified when I told each one of them that Warren would definitely not give an exclusive interview to any other paper. I figured I was safe on that promise.

My next task that day was less enjoyable. I had Emilio meet me in my office to discuss the health club. I told him I could not agree to cosign any lease and that he would have to look for another place that did not require that. He was embarrassed and swore to me that his financial problems were minor.

"I just got carried away last Christmas. I had too high a credit limit on my credit card. I only missed one payment." The litany of excuses was extensive.

I stopped him. "We all have money problems at one time or another, Emilio. Just keep looking for another place. One where I don't have to sign any leases."

"Okay. I'll make it up to you. I'll find a new site tomorrow. I won't work out with anyone until I find a place."

"Don't cut off your customers. We're going to need them soon enough. Take your time to get a good place. There is no hurry. In the meantime, give me my money back. I'll put it in my bank account, and we'll make some interest off it."

"Does this mean you're no longer backing me?" he said.

"Not at all. I just think we should earn some interest on the money if it takes a few months to locate a new place. I'm still behind you one hundred percent."

"Well, okay. I'll give you and your secretary free training sessions while I look. Kathryn helped me make some calls."

"No, Emilio." I was exasperated. "No free sessions. Keep the customers paying."

"Well, can I give Kathryn free sessions?"

"If you're trying to date her, there is a long list of boyfriends ahead of you. And she seems to fall for bad apples."

"Thanks for the advice. I'll take my chances," he said as he smiled at me.

———————

Three days later, I rode in the firm's car up to the Hart Senate Office Building to Senator Kelly's hearing. Riding in the car with me was Mark Waterman and Brad Charness and my special, surefire witness, Hugo the Human Destructo. It had taken days to convince Brad and Mark to let Hugo testify:

"Hugo is in enough trouble with the IRS as it is. They're ready to seize his house next week," Brad said.

"I'm amazed," I replied. "I thought you two would save his bacon."

"Nothing can save his bacon. He is going down. All we can do is cushion the blow. Maybe," Mark admitted.

"Then what does he have to lose by testifying? Look, how can the IRS seize his home right after he has testified before Congress? They can't. Testifying would probably protect him at least for a while."

"But there is no connection between his problems and Revenue Ruling 34-897."

"How do you know?"

"What?" Mark couldn't believe I was challenging him on a tax matter.

"How do you know? Didn't you tell me that his record keeping is a disaster? How do you know that there was no tax-free swap somewhere in the past? I bet there was."

"No way," Brad asserted.

"Let's ask him."

"You want to ask him if he was ever involved in a tax-free swap of his residence such that it triggered a valuation problem resolved by Revenue Ruing 34-897?"

"No. I want to ask him if he would be willing to testify against Revenue Ruling 34-897 if it would save his house and allow him to be photographed with US senators."

"Not fair."

"To whom? Personally, I think there might have been a tax-free swap in his past. I'm surprised that you're unwilling to give your client the best defense possible."

"It's not the best defense possible. It's only blowing smoke," Mark said angrily.

"Don't underestimate the value of smoke," I replied. "In fact, Washington is the only city where smoke is a widely respected work product."

When we explained the idea to Hugo, Brad and Mark were very careful to stress that Hugo could not lie in his testimony. I agreed. I also told him that he might be able to save his house from certain IRS seizure if he thought there was a tax-free swap in his previous financial dealings. After seconds of hard thought, Hugo assured me that there had to be such a transaction in his past. I looked at Brad and Mark.

"See," I said, "I knew Hugo had those problems. Please write the man some testimony."

When they finished writing the first draft of the testimony, I threw it away and started again. By then, Hugo had completely adopted the idea that Revenue Ruling 34-897 was the cause of all his problems. He gave me a great number of details to include in the testimony. Of course, I had no way of knowing whether he was making it all up or if his memory had improved. Hugo was a better actor than I thought.

As we rode to the Capitol, Hugo looked over the script (I mean, testimony). "Who wrote this?" he asked.

"Brad and Mark wrote the first draft, based on the information you provided us," I assured him.

"It's the best thing you ever wrote for me," he complimented them. Brad and Mark beamed. Hugo seemed particularly pleased that there were no difficult words. I had geared the vocabulary to him, and to whom he would be testifying before.

We arrived at the Hart Senate Office Building and made our way to the hearing room. Outside were four tables full of television equipment. Miles of wires ran into the room between boxes of components and control panels. There were small television monitors, sound mixers, quality controllers, buttons, and switches. Inside, huge glaring lights were posted around the room. Microphones were located at the witness stand.

The room was jammed. Photographers roved around, and print journalists sat at special press tables. As we entered, the media descended on us. Questions came from every direction as flashbulbs lit up the room. Not wanting to upstage our testimony, I loudly announced that Hugo would take no questions until after the hearing. That, of course, did not slow any of the reporters down. They continued to fire questions at us. We ignored them and made our way up to the table where the senators were going to sit.

Hugo was not just another professional wrestler. He was the premier wrestler in the country, having won the World Heavyweight Championship three times. More importantly, he had parlayed his prowess into a lucrative movie career, appearing in a number of blockbusters. He had also spent three years as the head of the President's Council on Physical Fitness during a previous administration. During that time he published a number of exercise books for both children and adults. He also created his own brand of vitamins. He handed out samples to fans on the street. In short, Hugo was an A-list media celebrity.

Senator Kelly had arrived and was waiting in a small holding room adjacent to the hearing room. Rob Fitzgibbons stuck his head in the door when Hugo reached the front of the room and told the senator that the star witness had arrived.

The senator emerged, walked over, and shook Hugo's hand. So many flashbulbs were going off that the room seemed to be illuminated by a strobe light. Everyone's movements appeared jerky. Hugo and the senator talked to each other quietly as the press mob continued to grow around them. They both stood there smiling and nodding to each other—two masters of public relations. Finally, some pesky reporter broke up the photo session by yelling out an incredibly rude question: "Senator, could you or Hugo explain exactly how this Revenue Ruling 34-897 works?" Hugo and the senator ignored the question. They parted and returned to their places for the hearing, the senator in the chairman's chair and Hugo at the witness table.

As I mentioned before, there are two types of congressional hearings. This hearing was not designed to get facts. Its sole purpose was to get the picture of Senator Kelly, along with Hugo, on every television news program and in every newspaper in the country. The facts of the issue were irrelevant. This was prime time.

The other members of the committee entered the room and took their places. No one wanted to miss a chance to appear before the American people. And talk about this serious issue.

Senator Kelly banged down the gavel. When he glanced up and noticed that one of the camera operators had missed the moment while adjusting his camera, the senator waited until the operator finished, then brought down the gavel again. The room quieted.

"The committee will come to order," he began. "Today the committee will examine a revenue ruling issued by the Internal Revenue Service that has serious implications for millions of Americans. Specifically, Revenue Ruling 34-897 may prohibit some taxpayers from taking the home mortgage deduction they are entitled to take under the law. The administration claims that this is a misreading of the law. It claims that once all the facts are known, no one will object to the ruling. That is why I have called this hearing. We want to get all the facts."

He leaned forward in his chair. "However, everything I have seen on this matter leads me to believe that the Internal Revenue Service should withdraw the ruling immediately. Everyone concedes that the ruling does, in fact, change the way that some taxpayers can take the deduction. I do not approve of this.

"The bedrock of the United States is the American family. Our government should do everything it can to strengthen the family. The home mortgage deduction helps do this. Families need homes so they can live together and grow. Taking away the deduction is a direct attack on the family. I was not sent to Washington to see the IRS hurt the American family. If that is the policy of the IRS and the Clinton administration, well, I apologize, but my loyalties are not with the president but with every American mother and father."

Finishing with a flourish, Senator Kelly asked the members of the committee if they had any opening statements. Each and every one of them did. Each praised Senator Kelly for holding the hearing. Each talked about the great courage the senator showed by taking on the IRS. Each was looking to get all the facts before deciding how to vote on the legislation to overrule the IRS. But each fully endorsed the legislation and trashed the IRS. They were all in great form. Their speeches were well written and well delivered. Each contained a catchy phrase, in hopes of landing on the evening news. It was sound-bite heaven.

When all the senators had spoken, Senator Kelly introduced the first witness.

"For today's hearing, we asked the secretary of the treasury to testify. Unfortunately, he was called away to Europe suddenly. He left last night. The deputy secretary is also unavailable. I felt this hearing was too important to delay until they returned. Many members of the Senate are looking to this committee for guidance on this important bill. Therefore, we are proceeding today by receiving testimony from the administration from Mr. B. Wayne Smith, the deputy assistant secretary of treasury for domestic finance. Welcome, Mr. Smith. Please proceed with your testimony."

Mr. B. Wayne Smith looked to be all of twenty-three. He had probably been an envelope stuffer in the last campaign, then landed a safe job where he thought no one would expect him to make a decision or take a chance. But now, since no one of real authority in the department had any desire to be humiliated by a Senate committee, Mr. Smith was representing the president of the United States before 178 reporters, 12 hostile senators, and 8 television cameras. Mr. Smith had just been promoted from the farm league to the big leagues.

He was so young, and under such stress, that his voice cracked. "Good morning, Mr. Chairman, and members of the committee," he read from his prepared testimony. "I appreciate the opportunity to appear before you today . . ."

It seemed that the congressional hearing was the last place left on earth where the murder victim was supposed to thank the murderers.

But Mr. Smith was not going willingly to the slaughter. He knew that he would be killed on an emotional level, so he tried a different tack. His testimony was based on facts, and the most boring facts he could find.

"In 1978, the Congress passed the Tax Reform and Taxpayer Improvement Act. That act contained a provision, section 1107 (b) (1), which requires taxpayers to value their property, in the event of a tax-free swap, under a new method. This new method was spelled out in section 2354 of that act. That section reads as follows . . ."

Senator Kelly looked bored. Then, to his dismay, he realized that the press was also losing interest. He was in a quandary. The administration was entitled to state its case, even if it did so in a boring manner. He couldn't just cut the witness off. But he couldn't let the witness continue, either. He was caught between the rock of senatorial courtesy and the hard place of the success of his hearing. He leaned over to Rob and whispered, "Turn on the timer light."

The timer light is a contraption with three lights connected to a timer. One light is green, another is yellow, and the last is red. At most hearings, public witnesses are given five minutes to testify. To keep them from going over their time allotment, the timer is used. During the first four minutes, the green light is on. With a minute to go, the yellow light goes on. When the time is up, the red light flashes. The chairman then asks witnesses to conclude their testimony. In deference to the president, the system is rarely used with administration witnesses. But Senator Kelly had no intention of letting a twenty-three year deputy assistant secretary ramble on until the press left.

Mr. Smith glanced up when the light first went on. Then he gamely continued reading his testimony. "Thus the revenue ruling eliminates the information gap and provides the taxpayer the method to adjust the basis of his property values . . ."

The second the red light flashed, Senator Kelly interrupted Mr. Smith. "Thank you for your testimony, Mr. Smith. I have a few questions. Are you saying that Revenue Ruling 34-897 is in direct response to a congressional action?"

Mr. Smith nodded. "In a way, Mr. Chairman. As I stated in my testimony, Congress passed the Tax Reform and Taxpayer Improvement Act of 1978 . . ." He began to restate his testimony, saying that the ruling was written to clarify tax laws—tax laws passed by Congress. Senator Kelly had no intention of letting the floor get away from him again. He interrupted Mr. Smith midway through the answer.

"I understand your contention that the ruling was in response to congressional action, but I can assure you that this member of the Senate never would have passed any law that threatened the American family. I suggest that you look elsewhere for blame for this fiasco."

Senator Kelly wasn't the smartest man in the world, but he understood that he couldn't let Mr. Smith answer any more questions. The rest of the senators felt the same way, and the committee soon dispatched Mr. Smith. After he left, Senator Kelly continued.

"Our next witness is a man who has been directly impacted by Revenue Ruling 34-897. He is an entertainment professional, but he is not here just because he starred in a number of blockbuster movies. I have strict personal rules against allowing just any Hollywood celebrity to testify before this committee," he lied. Senator Kelly would let any star testify before him at any time. He went on, "He is a man with a personal story to tell, one that will shock the members of this committee and the public. He is well known as Hugo the Human Destructo, and we welcome him here today."

It is the usual practice to use your real name when testifying before Congress. This posed a problem for Hugo. His real name was Jeff Maysent. Hugo did not think this was an appropriate name for a man who specialized in the bent-knee back-breaker wrestling hold. Therefore, Hugo refused to testify until I could work out a deal with the committee beforehand to let him use his stage name.

Hugo moved up to the witness table. I joined him, along with Mark and Brad. The bulbs started flashing again as the photographers moved around the room, snapping pictures. The crowd, which was large and noisy, quieted as Hugo began to speak. At the front of the room, the timer light was switched off. There was no need to hurry the star witness.

"Mr. Chairman, members of the committee," he began. "I am here today to expose a serious injustice. The Internal Revenue Service is preparing to seize my home in California. I do not know if it will happen today or tomorrow. I do not know where I will sleep when I return from this trip. I was advised by my friends to stay in California and fight the agents when they arrive to seize the property. But I thought it was more important to appear before you today to tell you my story. I do not know if you can help me. I only want you to help other innocent people from going through what I have had to face over the last two years."

Senator Kelly interrupted Hugo at this point. "We will do everything we can to help you as well as all innocent victims."

Hugo nodded in grateful recognition of the senator's offer of assistance. Looking serious, he continued. "Several years ago, I purchased some vacant property to build a house on. I was excited about the prospect of building my dream house. But my work commitments, and the time I spent on the President's Council on Physical Fitness, precluded me from having the time to build it.

"Imagine my surprise when I found that my dream house already existed. I found the house two years ago. Although it had been built for someone else, it was the perfect house for me. When the house went on the market, I knew I had to have it.

"As you know, there was a depression in real estate a few years back. I was unable to sell the property I owned in order to buy the house I wanted. Fortunately, an enterprising real estate agent knew about a potential buyer for my lot that was having cash problems. After many hours of work, he was able to arrange for a complicated multi-party land swap. I swapped my land and, after many steps, I acquired my house. It has been my house for two years. I live there with my wife and children. We want to stay there forever.

"Earlier this year, the Internal Revenue Service began an audit of my financial affairs. As you might imagine, they are very complicated. I am in the entertainment business, the health care business, and the vitamin business. I travel extensively around the world, sometimes on business, sometimes to carry out the important work of promoting physical fitness. It is difficult even for me to determine all my financial affairs. Frankly, it is not my job to keep books. I believe that God put me on this earth to help all people, but especially children, learn the value of physical fitness and good nutrition.

"Mr. Chairman, I admit that I am not the best record keeper. I admit that I do not always keep receipts. I was not surprised when the IRS questioned some of my business activities. But I was shocked when the IRS began to look into the details of my home swap.

"The swap was put together by real estate experts. They did the best job they could of determining the value of several different pieces of property. But the IRS started questioning the transaction. They said they were using Revenue Ruling 34-897 to assist them in their effort.

"Then they told me that because of the ruling, I owed more taxes. They want the money now. But because of my travels and other charitable work, I do not have the money to pay the taxes I owe.

"Today, I face losing my home. Part of the reason this will happen is due to Revenue Ruling 34-897. Tax experts have told me the ruling is only technical. It is not technical to me. I've been told that it only clarifies the law. I do not think that Congress intended for my family to live on the street. I've been told that it only affects a few people every year. Does that mean that it is all right for me to lose everything I treasure?

"Mr. Chairman, do not let this happen to anyone else. I will be okay, thanks to my friends. But other people may not be so lucky. They may lose their homes and have nowhere to go. I ask you to see that Revenue Ruling 34-897 is repealed."

Hugo had tears in his eyes as he finished. He had learned to fake them during his wrestling days. But no one questioned that they were real that day. The man was going to lose his house because of Revenue Ruling 34-897. The ruling was no longer an esoteric debating point. It was causing harm to innocent taxpayers, just like the Citizens Against Tax Injustice had warned it would.

In reality, Revenue Ruling 34-897 was only a very small part of Hugo's problem, assuming there was a tax swap. The primary reason the IRS was seizing Hugo's home was that he never paid any taxes at all. It may have been true that the IRS used the ruling to increase the amount that Hugo owed, but it was really irrelevant. By Brad's best guess, Hugo had made over $47 million in the previous seven years and had not paid one dime to the Internal Revenue Service.

No one but Brad, Mark, and I knew the depths of Hugo's problems. By now, Hugo was convinced that all those problems stemmed from Revenue Ruling 34-897. Brad and I had tried to discuss the situation truthfully with Rob and Senator Kelly before the hearing, but their eyes glazed over from Brad's description of the transactions. And it really didn't matter. The senator was uninterested in details when he had a genuine media star for his hearing.

The room remained silent while everyone considered Hugo's plight. At that moment, every person in the room was afraid of losing his or her house to the Internal Revenue Service. If I had taken up a collection right then and there, I probably could have raised thousands of dollars for Hugo.

Senator Kelly broke the silence. "Thank you for your testimony. Your willingness to appear before us today, when your house is in danger of seizure, shows the depth of your commitment to this issue. I do not have any questions. I do not think I can add anything to your stark and brutal testimony. Thank you for coming today."

"Thank you, Mr. Chairman." Hugo choked back the tears.

"Mr. Chairman, Mr. Chairman," one of the other senators called out. "I only have one suggestion. I think we have a duty to protect this man's home from the Internal Revenue Service. I plan to write the IRS today and tell them we intend to pass legislation to repeal Revenue Ruling 34-897. I will direct them not to seize this witness's house while the legislation is pending. I hope you will add your name to that letter."

The room broke into loud clapping and cheers. Senator Kelly banged his gavel forcefully. "There will be no clapping, cheering or other disruptive noises from the public. This is a serious hearing." The senator was clearly furious that he had not thought of the idea. If he had, he would have let the cheering continue for a long time. "I would be delighted to sign the letter," he said curtly.

Hugo just shook his head in disbelief at his good fortune.

———————

Two days later, I was reading the press clippings in my office. The hearing had been featured on all almost every news channel, including the network news. The newspapers and weekly magazines had extensive coverage as well. As I savored my feats of the week, I received a call from Russ Ratto. He was calling from Congressman Conlin's office. The congressman, as chairman of the House Ways and Means Committee, had just returned from the White House where he had been discussing pending legislation with the president.

"I thought you would want to know that Congressman Conlin discussed Revenue Ruling 34-897 with the president," Russ announced.

"What did they decide to do about it?"

"They agreed that the effort to repeal the ruling is total bullshit."

"Russ, you offend me," I said in mock horror.

"But they also agreed that they don't have a prayer of stopping the legislation to repeal the ruling. The president agreed to sign the bill when it reaches his desk. In fact, he told the secretary of the treasury not to enforce the ruling in the interim."

"That's great news."

"The White House even plans to release a statement in favor of the legislation."

"As well it should. It's about time the president got on the side of the average American."

"You mean like Hugo the Human Destructo?"

"Exactly, an average American."

"An average American who makes millions of dollars a year and is represented by Johnson, Woods & Hart."

"Something like that. By the way, did the congressman also tell the president that while he is rolling over and playing dead for us, we also want him to roll over on the Hand Towel Equity Act?"

"The president will veto the Hand Towel Equity Act so fast it will make your head spin."

"Maybe I should get Warren Ford to endorse the Hand Towel Equity Act."

"You sure are full of yourself, today. Enjoy it. It won't last." He sounded surprised at my cockiness—but also tired.

"You know, in the rodeo, it's a win if you stay on the horse for eight seconds."

"Well, I'd say you have been there for about seven. No one ever stays up for long in Washington."

I didn't want to alienate a good friend, so I said, "You're probably right, Russ. Just let me enjoy my win for a day or two." Russ agreed and hung up.

Of course, I had no intention of ending the ride. Warren Ford and I were on a roll, and I was going to keep it going. The president had conceded on Revenue Ruling 34-897. Too bad; I'd wanted to ride that issue for a while longer. I would just have to find another one. And in the meantime, I decided to reward myself and the firm with another bill. I prepared a bill for another $100,000 and sent it down to accounting. The total was now $750,000. I was on top now, with the president and Congress bowing to the will of Warren Ford. I was confident that with all the press, the scam would finally start bringing in lots and lots of money—and if not, that some bank would continue to lend money to Jason based on the bills.

I had to inform the members of CATI about our victory. A newsletter was overdue, so I decided to write one. I wanted it out before the press got wind of the president's concession on the legislation from the White House. I picked up a sheet of paper and wrote the lead story, "Victory in Washington." I discussed the hearing and the pledge by the president to sign the legislation. I told the members how the victory was due to their efforts and support. I laid out how the letter-writing campaign had stirred the Congress to act and the president to cave on Revenue Ruling 34-897. I congratulated them and praised them.

It took me three pages to write the story. The newsletter usually ran four pages, with the back page devoted to fundraising appeals. Another feature I always included was a letter from a member. I decided to put a letter on the last page and to include an insert with the fundraising appeal. It would be a slick addition to our most important newsletter. Finally, I might raise some money.

I shuffled through the letters I had received from the CATI members, hoping to find one to include. Usually I had one ready to go, but I had been so busy preparing for the hearing that I let the task slip. I started reading the letters but found none that I liked. I read through the stack twice. This was going to be a great newsletter—the announcement of our victory over the Internal Revenue Service—and I was not going to spoil it with a boring letter on page four. Also, I had decided to really hit the members with a big fundraising appeal, and I wanted another dramatic issue to grab them. But there were no good letters.

I rose and paced. It was my moment of triumph, and I couldn't lose it.

I finally decided to make up a letter. I had a momentary doubt about the wisdom of this, but it didn't last very long. Hadn't I just brought down the White House? Didn't I orchestrate the best hearing in the Senate since the beginning of the republic? I decided to proceed.

Not bound by the facts, I allowed my imagination to flow. I decided to try to top the Revenue Ruling 34-897 issue. I wondered what could throw more fear into average Americans than losing their house. There was only one answer: to be thrown in jail falsely. My mind kept flowing. Then I picked up a piece of paper and wrote.

Dear Mr. Ford,

I am a fourteen-year-old boy living in a large city. Last night the federal marshals and agents of the Internal Revenue Service came and arrested both of my parents. When I heard them come in the door, I hid in the closet.

I heard the IRS agents tell my parents they were guilty of tax fraud. They kept calling them Mr. and Mrs. Spees. That is not our name. There were some people called Spees in our neighborhood, but they were very bad and they left in the middle of the night a week ago. I think the IRS made a terrible mistake. My parents have never done anything illegal.

I have not heard from either of them for days. I am living alone. Please help me. I need your help.

(name withheld by request)

That would scare any parent, I thought. It was a fitting end to the newsletter.

Walking out to Kathryn's desk, I found a note telling me that she was working out with Emilio. Wanting the newsletter to go out in the morning mail, I wrote her a note, giving her specific instructions to get the newsletter printed and mailed, and to include a fundraising appeal I had previously written as an insert. I left the material on her desk.

It was late in the day, and the office was clearing out. I was still basking in the glow of victory. I strolled down to Jason's office. I wanted to talk about the Hugo hearing with him, but his office was empty. I walked in and sat at his desk. I would never have dared to do that before, but I felt I had arrived in the big leagues in Washington. I wanted to see how it felt.

Jason's desk was full of papers. Most of them contained financial data, along with some letters from banks. I didn't read any of them. I just sat there in Jason's chair as the sun set, feeling the power run through me. I loved being on top.

CHAPTER XI
YOU CAN'T ALWAYS GET WHAT YOU WANT

The next day I waited for Doug Dezube at the airport. He wasn't expecting me. In fact, I should have been at the office, making sure the CATI newsletter got out, but I felt great and wanted to share my joy by being the best lobbyist Dezube ever saw. I heard him bellowing to the guards as he pushed through the security areas. I smiled. Even Dezube wasn't going to spoil my mood. As he came through the security doors, he saw me, yelled out my name, and smiled. There is nothing a client enjoys more than total attention from a lobbyist.

Then his look changed. He realized that I would not have been there unless I had something important to tell him. Probably something bad. It was all bad news these days.

"What's the matter?" he asked.

"Nothing at all. I came to meet you because we have a meeting with Senator Kelly in twenty minutes. There wasn't time for you to come to my office first." That was only partly true. I wanted to see Dezube's face when I told him we actually had a congressional meeting without either begging or bribing some reluctant staff person.

He rewarded me with a renewed smile. "Isn't Senator Kelly one of our supporters?"

"Right now he is our only supporter in the entire country."

"And he wanted to see me?"

"More or less." I didn't have the heart to tell Dezube that Senator Kelly didn't remember him or the Hand Towel Equity Act when I mentioned it to him. But the senator was very pleased by the Revenue Ruling 34-897 hearing and would have agreed to see me for any reason. My stock was so high I could have taken the penis slasher in with me.

We caught a cab to the Capitol and made our way to Senator Kelly's office. Rob Fitzgibbons was waiting for us, wearing another cheap suit. I introduced Doug to Rob, and we waited for the senator.

After a few minutes, we were ushered into the senator's office. He was behind his desk. He saw me and rose with a big smile, extending his hand to me. "It is good to see you, Mr. Brewster." Then, turning to Dezube, he said, "And this must be Warren Ford. I have looked forward to meeting you. Welcome."

"Actually, Senator, this is Doug Dezube," I said quickly.

"Of course, Mr. Dezube, it's good to see you. How is Mr. Ford? Do you work for him?" Dezube looked confused. Seeing that, the senator looked confused. Rob looked scared, knowing that he hadn't prepared the senator and that he would hear about it later. I tried to get the meeting back on track.

"Senator, as you remember, Doug is the head of the Hand Towel Trade Association. You introduced the Hand Towel Equity Act earlier this year. We wanted to discuss the future of the bill with you. We discussed my coming in the other day after the hearing. By the way, Doug saw your magnificent hearing on the Revenue Ruling 34-897 bill, and he told me that he was glad you were on our side."

The senator recovered. "Of course, I remember now. Doug, how are you?"

"Fine, Senator, fine." I knew that by lunchtime Doug would have forgotten the confusion and convinced himself that Kelly requested the meeting. It was good to have clients with a strong power of denial.

I decided to warm the senator up a bit more. "Senator, you sure got great coverage on your hearing."

"Thank you. It is an important issue, and I am glad we made an impression on my colleagues as to how necessary the bill is."

"You certainly did that. I was told by my friend in Congressman Conlin's office that the White House has instructed the Internal Revenue Service to stop implementing the ruling."

"That's not good enough for me. I want that bill passed."

"The president will certainly sign the bill. He couldn't face the political heat if he vetoed it. It's a credit to the job you did."

The senator smiled. "I think you're right. The bill will get signed." He turned to Doug. "What can we do for you today?"

"Senator, as you know, you introduced the Hand Towel Equity Act earlier this year," I answered. "Since that time, some opposition has developed. The opposition may be due, in part, to a lack of understanding."

The senator interrupted me. "Do you think we should hold a hearing, a really first-rate hearing?

"No," I quickly responded forcefully. I knew that a hearing would get lots of press coverage, but all of it would be against the bill. The administration would love to trash one of Kelly's bills to get back at him for the revenue ruling hearing. Every opponent of the bill would come out of the woodwork. Most would make a good impression. A hearing would be a disaster.

"Well, then, what do you suggest as an alternative?" the senator asked. Legislative detail work was not his strong suit. In fact, he had never gotten beyond the hearing stage with a bill.

I had an answer. "Rather than hold a hearing, which will give your opponents a forum to disagree with you, you should go straight to the Senate floor. The president says he has problems with the Hand Towel Equity Act. In fact, Senator, there is a veto threat on the bill. But you can get around it if you add the Hand Towel Equity Act to another bill. Add it to a bill the president doesn't dare veto."

Even the senator saw where I was going. Rob had a big smile on his face. "You wouldn't be suggesting that I add the Hand Towel Equity Act to the bill to repeal Revenue Ruling 34-897, would you?" he asked.

"Exactly." I smiled. I was the master of the world. An expert manipulator. The puppeteer in the show that is our government. I had it all, except the money, and that was sure to follow.

The Senate has a unique method of operation. When a bill is on the floor for debate, it is permissible to add another legislative provision even if the two have nothing whatsoever to do with each other. The Senate can be debating a bill to create a water project and amend it with a section that calls for better oversight of foreign aid funds. Or with a provision that calls for new pollution devices to be added to coal-fired power plants. Almost anything is possible. Once Senator Kelly added the Hand Towel Equity Act to the revenue ruling bill, the Senate would probably vote both down. That was fine with me. It would keep Revenue Ruling 34-897 alive as an issue for CATI. Warren Ford would blast the Senate and call for a major new fundraising effort to try again.

On the other hand, the Senate might just decide to accept the Hand Towel Equity Act if it was attached to the very popular Revenue Ruling Repeal Act. The president might make the same decision and sign the bill into law. It was a long shot, but it was the only shot we had to see the Hand Towel Equity Act enacted.

Thankfully, Dezube had been quiet during this discussion. He obviously felt left out as he suddenly blurted, "You know, Senator, we have done your work for you. We're a resource for you and your staff."

The senator, Rob, and I all looked at Dezube. Each of us wondered what the hell he was talking about. He then made himself clear. "I haven't been following this Revenue Ruling Repeal Act, but I don't want it dragging down the Hand Towel Equity Act. Are you sure it is a good idea to combine those two bills?"

Good, Doug, I thought. *You are afraid that a bill that will probably pass the Senate by a vote of ninety-five to five and has a firm commitment from the president to be signed into law may endanger the fate of a bill that the president has sworn to veto and has the active opposition of everybody in the world not sitting in this room.*

But rather than point out that my client had said dumbest thing imaginable, I said, "Doug's point is well taken. You don't have to add the Hand Towel Equity Act to the Revenue Ruling 34-897 bill. You can offer it to any bill. It just seems to me that those two bills were meant to be together."

We left the senator to ponder our suggested strategy and went to visit offices where Dezube had not yet offended the staff. By midafternoon, he was back on a plane and I had caught a cab back to my office. I felt very satisfied about my work that day. I actually hoped that the Senate decided to kill both bills. I hated to let go of Revenue Ruling 34-897. I had violated a cardinal rule of lobbying— never solve a problem. Maybe I wasn't as good as I thought I was. Charlie Nagle would have found a way to keep the issue alive for at least another year or two. But on second thought, I decided that I *was* as good as I thought I was.

Returning to my office, I picked up the final version of the newsletter, which was lying on my desk. The story about the hearing looked very slick. The letter on the last page was heartrending. All in all, it looked like a super piece of propaganda. I was sure it would bring in hundreds of thousands of dollars.

As I picked it up to read more closely, the insert fell out. I figured it had to be the request for money. But instead, it was a reprint of another letter. The letter was from a man that had a fight with the IRS over whether he could depreciate the value of his dog since it was a potential television star. There was no fundraising appeal anywhere on the letter, or in the newsletter.

At first I thought it was a joke. But the more I looked at the insert, which was printed on the same quality paper as the rest of the newsletter, I realized that Kathryn had made a terrible, terrible mistake. I was furious. It was not like her to make an error, and her timing couldn't have been worse.

I charged out of my office and confronted her.

"What the hell happened?" I said, my voice tight.

Of course, she had no idea what I was talking about. She looked up from her work in surprise and shrugged.

I shook the newsletter in the air. "Have these newsletters been mailed today?"

She nodded.

"Where did you find this letter and why did you make it the insert?" I continued.

"Here in my file," she said softly. She showed me a file full of material I had asked her to keep for use in future newsletters. On top of the file was the original letter from the dog owner with a yellow sticky note attached, which read, *Hold for insert.*

I pawed through the papers on top of her desk and found the fundraising appeal I had intended for her to include as the insert. I handed it to her and watched as she read it. "Without this, the newsletter won't raise a dime. With it, it would have finally gotten us out of the hole," I said to the only person who knew the real financial situation.

Her bottom lip began quivering as she realized the magnitude of her mistake. I felt sorry for her, but I was still too angry to back down. I stamped back into my office and slammed the door.

About an hour later, there was a knock. Emilio entered and

reminded me that we had a workout session scheduled. I figured the exercise would do me good, so we headed to the gym. There we discussed the future of the health club. Emilio told me about his efforts to locate another site and to keep the equipment order current. I was pleased by his desire to keep the process moving. However, I reminded him that I had asked for my money back to hold for safekeeping. He looked disappointed, and I felt a bit guilty. I still fully intended to invest in the club, but there was no reason to waste the interest in the interim. He handed me a personal check for $10,000 as we left the gym.

"You know, Kathryn is pretty cute," he said on the street.

"Maybe, but she can sure be a bimbo sometimes," I said.

Emilio looked surprised. "I thought you two have worked together for a long time."

"We have, but she made a bad mistake this morning. Maybe she's falling in love. Maybe she doesn't like it on the seventh floor. Maybe she is having trouble dealing with all the responsibilities of the Citizens Against Tax Injustice. I don't know."

Emilio looked at me closely. "She knows everything about the tax group?"

"Everything. At least, she does when she pays attention."

"You are really down on her."

I realized that my anger would pass and I would regret saying anything further.

"You're right. She is a good secretary."

"And she looks great in workout clothes."

"Maybe. Anyway, when we open the health club, there will be hundreds of beautiful women joining, and they will all look good in workout clothes. I can't wait."

"Cool beans."

———

Returning to my office with my head cleared, I swept by Kathryn.

"I'm sorry," she said.

"I know. But it is a huge mess. We'll have to figure out another way to get the funds in."

She agreed. "It would be nice not to worry about that."

"No kidding, Kathryn. Thank God no one knows everything but

you and me. No one knows that we have no money, and no one will know that you left out the fundraising appeal. We'll have to cover for each other."

Entering my office, I was met by two Republican activists, Allan Katz and Mike Abrams. Their job was to organize fundraising in Washington on behalf of the Republican Party for the upcoming midterm election. They did it because it was a job, but also because they were the most rabid Republicans I knew.

"We need you to help raise money," Allan said. "We need to get the White House back, and the midterm elections are the first step."

"We want you to open your Rolodex up for us," added Mike.

"I'll be glad to help, but I don't know that many people. And everyone I do know has already been hit up to help. We spend our days calling each other."

"We do have other people, but you are a real mover and shaker," continued Allan.

"How many have you told that to today, Allan?" I asked.

"Richard, I am offended. We are looking to you to help in our salvation."

"Don't you want the White House back?" Mike tried a different tack. "It takes money to throw the Democrats out. Remember, they're taxing you to death just so they can spend government money to create new Democratic constituencies."

"I can't argue with that. Okay. I'm broke, but I'll try to find some money for our party. Anything else?"

"The issues group would like you to help them, too," said Allan.

"What would that entail?"

"There would be a meeting once a week to hash out ideas our candidate can use in the election. In addition, you might be asked to write a few position papers."

"I don't have the time," I protested.

"It's not that demanding. Besides, it's for a great cause," said Allan. "I just can't stand the Democrats."

"I won't argue about the importance of the cause, but I just don't have a lot of time to devote to a political race right now."

"You used to be an animal," said Mike, "working twenty-four hours a day for the party. Remember when we wrote that position briefing book for Governor Reagan?"

"That was a long time ago," I said. I sat back in my chair. "I wish I could do more for the party. I wish I could spend more time at work. Jason has made me one of his chosen boys, but I am sure he wants me to work more hours. I want to open a health club. But most of all, I want to spend more time with my children. My philosophy is simple: Life is managed guilt. I can never meet all the demands people place on my time. I can never meet all the demands I place on my myself. I just make the best call I can each day, realizing that no one, least of all me, will ever be satisfied. I wish I could do more."

"Hey," said Allan, "I can't argue with that. But what do I know? However, if there is anything you can do, please call us. We particularly need help preparing some issue papers mapping out the Republican strategy on trade."

"Why do you need help on that issue?"

"The president's trade position against the Chinese is very popular. I wish we had something to counteract it."

"The Chinese rejected the American position," I replied. "It will be a great embarrassment for our country when the news about it gets out."

They both leaned forward intently. "How do you know that?" they both asked.

"The Chinese wrote the US government a letter rejecting our claims."

"How do you know that?"

"I have a copy of it." I looked around my desk, found the letter that Walker Dudley had given me, and handed it to them. They read it with great interest.

"This hasn't been in the papers," said Mike. "When it comes out, it will be a black eye for the administration."

"Well, if I have a copy," I replied, "there must be hundreds of other copies around town. Nothing stays a secret for very long in Washington."

"Well, this is still a secret. Can we have a copy?"

"If I give it to you, do I have to raise money?" They looked at me as if I had said the dumbest thing in the world. In Washington, this was the dumbest thing to say. I backed down. "Just kidding. Sure, take a copy."

After they left, I went through the mail. I found a personal letter to Warren Ford from Charles E. Nagle. I opened it and found the best evidence yet that CATI had become a force to be reckoned with in Washington. In the letter, Mr. Nagle offered Mr. Ford his heartiest congratulations on the recent successes of CATI. He went on to offer the services of his firm and himself, Charles E. Nagle, to lobby on behalf of Mr. Ford.

Of course, I understand that you are currently represented by the firm of Johnson, Woods & Hart, the letter went on to say. *You have chosen a top-notch firm. However, if you find yourself in need of further Washington representation, our firm would be delighted to discuss the matter with you.*

I enjoyed reading the letter and looked for someone to share the moment with. Unfortunately, I wouldn't be able to explain to anyone why I was opening Warren Ford's mail, marked *Personal and Confidential.* Kathryn was nowhere to be found. She was certainly not at her desk. I assumed that she was in the bathroom, preparing for another date with Don, or Sam, or someone else. I tried calling Barbara, but she, too, was out of the office. I just had to savor the recognition of the arrival of CATI. A letter from Charlie Nagle, trying to steal it as a client, was the most concrete evidence of my success to date.

My joy was short-lived. The next day, I arrived at my office to find Kathryn looking scared. "Jason's looking for you, and he's mad."

"Why?"

"I don't know, but he came over here personally this morning. He told me to send you right to his office as soon as you got in."

As I approached Jason's office, I heard him muttering. Swinging around the door, I saw him sitting at his desk, staring at the *Washington Post.* He saw me and blurted out, "What the hell is going on?"

"I don't know what you're talking about."

"Have you seen the *Post* today?"

"Not all of it."

"Well, look," he said, his voice tight, pointing down to a story in the Style section. His hand was shaking. The story was very short. It was buried in a long string of pieces about the comings and goings of the Washington elite. The offending blurb read,

Super issue combines with super lobbyist. Fall is the time for clients to review the performance of their Washington lobbyists. The new citizens group, Citizens Against Tax Injustice, has been in contact with super lobbyist Charlie Nagle, regarding hiring him for special projects. No switch yet from current firm, Johnson, Woods & Hart, but watch for developments.

I was stunned. But I was also impressed with Charlie Nagle. He managed to get his name in the press again, attached to yet another hot issue. The story was true. Only it failed to mention that it was Nagle who had initiated the contact. I read the story again, awed by the skill involved. Then I remembered Jason was standing next to me and that he wanted an explanation.

"How could you let this happen?" he yelled. This was out of character for Jason. He usually preferred to show his displeasure with withering sarcasm.

"It's nothing."

"What do you mean?" he thundered.

"I talked to Warren Ford yesterday. He told me that Charlie Nagle wrote him. He has no intention of switching firms."

"What about special projects?"

"He has no intention of using any firm but ours for anything."

Jason was not satisfied. "Let's get him on the phone."

"What?"

"Let's get him on the phone and confirm that he is not going to use Nagle."

My heart was pounding. "Don't you trust me, Jason?"

"I trust you. I don't trust Charlie Nagle. Get Warren Ford on the phone."

"It's still early in Chicago."

"I don't care. Call him."

"I need to get the number from Kathryn. I'll be right back," I said as I started to move out of the room. He picked up the phone and pressed her interoffice number. I grabbed the phone away.

When she answered, I said, "Kathryn, will you please give me Warren Ford's number?"

"Huh?"

"Yes, the number in Chicago." I nodded to Jason.

"What number in Chicago?" she asked. There was an edge of panic in her voice.

"It's there on my Rolodex," I said calmly, hoping my leadership would reassure her.

"There is no Warren Ford."

"Yes, yes, I know." I turned to Jason. "She's getting it."

I reached for a piece of paper and started writing. "Good, that's right . . . 312-922-9656, thanks." I hung up before she could say anything further. Jason took the paper with the number and started dialing. He pushed the speaker button on his phone. He finished dialing, and we heard ringing on the line. Finally, after several rings, the phone was answered with a muffled "Hello?"

"Warren Ford, please," Jason asked.

"You have the wrong number," came the sleepy reply.

"Is this the office of Citizens Against Tax Injustice?" I interjected.

"No."

"Is this the home of Warren Ford?" asked Jason.

"No," the voice answered with rising anger. "You have the wrong number." He hung up.

I stood there for a second, trying to look surprised for Jason. "That bimbo gave me the wrong number. I'll go get the right number myself." I marched out of the room before he could stop me.

I returned to my office and sat down. It had been a close call, and it took me a minute to calm myself. Then I called Kathryn into my office and dictated a letter from Warren Ford to me.

Dear Mr. Brewster:

This is to confirm our conversation of last night, when I assured you that the Citizens Against Tax Injustice has no intentions to use other counsel at this time. We are pleased with the work of Johnson, Woods & Hart, and we are particularly happy with the outstanding service we have received from you. While other Washington firms have contacted us, we do not have any plans to use them.

Yours in Freedom,
Warren Ford

"There, see? It's all going to be all right," I said to Kathryn. She smiled, but I could detect the strain.

After Kathryn typed the letter, I walked it back down to Jason's office. He was still in a sour mood. He, too, was working on a memo.

"I got Warren Ford on the phone and he confirmed that he wasn't interested in any other firm," I said. "So I got him to write me a letter to that effect. Here it is." I handed it to Jason.

Jason took the letter and read it twice. For the first time that day, I saw him relax a bit. "Let's get this over to the *Washington Post*. That will fix old Nagle's wagon," he said.

Panic swept over me again. I knew the *Post* would try to confirm the letter. "I don't know about that," I said. I didn't want to push my luck.

"Why not? It would show Nagle to be the bullshitter that he is."

"The *Post* knows he's a bullshitter. That's why he gives them such great stories."

"I think we should release this letter."

"No!" I said sharply. Jason looked at me with curiosity. Then he looked back at the letter. As he read it again, he tensed up. Then he looked back at me for a long time.

"This was written here," he said slowly.

"What do you mean?"

"The letter doesn't have any fax markings on it, and it couldn't have come through the mail. This was written here."

My heart started pounding. I was convinced it was audible from the hall. In the next split second, several thoughts flew through my mind. There had been no need for the letter. I had written it because I thought I was so clever. I thought I was fooling everyone, that I was smarter than everyone. I had been so proud of myself that I forgot the letter was supposed to come from Chicago and not Washington. Now I had to dig myself out of a ditch I had put myself in unnecessarily.

"Warren Ford dictated the letter to me," I stammered.

"Did he tell you to sign it too?" Jason asked.

"Yes."

Jason bored in on me. "What's going on here?" he asked. He peered straight into my eyes and waited for an answer.

My mind was still in total confusion; on a high from my success thus far, I never anticipated getting caught. Now I was unable to think up another story to get me off the hook. Jason stared, waiting. The silence pressed in on me. Finally, I just started talking, not really knowing where I was heading.

"Jason, Warren Ford and the Citizens Against Tax Injustice owe this firm over $750,000 in fees so far this year." That was a good beginning, but I had no idea where to go next. Jason nodded in agreement with that point but kept watching me for more information. I couldn't think of anything. The silence grew again.

Then, half in defiance, half in surrender, I said, "Do you really want to pursue this and perhaps lose a good client?"

"What do you mean?"

"I mean, you have promised the banks that the fees from this client are good and will be collected. You did that based on information from me. If I have an idea that the bills might not be good, and if I told you, wouldn't you be ethically required to inform the bank? Do you really want that knowledge?"

"You told the bank the same thing."

"I know, but I am a nothing. You are Jason Johnson, and it is your word that they rely on, not mine."

"Do you think the funds will actually come in?"

I hesitated only a minute. I was so far into the whole scam that I couldn't find a way out of it. "Yes, I think that now that we have had a hearing and a major legislative victory, the money will come in. But in the meantime, do you really want to know everything? It might jeopardize the whole situation."

He regarded me silently for a long time. "No. I guess I don't want to rock that boat," he said. He handed me his memo. "I am distributing this tomorrow."

To: all Partners
From: Jason Johnson
Subject: Monthly Draws
Personal and Highly Confidential
Not to be shared with Anyone

Due to a temporary difficulty with the bank and with a shortfall in collections, all partner's draws will be reduced by 50% this month. This is a very temporary situation. We expect to resolve this matter in the very near future once we get all our bills paid by our clients.

I handed the memo back to Jason. He continued to look at me. I could tell he was torn between his desire to know everything at Johnson, Woods & Hart and his need to know nothing that he would have to report to the banks. I bet that no other junior partner had ever put him in such a fix, and he wasn't happy about it. It killed him to know that he had to let the matter drop.

On the other hand, I was angry now. I resented taking a salary cut. I bet the firm plane was still on the runway, and I saw the arrangement of fresh-cut flowers sitting on Jason's credenza. Sure, I was part of the problem, but not nearly all of it. We stared at each other for another minute, and then I started to leave. Jason looked away.

As I left, I said over my shoulder, "I don't think we should send this letter to the *Post*." Jason grumbled something unintelligible, but I knew that he had acquiesced.

CHAPTER XII
THE LONG AND WINDING ROAD

The next morning, the very confidential memo from Jason was in a sealed envelope in my in-box. I read it again with disgust. At least I had gotten the check back from Emilio and deposited it in the bank the night before. I had held it a few days but now needed the money. The health club would have to wait while I paid my bills.

Kathryn came into my office and closed my door. "Will I still get paid?" she asked.

"Of course," I reassured her. "What makes you think that you won't?"

"I just heard that the partners are taking a fifty percent pay cut. When the big guys get hit, the little guys usually get hurt too."

"Don't be silly. We're just having growing pains. We need to cut some expenses until we catch up with our income. It will all be over soon." *So much for confidentiality*, I thought.

About an hour later, I received a phone call from Russ Ratto. "I thought you might be interested to know that the Senate leadership has just decided to consider the bill to repeal Revenue Ruling 34-897 this afternoon."

"Thanks, Russ. I'll watch the vote on television. This is fairly quick action by the Senate. The House only passed it last week."

"Well, they decided that they couldn't take the pressure from all their constituents screaming for the repeal of the ruling. They want the bill out of Congress and on the president's desk as soon as possible."

"Remember when you told me that Revenue Ruling 34-897 was a nonissue. Remind me again, what was the vote in the House on the bill?" I asked him.

"The vote was 414 to 20 in favor of passage. But did you notice that my boss did not vote for the bill?"

"That's because your boss has integrity and actually understood the ruling and the bill. Also, he has the best staff in Congress. Thank God there aren't many others like him in the House."

"Apparently there are nineteen others."

"I'm glad you're working for one of them. Seriously. Thanks for the heads-up."

"I felt you could use some good news, since you're taking such a pay cut this month." He hung up.

I wondered when the press would start calling. So much for secrets. I was determined to sit in my office for the day, until things blew over a bit. By tomorrow, the firm's financial difficulties would be an old story. I didn't even want to walk out into the hall. If I did, I knew I would be met by stares of fright from the support staff. If I ran into another partner, we would immediately start talking about how we never approved of all the spending done by the firm even though we voted for every expenditure when they were brought up separately. Jason might have been guilty of mismanagement of the firm, but he had lots of accomplices. I wanted to avoid all such encounters.

As I sat in my office, watching the Senate on television, I got another call. This one was from Sheila Reynoldson, the staff member managing the FDA Improvements Act, the bill to authorize the FDA to review Dr. Garrity's medical evidence and the chicken pox vaccine.

"The Senate is passing a bunch of noncontroversial bills today. We were just told that the list includes the FDA bill. I thought you'd want to know," she reported.

"Thanks, Sheila. I appreciate it."

"We don't expect any problems on the floor. It should all be over in a few minutes."

"Thanks to you."

"No. Thanks to you. You have helped keep the passage simple. It's been a fun bill to work on."

"After it passes, do you want to call Dr. Garrity, or do you want me to call him?"

"We would like to call him."

"I will see what I can do."

"Thanks. By the way, I hope the story about your firm isn't true."

"What story?"

"That your firm is going bankrupt."

"Oh, that story. It's untrue. I thought you were talking about the story that our firm is suing Charlie Nagle because he gave the daughter of one of our clients a sexually transmitted disease."

She gasped. "What? Is that true?"

"Sorry, I've got to take another call. Good luck today on the Senate floor." I could hear her protests as I hung up. Smiling, I figured that made me even with Nagle for the CATI story in the *Post*.

I called Garrity as soon as I hung up with Sheila, before the bill reached the Senate floor. It is a fundamental rule that clients need to hear good news from their lobbyists. "Doctor, I have good news," I said when I got him on the line. "The Senate is bringing your bill to the floor today."

"That's wonderful news."

"They don't expect any problems. It should sail through the Senate."

"Bless you."

"After it passes, the senator's office is going to call you. They will tell you that the bill has passed. Try to sound surprised, okay?"

"All right. Thank you, Mr. Brewster."

"Think nothing of it, Doctor."

There was a long silence. "Is there a problem, Doctor?" I asked.

"I was just wondering . . ."

"Wondering what?"

"Well, I was wondering if the fact that I haven't paid you in months is one of the reasons your firm is having such financial troubles . . ."

After I got him off the phone, I decided I had to get out of there. I would go up to the Capitol to watch both my bills pass. It would be rewarding to see and had to be better than taking phone calls. As I stood to leave, Barbara Lehman came into my office. Already exhausted by questions about the firm's finances, I asked, "Are you here to ask me about your job?"

"No."

"About your salary?"

"No."

"You have no questions about the firm's finances?"

"Only one. Can I still use the firm's credit card to go to lunch today?"

I laughed. I was cheered to know that nothing changed Barbara's priorities. "Forget lunch," I told her. "I'm going to the Senate to watch some of my legislation pass. Come along with me."

"Can we have a drink if you are successful?"

"Absolutely. Maybe more than one."

"Great. I'm in." As we started to leave, she asked, "Not that I really care, but what bills are we watching?"

"The Senate has scheduled to consider the FDA Improvements Act and the Revenue Ruling Repeal Act. And Senator Kelly plans to add the Hand Towel Equity Act to the revenue ruling bill. I expect to have an excellent day."

"Sounds boring. But if you're buying, I'm going."

Before leaving, I called Rob Fitzgibbons to remind him that Senator Kelly was to add the Hand Towel Equity Act to the revenue ruling bill. Although he wasn't specific, he assured me they were ready for the day's events.

We took a cab to the Capitol and found seats in the Senate gallery. The Senate was in the process of passing a number of measures. It was a slow day, and most of the bills were routine matters. The galleries were fairly empty. There were almost no members of the press in the Press Gallery and only a few members walking on and off the Senate floor.

Barbara nudged me in the ribs. "There's your champion," she said, pointing to Senator Kelly as he came onto the Senate floor. Rob Fitzgibbons accompanied the senator. They walked back to the senator's desk and found seats. "I'm surprised he found his way to the Senate Chamber," Barbara whispered.

"Shhhhh," I hissed. "He is my hero today."

The assistant majority leader stood at his desk, managing the action on the floor. He called up bills one at a time. Once they were called up, he let any interested senator express his or her support for the measure. When everyone had spoken, he called for a vote on the bill. Each of the bills passed without a dissenting vote. All the bills had been fully reviewed by the leadership of both parties to ensure that there were no problems or objections. Any bill that faced a controversy was pulled from the schedule. They would be debated later. The idea was to process as much legislation as possible that day.

The assistant majority leader called up the bill to repeal Revenue Ruling 34-897. Barbara and I sat forward in our seats. Little did anyone know that the bill would be amended with the most hated bill currently in Congress—the Hand Towel Equity Act. The lazy afternoon proceedings were about to get exciting.

The assistant majority leader began to explain the bill. "This bill is designed to repeal a controversial policy proposed by the Internal Revenue Service. Specifically, it would abolish Revenue Ruling 34-897. There is a question about how this ruling would impact certain taxpayers. Rather than allow the ruling to stay on the books, causing confusion, this bill would eliminate it from the body of law guiding the IRS.

"The administration has indicated that it will sign the bill once it has passed the Congress. The bill passed the House by a vote of 414 to 20. I am unaware of any objections in the Senate. I urge that we pass it."

He paused and looked around the room. This was designed to allow any other senator that had something to say about the bill to stand up and be recognized. No one stood up. Senator Kelly remained in his seat, absentmindedly chatting with Rob.

"Where is your leader now?" Barbara asked.

"Probably asking Rob where he buys his suits," I said. Another minute passed. "Stand up, Senator. You're on," I whispered. The senator continued to chat quietly with his aide.

The assistant majority leader looked around the Senate chamber again. No one rose to make a comment on the bill. He turned back to face the presiding officer. "I move that we pass the bill."

The ranking Republican of the floor announced that there was no Republican opposition to the bill. He also urged that it be passed. "Now, Kelly, you boob," I whispered. The senator didn't move.

"Great choice of champions," Barbara said.

The bill to repeal Revenue Ruling 34-897 passed. It would be sent to the White House, where the president would sign it into law. The Citizens Against Tax Injustice had scored a major victory.

As the assistant majority leader paused and looked over his notes, Senator Kelly rose and addressed the presiding officer. He was recognized to make a speech.

"Mr. President, I wanted to say a few words about the bill we just passed. It repeals a very bad revenue ruling issued by the Internal Revenue Service. I held a hearing on the bill a short time ago. At that time we discovered that the ruling was being used to justify the seizure of a house of an innocent taxpayer. I am convinced that the record we created that day helped the Senate pass this bill.

"I had originally intended to add another provision to this bill. It also dealt with a serious injustice in our society—the illegal importation of hand towels. But I decided that this bill was too important to change in any way. The bill needs to get down to the White House as soon as possible and does not need to go to conference with the House. It needs to be signed into law so that the IRS will never use Revenue Ruling 34-897 to hurt a taxpayer again. So I will wait to ask the Senate to pass the Hand Towel Equity Act at a later time.

"I thank you for the opportunity to make these remarks."

With that, the senator walked off the floor. Rob continued to sit near the senator's desk, which was covered with papers.

"Beautiful speech," Barbara said, smiling. "But now you'll have to call Dezube and tell him that Kelly didn't bring up his bill today." She shrank back in mock terror.

The assistant majority leader continued to bring up bills for consideration. The wheels of legislation rolled on.

About thirty minutes later, he announced that the next bill to be considered was the FDA Improvements Act.

"Well, at least I am two for three today," I whispered.

"And you got the big one."

"Which one?"

"The tax bill."

"Yeah, it is big, but I am really proud of the next bill. It will actually help people."

She smiled. "Something new and different."

I smiled back. "Something new and different."

The assistant majority leader was explaining the FDA Improvements Act. He told the empty galleries how the FDA needed the legislation in order to review a new vaccine for chicken pox and additional vaccines to prevent other childhood diseases. The administration had testified in favor of the bill, and the House had passed it recently. He urged the Senate to pass the bill.

The Republican leader came on the floor. He announced that the Republicans also supported the bill. He too urged the Senate to pass the bill.

At that point other senators stood and expressed their support for the bill. Senator Kelly came back on the floor and watched the action for a minute. He turned to Rob and they had a lively conversation. As the chamber quieted, Senator Kelly rose and requested recognition.

"Mr. President, I, too, want to express my support for this legislation. It is an important bill for the children of America . . ."

Barbara nudged me. "With his support, it will surely pass. I think the rest of the senators were waiting for his blessing."

"With his support, the chances of passage probably went down," I responded. "Any bill he supports can't be all good."

"Maybe Rob explained it to him."

The senator continued his speech. "However, Mr. President, I have an amendment to add to the bill . . ."

I got a knot in the middle of my stomach.

"This amendment does not impact the FDA. In fact, it is irrelevant to this bill. However, as you know, the Senate rules allow me to add other provisions."

"What is he doing now?" asked Barbara.

"He's adding the Hand Towel Equity Act to this bill," I said, growing cold.

"Pretty slick."

"No, it's not. It will kill this bill. And it is important. The president will never sign a bill with the Hand Towel Equity Act added to it. This is the worst thing he could do."

"I didn't know he could even figure out the Senate rules. I wonder who gave him the idea?"

"Me," I said. I was very, very cold.

"My amendment is designed to correct another injustice. It is the importation of hand towels into the United States from third-world countries. These countries have very low standards of living. Their wage rates are far below the rates in America. By producing the towels under such conditions, they undercut American workers. This bill will increase the tariff on those hand towels."

He continued to describe the Hand Towel Equity Act. But as he was talking, there was increased commotion on the Senate floor.

Several senators were aware of the president's objections to the bill. Others opposed it for their own reasons. They had no intention of letting Senator Kelly get away with adding the Hand Towel Equity Act to the FDA bill.

When Senator Kelly finished describing the Hand Towel Equity Act, he offered it as an amendment to the FDA bill. It was now in play.

Several senators jumped up and immediately objected to consideration of the amendment. Cries of "Mr. President, Mr. President" rose from the floor as senators strove for the honor of blasting the Hand Towel Equity Act first. The presiding officer recognized one senator in the front.

"Mr. President," he began, "I am gravely concerned that the FDA Act, an important piece of legislation, will be jeopardized by the inclusion of the Hand Towel Equity Act."

"Right on," I whispered.

"The president has stated he will veto the Hand Towel Equity Act. Adding it to this bill could doom them both."

He went on to trash the Hand Towel Equity Act. He was rough, but not as rough as I wanted him to be. After he finished, other senators stood and joined the effort. But Senator Kelly refused to back down. He insisted that his amendment be added to the bill before he would agree to final passage of it. In the usual circumstances, the Senate could vote down the amendment and then vote on the underlying FDA bill, but not in this case. Many senators were away from the chamber that day. There wasn't a quorum. That was why the leader was moving noncontroversial bills.

It was a stalemate. As the debate grew more heated, it became clear that there was no easy or quick way out of the box. Finally, with great regret, the Senate leadership pulled the FDA bill from consideration. They moved on to other matters.

Senator Kelly stood and started to leave. As he did, he looked up into the galleries. He spotted me, smiled, and gave me the thumbs-up sign. Rob waved at me.

"It looks like the senator wants to talk to you," Barbara said.

"Let's sit here for a minute so we miss him," I replied. "If I meet the son of a bitch, I may cut off his penis."

A few minutes later, as we left, I saw Sheila in the hall. Her face was red with frustration. I went to her and offered my sympathies.

"I don't understand why Senator Kelly did that," she said. "I don't believe that he could develop that strategy by himself. Who came up with the idea?"

"It must be some real smart-ass too clever for his own good," I answered with total sincerity.

"Amen. Well, call me tomorrow. We can discuss a counterstrategy. I am glad you're on our side."

"Thanks. I appreciate your confidence."

"At least Dr. Garrity won't know what happened. I hate to think what this would do to him."

Believe it or not, I felt even worse. "Oh my God, Sheila. I forgot about Dr. Garrity."

"Let's hope he is in the dark about this until we can fix it."

"Yes, let's hope."

───────────

We rode back to the office in silence. Barbara knew that I needed to think about the mess we were in. A worthless, unnecessary bill had flown through the Senate, while an important bill had got caught in the legislative grind. Not only was it my strategy that had created the mess, but also now I was in the midst of a conflict. Attorneys cannot represent both sides of an issue. To do so brings down ethical sanctions that could cost me my license to practice law. The problem was simple. I had one client, Dezube, who had only one chance of his interests getting signed into law—staying firmly attached to the popular FDA bill. But another client, Dr. Garrity, had an equally important interest in getting the two bills separated. If I helped one, I would hurt the other.

I tried to decide whether to confide in Barbara or not. Somehow, I didn't think she had an interest in ethical issues, but I gave it a try.

"Barbara, did you understand all that happened in there?"

"I understand that you got your tax bill through. Isn't that your big meal ticket? Why aren't you jumping for joy?"

"Because that bill isn't really important. I would actually prefer if it dragged on for a while. It would be better for the scam."

"So, that's the scam bill? I wondered. Is it paying off big-time?"

"Not yet. Soon, I hope. While it would be fun to ride the Revenue Ruling 34-897 bill a bit longer, it is also pretty significant that we got such a big win. Either way, I think we have turned a corner on the scam. But that's not what concerns me. I have a bigger ethical issue between the Hand Towel Equity Act and the FDA Improvements Act."

She interrupted me. "What do you mean, you might have turned a corner on the scam? Isn't it a big success?"

"Well, it has lots of members and just passed a bill, but it hasn't exactly raised much money yet."

"Well, just how much exactly has it raised?" She was homing in on the crucial issue. I wanted to avoid answering that question. Instead, I wanted sympathy and advice on my ethical dilemma.

"Not too much. But what should I do about my conflict?"

She would not be distracted. "I don't know. Tell me how successful you've been with your scam."

"Well, it actually hasn't raised a nickel. The expenses have eaten up all the income." I smiled at her as I delivered the truth.

She didn't smile back. "You have spent hours and hours of time and effort and have nothing to show for it?"

"Not yet. But I think that is all going to change soon."

We had arrived back at the office. "How about that drink?" I suggested.

"Maybe. I'll see what else is on my desk," she said, although it sounded like "Maybe. I'll see if I get a better offer."

"Well, I'll come by your office when I get done," I said as she got off the elevator on her floor. I went up to my office. A note on my desk informed me that an emergency partners' meeting would soon be starting. There was also a stack of CATI letters. I looked through them. The first few letters were uninteresting. One man didn't understand why the IRS was after him even though he had not paid taxes in eight years. Others made the standard accusations that the IRS had seized the wrong bank account or made an accounting mistake.

The tenth letter was in faint but beautiful handwriting. It was from a Mrs. Mary Grant from Oregon City, Oregon.

Dear Mr. Ford,

God bless you and the Citizens Against Tax Injustice. I am an 83-year-old widow, living on Social Security. I own my own home, which I bought with my late husband in 1937. Those were difficult times but we knew the value of land and homes. It was hard at times to keep the house, but my husband worked two jobs and I took in mending and we had enough.

Now in the twilight of my life, I want to protect my home for my children and myself. They are good people and they all have fine families. I did not know about the IRS and its attempt to take away people's homes. I find it hard to believe, but I never understood the federal government. I want to do everything I can to protect my property and my family.

I am sorry that I haven't been able to send you any money before now. As I said, all I have is Social Security to live on. However, today I am sending you a check for $75. I will have to skip a meal or two, but it is worth it for my family. I know it is not enough to pay for all your special projects, and so I don't expect to receive a full membership. Just keep up your good work.

> God Bless You,
> Mary S. Grant

I felt as if a block of cement had hit me. I read her letter over and over, each time feeling worse, until I was consumed by guilt.

How could I have allowed people like Mrs. Grant to fear that they would lose their homes? She was in no more danger of Revenue Ruling 34-897 than she was of being captured by space aliens. Yet here she was, sending me her Social Security money to pay for protection she didn't need.

I felt like the man in the coffee shop after the storm. I was sharing the vision of my scam with innocent people and scaring the hell out of them. They were trying to protect their loved ones, and there wasn't even any danger.

I intended to find her check and mail it back to her immediately. I left the office quickly, knocking the letter to the floor in my haste. I looked for Kathryn at her desk, and then throughout the hall. But it was after closing time, and she had gone home. I went to her desk and searched through her papers. In one stack, I found a new contributors list with Mrs. Grant's name on it. I saw a deposit list to the bank that included her check. Finally I saw a notation that Mrs. Grant had been mailed the form-letter acknowledgment from Warren Ford, along with a request for more money. It was the only time in my life that I had prayed for a secretary to be inefficient, but Kathryn had covered all the bases.

I paced around the seventh floor, trying to shake the guilt. I felt terrible for the second time that day. Returning to my new, big office, I considered how my position at Johnson, Woods & Hart was built on the contributions of Mrs. Grant, who would now have to skip some meals to pay for the privilege of our representation. And worst of all, the firm wasn't even getting paid. Instead, it was going to stationery stores, print shops, the US Postal Service, and *American Magazine*.

Still feeling sick, I headed down to the partners' meeting. It was just starting. Jason had turned the meeting over to Bill Meyer, the office manager, to discuss the firm's finances. It was one of his usual smart moves. No one could understand the office manager because he had no idea what he was doing. His numbers didn't add up. They made no sense. His presentation was impossible to follow. Worst of all, we couldn't tell if the mishmash of nonsense was due to his presentation or to the fact that no one had a handle on the true financial condition of the firm. When the rambling had ended, the office manager looked up to answer questions.

Jason asked the first one. "The bottom line is that we need most of our cash to pay our overdue bills and the partners can't receive their full salaries this month, right?"

"Yes."

Jason shook his head, looking baffled. Then he asked, "How much do we have in accounts receivable?"

"Over $60 million." As he said this, I slipped lower in my chair. Over $750,000 of that money was owed by CATI. But I also knew I was not the only problem.

"And we have borrowed against some of those accounts, right?"

"Yes."

"So if we collected what was owed to us, we could pay off the banks and all our debts and the firm would be in great shape, right?"

"Right."

Again, Jason just shook his head. He actually looked sad. We had let him down.

Other questions were asked of the office manager.

"What are our expenses? Is there an accounting somewhere?"

"Do we still have the airplane?"

"How many offices are losing money?"

"Are we still thinking about opening an office in Paris?"

"How many partners are not pulling their weight?"

"What are our plans to cut back on expenses?"

The answers just increased the confusion. The office manager was getting flustered, which only made his presentation worse. He looked to Jason for help, but Jason just sat there, shaking his head.

Finally, the partners stopped asking the office manager questions. Instead, they turned their inquiries towards Jason. Jason listened politely but declined to answer them.

"I just don't have the information," he protested. "Besides, the only fact that keeps running through my mind is that we have millions of unpaid bills out there. Get the money in the door, ladies and gentlemen."

As the questions ended, they were replaced by suggestions of where to cut the firm's swollen budget. Despite Jason's focus on collections, we could also get the firm on a sounder financial footing by cutting out some expenditures. Several partners suggested a number of prudent cuts. Jason listened to each idea politely, and then protested that the problem was not with the firm's expenditures but with collections. Jason was clearly not in the mood to hear any criticism about the management of Johnson, Woods & Hart.

Finally, everyone ran out of steam. There was silence as we sat staring at each other. Since we were not going to adjust the budget, there was not much else to say. But then John Horn, the chief litigator, decided he needed to add his wisdom to the proceedings.

"The key to the continuation of this firm is loyalty," he said defiantly. "Without loyalty, we are just a bunch of individual lawyers and not worth a good goddamn. We need to stick together, and anybody that can't see that is a goddamn fool. We are a family, and it's about time to start acting like one. Let's stick together. If we start cutting expenses right and left, it will be every man for himself . . ."

As Horn continued to rant about loyalty, his voice got louder. We could see that he was delivering one of his famous closing arguments. As he wrapped up, he implied that anyone who still wanted to cut expenses was guilty of treason and should be immediately hung.

As he finished, the room fell silent again. We all looked down at the conference table. We were afraid to admit that we had heard the same speech from Horn so many times it had lost any meaning. But several of us were finally admitting to ourselves that Horn was simply full of bullshit.

In the quiet, Jason wrapped up the meeting. We all stood and left the room silently. After retrieving my coat and briefcase from my office, I ventured down to the fourth floor to try to find Barbara for our overdue drink. She was nowhere to be found. Disappointed, I went down to the garage, got my car, and started to drive home.

For a while I felt sorry for myself. I was in one of the premier law firms in the city, and I was going to have to cut back on my lifestyle. I still had no doubts that Jason would pull us through the financial mess because I assumed that most of the bills were good and not made up out of thin air like mine. Eventually I would get my salary back. In the meantime I was married to a spendaholic and had three kids to support. I lusted after a beautiful associate but had yet to get beyond the cock-teasing stage with her. I wanted it all—from the money to the power to the side dish of a redhead—and I wasn't there yet. Yes, I felt I had every right to feel sorry for myself. And I did. Until I remembered Mrs. Grant. Then I rode in silence and emptiness.

CHAPTER XIII
FOOL ME TWICE, SHAME ON ME

No one ever accused President Clinton of being a fool. He never had to learn the same lesson twice. And so, the next day, when the press confronted him in the middle of his morning jog, he was ready for them. I watched it all play out on the news.

"Mr. President," called out one reporter, "what about the situation in Egypt?"

The president smiled, waved, and kept running.

"How are you going to pay for your latest domestic initiative?" asked another.

The president held his hand to his ear to indicate he couldn't hear.

"Mr. President, will you sign the bill to repeal Revenue Ruling 34-897?" tried a third as the president rounded a bend. The president turned and ran back to the crowd of journalists.

"I will sign the bill into law as soon as it hits my desk," he said, jogging in place. "By the way, I had the secretary of the treasury do a little research about that revenue ruling. It turns out that the ruling was first drafted during the last administration. When we came into office, we had a chance to stop its release. Frankly, we didn't catch it, and it got out. We never would have initiated any ruling like this. But we can't catch all the mistakes set in motion by my predecessor."

"So you aren't angry with Warren Ford?" the reporter asked.

"I've never had the pleasure of meeting Mr. Ford, but no, I am not angry with him. He pointed out a mistake made by the last administration. I only wish he had caught it when the Republicans were in office."

The crowd of journalists laughed. As the president turned to start running again, another question shot out. "What are you going to do about the poor boy whose parents were mistakenly imprisoned by the IRS?"

Again, the president turned. "This situation, if it is true, is a gross miscarriage of justice. This morning I will direct Attorney General Reno to personally look into this case. She will use all the law enforcement tools at her disposal to get to the bottom of the matter. She will report back to me and I will report back to you."

"How can we be sure that the American people will get that report?"

"Will you let me forget?" he asked, smiling. The reporters laughed again.

The president resumed running. As he ran off for the last time, one of the reporters yelled, "I guess you don't want to get burned by Warren Ford again."

The president smiled and waved. "You got that right," he said over his shoulder.

———

My morning started when the cat bit my foot as I walked to the bathroom to shave. Blowtorch was the meanest, mangiest cat on earth. She hated everyone and everything except food and Elizabeth. Even Amy, at her young age, had learned to stay away from the cat. That day, Blowtorch was up early and roaming the hallway. She fell in stride with me. As I reached the sink, she slowly lowered her open mouth over my foot. At the last second, she bit down hard.

"Ow, ow, goddamnit," I yelled, waking the whole family. The boys came running out of their shared room. "What's the matter?" asked Matthew.

"Blowtorch bit me," I complained. Matthew started laughing. David told me that I had said some bad words. The cat stalked away proudly.

After that distraction, Matthew missed the school bus. I drove him to school and then got caught in a late-morning traffic jam. I was stuck behind an SUV, which prevented me from seeing anything down the road. As it grew later and later, I got angrier and angrier at Senator Kelly, Rob Fitzgibbons, Jason, myself, Barbara, John Horn,

Elizabeth, and everyone my life had touched over the past few days. My only friend seemed to be Warren Ford, and only because he never talked back to me.

So I was in a foul mood when I arrived at work. Everyone was talking in whispers, but I was too angry and preoccupied to inquire why. Kathryn tried to get my attention, but I didn't want to talk to her. I was upset again about the lack of money coming in from the scam, and I had not completely forgiven her for mailing out the wrong insert in the last newsletter. I stomped into my office.

On my chair was an envelope, which had been hand-delivered that morning by a private messenger. I picked it and started to toss it into my in-box until I noticed it was from Emilio. I had no idea why he would send me anything by courier. My curiosity overcame my bad mood, and I opened the letter.

Richard,

I need to notify you that the check for $10,000 I gave you is no good, and will be returned unpaid by my bank—however, if you redeposit it, it will be good. I'd like to talk to you. I'm sending you this via messenger as I wanted to notify you in confidence and didn't want to leave a message. Please accept my apology and let's plan to meet sometime soon.

Have you been working out? Let's get you going strong! I'll have a full workout schedule for you ready when I see you.

I've got leads on a couple of good places for the health club. Thank you for everything. I'm anxious to see you and I'll explain everything.

Emilio

"I'll kill the son of a bitch," I yelled. Then I walked out of my office and asked the support staff if they knew where Emilio was. I was barely controlling my fury. One secretary told me that her boss had an appointment to see Emilio in twenty minutes at a local health club. I thanked her and told Kathryn that I was going over there. She tried to tell me something, but I didn't listen and barged out. Two other secretaries tried to stop me as well, but I blew right by them.

I spent the next two hours looking for Emilio. He had rescheduled the appointment with my fellow partner. I went to three clubs that he regularly used with clients, but no one had seen him that morning.

Finally, at the fourth place, the manager was talking to him by phone. I asked to talk to him.

"What the hell are you doing?" I shouted at him when I got on the line. I hadn't bothered to identify myself, but he knew who it was immediately.

"Richard, I am terribly sorry, and terribly embarrassed. The check is now covered. Put it through the bank again. Today. I am terribly sorry. I just got confused about which account had the money in it. It's all straightened out. I am terribly sorry."

"What kind of a jackass are you?"

"I'm terribly sorry. It is all straightened out now."

The check was the main source of my income now, and I needed it very badly. "There better not be any problem this time."

"There won't be. It is covered. I am terribly sorry. I am terribly embarrassed."

The call continued like this for a few more minutes. I think he broke a world's record for apologies, and I finally calmed down enough to hang up. I left the club and went to my bank. I directed them to redeposit the check. It was another exceedingly hot day, and I was covered with sweat by the time I returned to the office. I was hot, angry, ripped off, and my foot hurt. Riding up in the elevator, I wondered what else could go wrong.

I soon learned. As I walked down the hall to my office, Kathryn approached and pulled me aside. She wasn't going to be put off any longer.

"There are two agents from the Federal Bureau of Investigation in your office waiting to talk to you," she told me.

"What?" I asked in disbelief. "What are they doing here?"

"They have some questions about Warren Ford. They have been here all morning. They wanted to see you, but when you ran out, they began talking to everybody else."

My anger quickly fled as my heart started pounding. I noticed that Kathryn wasn't doing very well either. "Did they talk to you?" I asked. She nodded, her upper lip quivering. "What did they ask you?"

Before she could answer, I heard my name being called by a strange voice. I turned and saw two agents standing at my office door. "I am Special Agent Keith Kennedy," said one of them. "This is Special Agent John Shank. May we have a few minutes of your time?"

I thought fast. I looked flustered and hot and had disappeared for two hours. I had to explain that behavior. I decided to try the truth.

"I am Richard Brewster," I said, shaking their hands. "My secretary tells me you have been here all morning looking for me. I apologize for not being here. You see, my business partner bounced a big check on me. I had to track him down and straighten things out. I am still a bit upset by the whole matter." I smiled at them as they led me into my office. They shut the door behind them.

"I see," said Agent Shank without emphasis. Clearly, I didn't have his sympathy.

"Mr. Brewster," Agent Kennedy began, circling the room as he talked to me, "we have been asked to help find the fourteen-year-old boy whose parents have been allegedly arrested by the IRS without cause. If the story is true, he is in danger and it could be a violation of the parents' civil rights. That is a federal offense. We know the newsletter that reprinted the letter was mailed from here. We would like your assistance in finding him."

"I'll help in any way I can," I replied. "I am sure that the parents are out of jail by now, so there shouldn't be any real problem."

"We'd like to see for ourselves," said Agent Shank.

"Do you have the name and address of the boy who wrote the letter?" asked Agent Kennedy. "They were withheld by request from the newsletter, but I assume that you have it."

"I'm sorry. I don't have it."

"You published a highly inflammatory letter without documentation of who wrote it?" asked Agent Shank.

"I was in a hurry that night. We had just completed a big day in the Senate . . ." I rambled on.

"Yes, we know. A bill designed, in part, to embarrass the president was passed," said Agent Shank, disapprovingly.

"Mr. Brewster, do you have the original letter?" asked Agent Kennedy.

"No."

"Where is it?"

"Warren Ford has it."

"Do you have a copy of the letter? A fax of it?"

"No."

"How did you get the letter in order to publish it?"

"It was read to me by Warren Ford."

"May we have Mr. Ford's address and phone number?"

"Of course. I'll get them for you."

I picked up the CATI file on my desk and paged through the documents. I knew the information wasn't there, but I had to put on a show for the agents. I flipped through the pages quickly at first, and then reaching the end of the file, I went through them again very slowly. They watched me intently. "The information doesn't seem to be here. I'll get them for you and will call you later."

"We have time, Mr. Brewster. We'll wait."

I left my office and got all the other CATI files from Kathryn's file cabinet. I walked back in and went through them in front of the two agents. Of course, I didn't find Warren Ford's address or phone number.

"The information just doesn't seem to be here," I said apologetically. "I hate to waste your time. I'm sure I can find the information, and I'll get it to you as soon as I can."

"Mr. Brewster, I thought this would be a ten-minute visit. I thought we would get the letter and be out the door. I thought it was all very straightforward. Now I am not so sure. There may be more here than I originally thought," said Agent Kennedy. "I want to understand. Is Warren Ford a big client of yours?"

"Yeah, I guess so."

"According to your bookkeeper, he owes the firm in excess of $750,000. Do you have other clients that big?"

"Probably not, although the American Hand Towel Association is quite large."

"But you have no record of Mr. Ford's address or phone number?"

"Not that I can find."

"Why aren't there any copies of mailed bills in the files? They would include an address, or at least a fax number," interjected Shank.

"There is no need to mail them. I just tell Mr. Ford how much he owes us. Then I submit the number to the accounting office."

"You mean he owes you over three-quarters of a million dollars but has never received any documentation from your firm?"

"Yes, it's been fairly informal to date," I lied badly. "Actually, I had no idea he owes us so much. We will start implementing a better record-keeping system immediately. I have wanted to for months, but Mr. Ford didn't think it was necessary."

"And you don't have the address and phone number of your biggest client?" Agent Shank returned to the basic point.

"Apparently it's not in the file. Actually, I can usually remember his phone number, but I am flustered today."

"Why?"

"Because my trainer bounced a big check. Look, I am sure that as soon as you leave, the number will pop into my head. I'll call you with it."

"Would anyone else in the firm have the number?"

"I don't know. I did try to call Mr. Ford one day from Jason's office—"

"We know. He gave us the number you used that day. We tried it. It went to a private residence. The person answering had never heard of Warren Ford."

"Jason kept the number?" I asked with shock.

"You wrote it on an important document. It was still on his desk. He gave it to us as soon as we identified ourselves." He leaned in. "We appreciate it when people cooperate with us."

"Well, it wasn't the right number. We tried it that day and it didn't work then either."

"He told us," said Agent Kennedy. He walked over and stood less than six inches from me. He was at least four inches taller, forcing me to look up into his face. "Mr. Brewster, let me be sure I understand what you are telling two special agents of the Federal Bureau of Investigation today," he said. "You manage one of the firm's largest accounts. In fact, you went out of your way to cut one of the more senior partners, and one well-respected political pro, off the account. The executive director of the client owes your firm over $750,000. He may have information relating to a serious crime. Yet you have no address or phone number for him and have no way to contact him. Is that right?"

"I am sure we have the address and phone number around here somewhere. I just can't put my hands on them right now. I'll get them to you as soon as I can."

The two agents glanced at each other, and then made to leave. They both handed me their business cards. "I expect to hear from you very soon," said Agent Kennedy.

They walked slowly out the door. I began to relax. I noticed that my palms were wet. I assumed that my upper lip was wet as well. The interview had been a disaster, but it was finally over.

Agent Shank stuck his head back in my door. "One more thing, Mr. Brewster. What does Warren Ford look like?"

"What?" I asked, stalling for time.

"Please describe Warren Ford."

"What does he look like?" I babbled.

"Yes. Is he tall or short, Black or White, balding or with a red beard? What exactly does your client look like?"

When the agents finally left, I sat in my office for a good ten minutes, trying to calm down. When I felt I could function again without shaking, I emerged into the hall. All the support staff stared at me. Three of the attorneys were also standing at their doors, watching. I calmly asked Kathryn to come into my office. After she entered, I shut the door again.

She was a wreck. The makeup around her eyes was streaked, her eyes were red, and her hands were shaking. I had to buck her up. I smiled at her, displaying a confidence I didn't feel.

"I can't believe the FBI is investigating us," she said, her voice quivering.

"They aren't. They're looking for Warren Ford."

"There is no Warren Ford! You are Warren Ford!"

"Well, you know that and I know that, but no one else does."

"The FBI does."

"No, they don't. I totally buffaloed them. They don't have a clue."

"Really?" She looked hopeful.

"Really. I answered all their questions. We probably won't ever see them again."

"When they came in, they just wanted to get a copy of the newsletter. But when you weren't here, they started talking to everyone and kept getting different answers. They got more and more persistent."

"Well, no FBI agents are going to get ahead of us. Just watch." I picked up the phone and dialed Agent Kennedy's number.

"Is Agent Kennedy there?" I asked when the phone was answered.

I knew he wouldn't have enough time to have gotten back to his office.

"He is not here," came the businesslike reply. "Can I take a message for him?"

"Yes. Tell him Richard Brewster called. I want to leave a message for him. I just talked to Warren Ford. He told me that the IRS had released the parents of the little boy in question two days ago. Everything is all right—"

"This is Agent Kennedy," broke in a voice. I don't know what technology he used, but I was surprised to hear him. "Could you repeat that message, please?"

Trying to recover, I said, "Certainly. Warren Ford just called me. He told me that the IRS released the boy's parents two days ago. The matter has been resolved."

"I'll be the judge of that. Did you get Mr. Ford's address and phone number?"

"No. I forgot to ask him for them after I got the good news."

"You forgot to get his name and address and phone number less than twenty minutes after you promised to get them for us?"

"Yes, but—"

"But now we are supposed to call off the entire investigation after this alleged phone call, with no way of verifying the information?"

"Yes." I smiled at Kathryn and gave her a thumbs-up. She smiled back, but there were still tears in her eyes.

"Mr. Brewster, did you at least get the location of the alleged IRS abuse?"

"I remember now that Warren told me it was in Chicago."

"Do you remember anything further?"

"No, but I will call you when I do."

"Please do, Mr. Brewster." He hung up.

I turned back to Kathryn. "See. It's almost over. There is nothing to worry about."

She wasn't convinced. "Please don't let them come back and ask me any more questions. I don't know what to tell them."

"I can't keep them from coming back. But if they do, don't tell them anything. Just find me and I'll deal with them."

"What will you do?"

"I don't know yet. But I'll think of something."

I left work early that day. For the first time in years, I relished the time I spent stuck in traffic. As long as I was behind a van or an SUV, I couldn't be investigated or ripped off. Whenever there was a choice of two roads to travel, I took the one with more cars on it.

At home, I walked in on Elizabeth and the children playing. Matthew and David were putting together puzzles while Amy kept reaching in and stealing the pieces. Elizabeth would retrieve the pieces and return them to the coffee table. She hadn't yet started dinner.

We were absolutely broke. Thanks to Emilio and the firm, we didn't have $200 in our checking account. I was under investigation by the Federal Bureau of Investigation. My firm was in financial difficulty. My most deserving client, Dr. Garrity, was threatened with a legislative catastrophe—one that I helped create. In short, my life was a shambles. So I did what any self-respecting lobbyist would do. I took the family out to dinner.

Twenty minutes later, we were seated in our favorite Chinese restaurant. Matthew was coloring the zodiac animals on the paper place mat. David was waving chopsticks in the air. Amy was throwing rice on the floor. Elizabeth and I tried to talk about our financial situation in our typical mature fashion. We had to decide whether to borrow money from her parents or mine to maintain our lifestyle.

In the back of the restaurant was a bar with a television. The evening news was on. Suddenly I heard a story about a lost boy in Chicago, and I turned to watch.

". . . and so the search goes on for the boy the police here now call the 'Home Alone 2' boy, who was left without supervision when the IRS arrested his parents. Coming on the heels of the Revenue Ruling 34-897 fiasco, it appears that the Internal Revenue Service is an agency out of control. The real question is when will the president do something.

"When asked today to comment, the president's spokesman said, 'We are concerned about the reports. President Clinton has directed Attorney General Reno to fully investigate this matter. Already the FBI has determined that the alleged arrest occurred in the city of Chicago. A task force of over two hundred agents—FBI, Justice

Department and the IRS—has been assembled to investigate the matter.'"

Then the newscaster put on his most concerned face, and finished the story by adding, "The only question is whether this case will be resolved before any harm comes to the boy. If it is not, it would be a major embarrassment to the president, who promised to reinvent government and make it more responsive to the American people."

Elizabeth looked at me. "Is that your case?" she asked. I nodded. Further conversation was interrupted when Matthew and David got into a fight.

We finished dinner and left the restaurant. Driving home, Elizabeth kept a close watch on me. I knew she wanted an explanation, but I didn't know how to begin. We spent the evening in an unusual silence.

That night, I couldn't sleep. I tossed and turned and worried. When my alarm rang, I was exhausted and on edge. I dragged myself into the bathroom and took a shower. Already it was a very hot day. The air outside was gray from all the pollution. Everything was covered in grit.

I drove to work in a tense mood. I prayed that I would have time to get to my office and think out my next steps before I had to face the world. But as I turned down the street where our building was located, I saw a crowd of journalists waiting at the front door. There were three television cameras and several other men and women holding notepads and tape recorders.

I slunk down in my seat, drove past them, and turned into the garage. As I pulled into my spot and climbed out of my car, I saw Jason standing across the garage, waving me to come over to him. He wore a puzzled expression.

As I walked over, he asked, "Do you know why all the press is outside?"

"I have a pretty good idea," I admitted.

"Does it have anything to do with the visit I received from the FBI yesterday?"

"Yes. The FBI is trying to find Warren Ford in order to find the 'Home Alone 2' boy. The press is trying to find him, too. Someone in the FBI must have tipped off the press. They know that we represent him and the Citizens Against Tax Injustice."

"Do we have a statement for the press prepared yet?"

"No."

"Then let's go up the back steps." Jason led the way. I followed willingly, grateful that he was going out of his way to protect me as well as the firm. It was the ultimate sacrifice for the dignified Jason Douglas Johnson to sneak up seven flights of stairs and bang on the fire door to get into his office.

"Where is Warren Ford?" Jason asked. We were passing the fourth floor. He was winded from the exertion.

"Do you want the truth?" I asked.

"Do I?" he asked back.

"Probably not."

"Will all this go away?"

"Not by itself."

"Then why don't you tell me the truth," he suggested.

"Warren Ford doesn't exist."

"Who is the client?"

"There isn't one. I created the whole thing. I guess it got out of hand."

"I would guess so," Jason said. "Doesn't this client owe us some fees?"

"Over $750,000."

"Will we ever collect a dime?" he asked.

"Not unless we get out of this jam. But when we do, I will get the members of CATI to contribute more money," I said, trying not to think about Mrs. Grant. "I'll ask for a special assessment."

"Then we better get out of this jam," said Jason, taking command. "What are the details?"

I filled him in as we stood in the fire escape. After I finished, he thought for a while.

"Our real problem is with the FBI," he said. "We just won't talk to them until they solve the case of the missing parents. They will determine that there was no arrest. It won't take long, probably just a day. Then they will go away. As for the press, we'll give them a good story and they'll go away, too."

"What will you tell them?" I asked. I already knew who the firm's spokesman would be.

"I will tell them that we won't release Mr. Ford's address and phone number. It is a matter of strictest attorney-client privilege."

I smiled in appreciation of his effort but said, "I doubt that attorney-client privilege extends to his address and phone number."

"Why not?" he asked, smiling. "Isn't he afraid of harassment by the Internal Revenue Service?"

I caught on. "Yes, he is."

"Isn't he afraid the IRS will throw him into jail on some trumped-up charge?"

"Absolutely."

"Don't we have to protect him . . . even at the risk of great sacrifice to the firm?"

"Yes."

"Don't you want me to tell the press, on national television, that Johnson, Woods & Hart, will go to whatever lengths are necessary to protect our client from harassment by the federal government?"

"Please." We were both grinning now. It was a game again. Jason was in his element. He would get the firm's name out in every media outlet he could. He would be in the national limelight. And he assumed that the FBI would quickly discover that there was no "Home Alone 2" boy and drop the matter. "This will all blow over by the day's end," he said, as banged on the fire door and waited to be let in. "Then you need to get some money into the firm from the client. I want you to focus on that problem. You know, the firm needs that money."

Back at my office, Kathryn was sitting at her desk with dark circles under her eyes. "Cheer up," I whispered. "Jason knows everything, and he'll take care of it." For the first time in two days, she looked relieved.

Three hours later, she poked her head into my office. "Agent Kennedy is on the phone," she said.

"Tell him I am not here."

"He says he knows you're in here and that you aren't on the phone." She looked terrified.

"He's just bluffing," I said but scanned the building across the street. "Tell him I will call him back."

"I don't want to talk to him."

I could see that she was in no condition to handle the situation. "I'll take it," I said, and hit the speaker button on my phone so she could hear our conversation.

"Richard Brewster," I started.

"I saw Jason Johnson's press statement," he immediately began. "It's bullshit. You know as well as I do that you can't hide Warren Ford. Not when the safety of a young person is at stake. I want his location."

"I would love to help, but it is a matter of strictest attorney-client privilege."

"Bullshit. Do you know that we have over two hundred agents and police officers looking for this kid in Chicago? What are you hiding?"

"I wish I could help you, but I can't."

"Listen to me. I hate wasting my agents' time. This could be resolved in ten minutes with your assistance. Without it, it will take a little longer. Get this through your head. I saw the CATI files on your secretary's desk. If you destroy or tamper with them, I will arrest you for obstruction of justice. In the meantime, I will get a subpoena for the documents as soon as I finish the paperwork. Then I will come and take them. Or you could make this easy. Just tell me where I can find Warren Ford—if he exists. If he doesn't exist, tell me who you are hiding and why."

"I can't help you. I wish I could."

"You are going to regret that answer," he said as he hung up.

I looked up at Kathryn. "Guess I showed him, didn't I?" She started to cry. "Don't worry," I tried to reassure her. "It looks bad now, but soon it will all blow over. They will figure out that there is no 'Home Alone 2' boy, and then they will all go away."

Kathryn wasn't convinced. She just kept shaking her head as she left my office.

I turned to my other problems. First I called my bank. "Was there any problem with the check for ten thousand I redeposited yesterday?"

"As a matter of fact, it bounced again."

I called Emilio's home and talked to his roommate. He was as angry as I was. "He packed up and left yesterday while I was at work. I have no idea where he is, and he better hope that I don't ever find him. He gave me a bad check for rent and the utilities."

Other calls around town elicited the same response. Emilio had dropped out of sight, owing everybody money. He wrote enough bad paper to cover a large wall. But I was far and away the biggest sucker.

I watched the news channels throughout the day. Unfortunately, it was a slow news day, so the stations continued to give updates on the search for the "Home Alone 2" boy. By midafternoon, they were reporting that the case had now turned into a search for Warren Ford, who held important information. Jason's statement to the press was reported over and over. At least I did my part to get him, and the firm, publicity.

The story continued to grow. By evening, the case had become fodder for the radio talk shows. The issue was framed simply. Warren Ford was a true patriot, running for his life from the IRS. Or he was a coward, threatening the life of an innocent child. Our firm was front and center in the discussions. We were either the last bastions of freedom fighters on earth or a bunch of sleazy lawyers hiding a criminal. The comments from the callers ran the whole gamut:

"I understand that the Internal Revenue Service has issued a shoot-to-kill order for Warren Ford . . ."

"Warren Ford has already been taken into custody by the FBI. They are afraid to tell us because loyal Americans would storm the building where they are holding him . . ."

"I have known Warren Ford for years, and I can assure you that he would do nothing to harm anyone . . ."

"Warren Ford is the leader of a cult that engages in child sexual abuse. He is hiding to avoid prosecution . . ."

"Warren Ford is a member of the mafia . . ."

"Warren Ford is in hiding ever since his wife cut off his penis . . ."

"Warren Ford was standing on the grassy knoll in Dallas on November 22, 1963 . . ."

Just when I thought the day couldn't get any crazier, Jason walked into my office. He sat in a chair across from my desk. For the first time ever, he looked haggard. His coat was off, and his shirt was wrinkled and damp.

"You looked great on television," I said.

"Thank you," he said with a very slight smile. "Unfortunately, my statement doesn't seem to have worked. The feds and the press are still all over us. What is going to happen next?"

"I had hoped that the FBI would give up looking for the boy, declare victory, and go home."

"I thought so, too. We could have lasted for a day or two until they ended the search. But I am beginning to have my doubts that they will back off until they have heard from Warren Ford. I've been talking to my friends around town, and they say the White House really wants to run this one down to the ground. They want proof the boy is safe, and they want Warren Ford to acknowledge it, too."

"Haven't they checked their arrest records and found there was no such arrest?"

"Yes, they have been checking. They are about 99.9 percent sure. But they are not 100 percent sure. And they don't trust Warren Ford. They are afraid he will make a big splash if they are wrong. They really hate him after some revenue ruling bill, whatever the hell that is."

"Oh yeah. That."

"They won't relax until he admits he made a mistake. Is there any way we can throw them a bone? Let them know that Warren Ford will not bite them in the ass if they announce that the case is closed?"

"I've been thinking about that all day," I lied. I just assumed that Jason would fix everything. "Maybe we should just admit the letter was a hoax or that Warren Ford doesn't exist—"

I didn't get to finish my thought. "You can't do that," Jason said. "If you do, your tax group would collapse. The banks would be all over it. They would demand repayment of all the money they loaned us based on the bills."

"How much did the firm borrow against the CATI bills?" I asked, hoping it wasn't much.

"All $750,000," he admitted.

"Oh my God," I said. "I'm not sure I understand. The banks loaned us that much based on a client that had never paid us a dime?"

He nodded. "You're good, Jason," I said with real admiration. He smiled weakly. "But I guess the loans are really based on all our accounts receivable. The other bills must be good. Am I right?"

Jason looked sick. "We can't let this unravel. If they find out one of our clients is a fake, they'll demand repayment of the $750,000, and they will want to see our other accounts."

"So, I take it there are other questionable bills we used as assets?" I asked, with a growing sense of doom.

Jason nodded again. "Several. But the others are based on real clients at least. They're just slow payers or are contesting the amounts. It wouldn't be a problem if we had a reserve for bad debts.

But we don't. We borrowed every dime to keep growing. It's only a problem if we get caught. If we have the time, we can collect on our good clients and pay off the bank debts. No one will be any wiser. We just need to keep up appearances. But we can't let the banks know any of the debts are bad. Things would quickly fall apart."

Before I could say anything further, Kathryn buzzed me on my interoffice phone to tell me I had a call. "Not now, Kathryn," I said with annoyance.

"It's Emilio."

I grabbed the phone. "Where are you?" I yelled.

"I am waiting for you at the Potomac Pub. I wanted to come to your office, but there are police and press all over the place."

"Stay right there. I'm leaving now." I hung up, grabbed my coat, and ran to the door. "I'll be back later," I said over my shoulder to Jason, who had a look of shock at my sudden departure. He was not used to such behavior from the younger attorneys.

I arrived at the pub in less than five minutes, soaked and panting after running through the heat. I looked around for Emilio but didn't see him anywhere. I sat at a table and waited, shivering in the chill of the pub's air-conditioning.

After ten minutes Emilio entered and sat at my table.

"I thought you said you were already here," I accused him.

"I was, but I left. I wanted to make sure that you would come alone."

"Where is my money?" I asked, my voice tight.

"I don't have it."

"What did you do with it?"

"I used it to pay off some debts. If I didn't pay certain people off, they were threatening to go to the police."

"Why? Did you steal from them too?"

He dropped his gaze to the floor. "I'll tell you the truth because you trusted me and because you wanted to be partners with me. Last summer I housesat for one of my clients. I don't know why I did it, but I used his credit cards and his money machine cards. I loved living his lifestyle. I ran up several thousand dollars in debt in his name.

"When he came back from vacation, I knew I would be in real trouble. I went to him and confessed to my actions. I promised to pay him back. He agreed not to go to the police if I did.

"Then, I met you. You actually trusted me and wanted to work with me, as a partner and not as an employee. It was my big break, and I didn't want to blow it. But I was afraid that if you found out about my past, you would not want me to be your partner. I had to keep the people from last summer from going to the police or to you. So when I got your check, I used the money to pay them off.

"I intended to order the equipment for the health club and then pay for it over time out of my share of the profits. You would have never known. But then you asked for your money back."

"It must have scared the shit out of you," I said, choking back my anger.

"Not really. I just opened a checking account at another bank. I wrote a check to the first bank. I hoped that the check I wrote you would clear before the check I wrote you on the second account bounced. Sometimes the timing works."

"Let me get this straight," I interrupted him. "You wrote a bad check to cover the check you wrote to me, hoping that I would get paid during the period of the float."

"Yeah. Usually the banks put holds on the money until it clears, but sometimes they don't. It was my only option. But the timing was off and it didn't work."

"What would have happened if I had been paid? What about the banks?"

"I would have gone to see them and promised to pay them back. There is so much bank fraud that the FBI would never investigate a case of $10,000. The only hope the banks had for a recovery was if I paid them back."

"So, where are we?"

"I owe you the money. I will pay it back. I will pay you $500 a month until I have paid you back all the money I took."

"Why should I assume I would ever get paid?"

"Because you trusted me."

"And you must have laughed all the way to the bank. Did you think I was the dumbest person you ever met?" I said.

"No. You trusted me. You are the first person that wanted me to be your partner. I will pay you back."

"I still think I should turn you in to the police."

His eyes went wide with fright. "Don't do that. I am not a bad person. I just had a few bad breaks. I will pay you back."

"I don't want to see you go to jail. I just want my money back. If you pay me, I'll forget this ever happened." Then I leaned in and tried to look menacing, "But if you try to ignore me, I will go to the police. I know a lot of people in the law enforcement community in this city, and I will get you if I have to. I was talking to an FBI agent just yesterday. Do you understand?"

He nodded, but unconvincingly. What a joke it was for me to threaten him. He understood the criminal justice system—what he could get away with and when the police would actually handle a case. I looked at him. He looked at me. He probably knew that the DC police were too overwhelmed with work to chase down a bad check case for $10,000. He was humoring me because he knew I would never get any assistance from the law enforcement community.

If they wouldn't help me, my only hope was to get him to pay me back. To do that, I had to scare him some more.

I gave him my toughest look. "Emilio, you correctly noticed that our building was surrounded by law enforcement agents. Well, they were there to get you. I reported you as soon as the check bounced. I know a few things about police work, and I got them interested in the case. They want your ass. And I am prepared to deliver it to them."

He looked impressed, like he had underestimated me. I had his full attention.

"Should I tell them where you are, or do we have an understanding?" I asked.

He reassured me. "I would pay you back even if you didn't alert the police. You trusted me, and I will never forget that. I will pay you before I pay anyone else. I will pay you in cash. I will pay you every month. If I ever miss a month, you can call the police and deny that you have ever gotten a payment."

"Give me your address and phone number," I said.

"No."

I shrugged. "Then I guess that we don't have a deal."

"What then?"

"I go back to my office and tell the police that I just met you. They will pick you up tonight."

"I can't pay you if I am in jail," he said quickly.

"You probably won't pay me anyway."

He hung his head. "Yes, I will," he insisted.

"Give me your address and phone number," I insisted. "Then if you miss a payment, I can have you picked up."

"I won't miss a payment. I told you. But you have to give me a chance to raise the money."

"Give me your address and phone number. Do we have a deal or not?"

He looked defeated. "Okay," he mumbled. He took a napkin off the bar and wrote out the requested information. He slipped it to me. "I'm sorry," he said. "I never intended this to happen. I am not a crook. I just had a few bad breaks. I'll pay you back."

I was in no mood to be warm and fuzzy. "I better see the money on schedule."

"You will." He left the pub.

I sat and contemplated my day. It had been a disaster by any standards. But I had buffaloed Emilio, telling him that the police were there to get him. Maybe I could survive the FBI investigation as well.

I wondered how Charles Nagle would handle the mess my life had become. According to legends, he had gotten out of worse ethical and legal binds on a number of occasions. If he could do it, so could I. But I was angry and tired. I sat there for a long time. I ordered and drank five beers.

Finally, I decided to go home. I stepped out again into the oppressive heat of the evening. By the time I walked the few blocks to our office building, I was hot and sweaty again. I pulled my tie down and unbuttoned my top shirt button. It was a major breech of Jason's dress code, but I didn't care. In fact, I hoped he would notice and so deliberately walked by his office, even though it was long past closing time.

Jason's office was dark except for a single lamp on Jason's desk. And there I saw Barbara, hunched over, reading his papers.

"What are you doing here?" I said. She jumped back, clearly startled by my voice. She looked at me with wide eyes.

"Richard, are you alone?"

"Yes. But what are you doing?"

"Looking at Jason's papers. Walker told me Jason has a list of associates that he is going to let go to save money. I wanted to see if I was on it."

"Walker said that?" I asked. She nodded. "That's bullshit. I would know if we were letting people go. Jason isn't trying to save money. Actually, it wouldn't surprise me if he hired two new associates next week just to prove some dumb thing."

She smiled. "Why did Walker say that?"

"He was probably trying to scare you so you would sleep with him for protection, you know what I mean?"

Her smile got bigger. "How do I know you aren't trying to reassure me so I'll sleep with you?"

"You mean, kind of like a thank-you."

"Exactly."

I stepped closer to her. "Would it work?"

"I don't know, yet." She took my hand and led me over to Jason's couch. We sat down together, and I put my arm behind her head. My brain was spinning from the heat, the alcohol, and her presence. I had to sit there for a moment to quiet my roiling insides. She leaned her head against my arm and scrunched closer. We were both silent, sitting on Jason's power couch.

"This feels nice," she whispered, turning her head to me.

"It certainly does." And I kissed her. Once. Twice, long and deep. My head was spinning again, and, of course, I was as hard as a rock. I let my fingers move down her shoulders to her breasts. My head swirled as we kissed. It felt wonderful, but most of all, it felt . . . wrong.

I should not be here, I thought. *This is all wrong. This woman is not a toy. She is not part of the game—a status symbol to be accumulated by a successful Washington insider*. Of course, while these thoughts raced through my head, my hands had managed to unbutton her blouse and unhook her bra. As her clothes fell away, I saw that she was covered in freckles and had the most beautiful, shapely breasts I had ever seen. They were stunning.

But as she came out of her clothes, she too tensed up. She stopped kissing me and moved away. I couldn't clearly see her expression for two reasons. First, the room was dark and murky, illuminated by only one small desk lamp. But mostly, I was fascinated by her body and kept my eyes on it.

"I think we should stop," she said simply.

"Did I do something wrong?" I asked.

"No. Not tonight. You are fun to be with. But I have never slept with a married man. I thought you might be the first, but I don't want to go further."

A wave of relief swept over me. Then I got mad. It was one thing for me to have doubts, but it pissed me off that she had them. "What do you mean?"

"I mean I don't want to go down this road, at least not tonight. It only leads to pain." She raised her arms, covering her breasts. Of course, she made sense. She was absolutely right. But I was drunk, I was mad at the world, and I wanted her to want me so I could say no.

"Then why have you been coming on to me?"

"It's my style, my thing. Besides, you have been coming on to me, too."

"So has every man in the firm. And you encourage it. Every man in the firm is worried that some other man will get there first."

"And which man has worried about more than getting laid by me? Who wants more than that with me?"

I had no answer for that. So I focused on the bigger issue for me. "So, you haven't slept with Walker?"

"No."

"And no one else in the firm?"

"No."

"You just lead everyone on but never deliver?"

She looked very angry. "I resent that you only think of me as someone who should deliver, but to answer your question, no, I have not slept with anyone in the firm yet."

"Wow, you are a better lobbyist than I thought."

She scowled at me, picked up her clothes, and left the room.

CHAPTER XV
MISSING IN ACTION

got up early the next day to see the *Today Show*. I had missed the late-night news the night before, and I prayed that a satisfactory conclusion had been reached in the "Home Alone 2" boy case. But it was not to be.

It was the last story on the seven o'clock headline news. "The 'Home Alone 2' boy story took an unexpected turn yesterday. After reviewing all the arrest records in the Chicago area, the Federal Bureau of Investigation determined that there was no arrest like the one featured in the Citizens Against Tax Injustice newsletter. The FBI is now convinced that the whole matter was a hoax. Federal officials are currently looking for Warren Ford, the executive director of CATI. The location of Mr. Ford is unknown to all but his lawyers, the Washington firm of Johnson, Woods & Hart. They have refused to assist law enforcement officials in locating Mr. Ford."

At this point, they ran the tape of Jason's statement to the press from the day before. We'd both assumed that once the FBI determined there had been no arrest, they would call off the investigation. We did not anticipate they would go the next step and investigate Warren Ford for fraud. In that light, Jason's statement looked worse.

The story concluded when the newscaster said, "The investigation is continuing."

Katie Couric broke in with her comments. "I can't believe that any respectable firm would hide the perpetrator of such a foul hoax. Is that what we call justice today?"

"Thanks, Katie," I said sadly. She had been my favorite newsperson until that moment. I had met her once, at a wedding, where we spoke briefly and shared a dance. Ever since that time, I had referred to her as my personal friend. Now she was twisting the knife in my back, the knife that Agent Kennedy placed there.

Within three minutes, my phone rang. It was Ed Topp, the head of the communications section and Jason's biggest rival in the firm. "Isn't Warren Ford one of your clients?"

"If you will remember, Walker Dudley claimed half of the credit for the client," I responded. I was tired of the day already. Despite the air conditioner, I was sweating.

"But are you responsible for it?"

"Yes," I admitted.

"Why did Jason give a statement to the press on the case yesterday?"

"He was helping me."

"Is that all?"

I blew my cool. I was convinced that Topp was only looking for dirt to throw at Jason. I had no intention of giving him any. "What's your point, Ed?"

"I was just wondering why Jason is so defensive about this case. If it was me, I would have given all the files to the FBI and helped them locate this Warren Ford."

"Would you throw me overboard to the FBI as well?" I asked.

"Well, yes, but it's not that simple," he said. He started a long explanation of his reasoning, but I hung up on him.

————————

When I arrived at my office, several people were milling around, including Jason, John Horn, a few US marshals, and FBI agents Kennedy and Shank. Agent Shank saw me coming first. Shaking with rage, he stalked towards me and asked, "Where are the files?"

"What files?" I asked.

"You know exactly what files I mean. The Citizens Against Tax Injustice files. They were here a few days ago."

Agent Kennedy came up and took control of the situation. It was a version of the good cop/bad cop routine. Only this time, Agent Kennedy wasn't much of a good cop. He was angry too. "Mr. Brewster, I have a subpoena for all the files of the Citizens Against Tax Injustice. May we have them, please?"

There wasn't any point in arguing. Jason and several of the firm's highest priced legal talent stood by silently. I knew they would have stopped the proceedings if there were any way to do so. I went to Kathryn's desk. The files weren't there.

"They were right here," I said, looking for them.

They weren't in the file cabinets. They weren't in my office. They weren't in the central file room. They weren't anywhere in the building. After three hours of searching, we all gave up looking.

The CATI files weren't there.

Agent Shank stomped over and stood with his face two inches from mine. His eyes narrowed, and I felt his breath on my face as he spit out, "What have you done with the files?"

"Nothing," I said honestly.

"Where are they?"

"I have no idea. Look, I may be a smart-ass, but I know when to stop. I have no idea where the files are. They were here last night when I left."

"Do we have to get a warrant to search your house?"

"No. Go out there and look for yourselves. I give you my permission to search my house. You don't need a warrant. My car, too. And Jason's house." Jason started nodding at this point. "The files aren't there."

"Does your secretary have them?" Agent Kennedy asked.

And then I realized—Kathryn wasn't there either. I had not focused on her after I saw the FBI agents. I asked around, but no one had seen her all day. Calls to her house and her parents' house brought no results.

Kathryn had disappeared with the CATI files. And I was left facing the FBI. I looked at Jason. He met my eyes and shook his head slightly. I knew what he wanted me to do. If I admitted that Warren Ford was a figment of my imagination, it would be out on the streets in less than ten minutes. Within twenty minutes, the banks would be screaming about CATI's bills, which they had loaned the firm money against. We would have to come up with almost three-quarters of a million dollars overnight. We didn't have the money. We had to continue to bear the wrath of the FBI and the press. I shouldn't have created the client and the bills. But Jason shouldn't have borrowed against the accounts receivable. We were in this together. I turned back to face the agents.

An hour later, after I convinced them that I had not ordered Kathryn to disappear with the files, the federal agents finally left. Jason called an immediate emergency meeting in his office with most of the senior partners and me. Once assembled, he got right down to business.

"We are now the target of an FBI investigation. They think we are hiding Warren Ford. Warren Ford, in turn, is wanted for questioning regarding fraud. The press is camped outside our offices and won't go away until this matter is over. The files in question are missing, along with one secretary, who either has a misguided sense of loyalty or a guilty conscience. I hope we can pull together and get through this crisis. For once, let's not fight between ourselves."

John Horn spoke next. "Jason tells me this is a matter of attorney-client privilege. We will never reveal the whereabouts of Warren Ford until he tells us it is all right to do so. As the senior litigator in this firm, I am taking responsibility for this case as of today." He turned to me. "Do you have any problems with that?" he asked me.

"No," I said. "So you think we should protect Warren Ford?"

Horn puffed out his chest. "I won't reveal his whereabouts until he calls me personally and tells me to. Tell him that, will you, when you talk to him next. I want to hear from him personally when it is okay to release his location."

"You got it, John," I said gravely. Despite the seriousness of the situation, Jason was having trouble suppressing a smile.

"How did we end up with this client?" asked Ed Topp. "The firm shouldn't have accepted such a flaky client."

Although Jason knew exactly how flaky the client was, he wasn't going to give Topp the opportunity to point fingers. "That flaky client owes this firm $750,000. It's far more than any client you have brought in. Are you really suggesting that we would turn such business down even if you ran the show?"

"We could afford to if we didn't have such cash flow problems," Ed responded defiantly.

"We wouldn't have such cash flow problems if you didn't insist on bringing on so many of your friends," Jason shot back. "None of them are covering their salaries."

"It's only a matter of time."

"Well, that $750,000 will give them, and you, that time." There would be no backing down. The bulls were out in the field, trying to gore each other. The Warren Ford matter was just the excuse. It was reassuring in a way to know that no matter how bad things got, the firm's leadership would continue to trash each other.

That night, as I walked through the parking garage, I found Agent Kennedy leaning on a post next to my car. He waited until I got closer, then walked over to intercept me.

"Warren Ford doesn't exist," he said to me, his voice quiet and controlled. "I know that and you know that. This whole Citizens Against Tax Injustice is one big fraud."

"That's not true. It is a full-fledged, legitimate organization. It served an important function in the fight against Revenue Ruling 34-897," I said defiantly.

"That was a bullshit exercise," he snapped. "There was nothing to it. It brought you fame and fees. And it embarrassed the president of the United States. A president of the other party. You were very clever."

"Not as clever as you are giving me credit for."

"Have you seen the news tonight?"

"No."

"The White House announced that it agrees with the FBI conclusion that the 'Home Alone 2' boy letter was a hoax. The president said he was satisfied that there was no boy in danger. He also pointed out that Warren Ford had discredited himself and the Citizens Against Tax Injustice.

"Attorney General Reno has instructed the Justice Department and the Federal Bureau of Investigation not to waste any more time on the matter. They won't.

"But I will. Thousands of hours of agents' time were wasted running down your phony letter. I will see that you pay for your irresponsible actions. I will make a case against you for fraud.

"You can help yourself by talking to me. I realize, Counselor, that you don't have to. It's your decision. But the longer you avoid me, the more time I will have to investigate. I will find out the truth, and I will arrest you."

Without waiting for a reply from me, he turned and strolled

away. Halfway to his car, he turned back once again and said, "By the way, the president vetoed the revenue ruling bill today. No one in Congress seems interested in trying to override the veto. Congratulations on your effort."

CHAPTER XVI
GOODBYE, DEZUBE, TUESDAY

In some ways, Agent Kennedy was right. In other ways, he was wrong. The White House ordered federal law enforcement agencies to continue the search for Warren Ford, but without the immediate danger of the "Home Alone 2" boy, everyone relaxed considerably, and most agents turned to other matters. The media circus did subside.

But not entirely. It was too good a story for the press to abandon entirely. A few reporters continued to stand outside our building. They continued to call members of the firm, looking for someone to tell them where Warren Ford was hiding. Their calls were directed to the support staff and the younger attorneys. The press hoped that one of them would be a chink in the firm's united front. Fortunately, no one knew anything except Jason and me. But the constant scrutiny kept the tension high. It was unneeded in a firm with squabbling senior partners and financial difficulties. Everyone was a nervous wreck.

We all tried to get on with our lives. I, especially, was tired of the roller coaster ride that my existence had become. I kidded with my partners that I was tired of trying to catch the spears life kept throwing at me. They said they felt the same way.

The only partner who seemed strengthened by the whole episode was John Horn. He told everyone that the matter had quieted down only after he took control of the case. He hinted that it wouldn't have been such a fiasco if he had been in charge of the matter from the beginning. "Things are finally under control," he announced at one partners' meeting. "In fact, Warren Ford hasn't even felt the need to call me. It is all under control." And whenever Horn made those pronouncements, Jason would praise him.

In silence, I tried to carry on. I knew that Agent Kennedy was watching me. I couldn't see any of his handiwork, but I was convinced he was out there. I even drove on quiet back streets on my way to and from work, to see if I was being followed. I never saw anything, but I was not reassured. I assumed that he had put a homing device on my car.

In the meantime, the attorneys at Johnson, Woods &Hart had to make a living. Donations to CATI, as might be expected, were nonexistent. CATI needed Warren Ford to solicit donations. And as the press let everyone know, Warren Ford was in hiding. I couldn't bring him back with the FBI searching for him. If I used his name for a citizens' alert, Agent Kennedy would have swept down and seized all the copies, and me as well.

Without CATI, I needed to work on other business. Fortunately, I always had Doug Dezube.

A few days later, he swept into town unannounced. He stormed into my office at 9 a.m., already raging. He was a full troll that day.

"Let's go see that idiot," he demanded.

"Who?" I asked in genuine curiosity. I wanted to know who qualified as an idiot to Dezube.

"Senator Kelly, that brain-dead boob."

"What did he do to make you so angry?"

"He stuck my Hand Towel Equity bill on some goofy FDA Improvements bill."

"What's wrong with that? It was our general idea."

"They have nothing to do with each other. I don't want my bill dragged down by some technical health matter. The Hand Towel Equity Act is about jobs."

"So you want me to get Senator Kelly to pull the Hand Towel Equity Act off the FDA bill?"

"No, I want you to get him to pull the FDA bill off the Hand Towel Equity Act."

"Are you sure?"

"Yes. Am I being unclear? I can't believe that clown tried to combine those two bills."

We called the senator's office but learned that he was unavailable to meet with us on such short notice. We were referred to Rob Fitzgibbons, who agreed to see us. We took a cab up to the Capitol.

When we got in to see Rob, Dezube explained everything to him. "I know we agreed on a strategy, to add the Hand Towel Equity Act to another bill, but I meant for the senator to add it to a good bill. Who cares about the Food and Drug Administration and its regulatory powers over vaccines?"

Rob was defensive, sweating under another polyester suit. "We thought the FDA bill was a perfect place to add your Hand Towel Equity Act. It was going to pass and had the support of the House of Representatives and the president."

"If it was such a perfect place, why did the Senate leadership defer consideration of the bill after you added the Hand Towel Equity Act?"

"I think it was because we caught them unaware. It will get sorted out in the near future."

"I don't want to wait. I want the senator to withdraw the Hand Towel Equity Act from the FDA bill and to add it to another bill—one that focuses on jobs."

I should have argued against this idea. It was the only hope Dezube had of ever getting his bill enacted into law. But I needed to win one. I needed to feel good about something I did, and I wanted to see the FDA bill get through Congress. Without the Hand Towel Equity Act amendment, the FDA bill would sail through. The FDA would work with Dr. Garrity to get his vaccine for chicken pox reviewed and tested. Millions of American children would be spared from the disease if the vaccine worked. It was the right thing to do.

Rob continued to argue that the senator had done the right thing, but Dezube kept insisting that the senator withdraw the amendment. During our discussion, the senator himself walked past Rob's office. Dezube leapt up and grabbed the senator's jacket.

"Senator, we are trying to convince your staff that you should withdraw the Hand Towel Equity Act from the FDA bill. Mr. Fitzgibbons doesn't seem to agree with us, but we feel that it would be better as part of a jobs bill and not as part of some health bill. Remember, we are talking about American workers here."

The senator stopped and thought about what Dezube had said. He started to nod. Rob piped up to defend his handiwork. "Remember,

Senator, we felt the FDA bill was a good bill to attach the Hand Towel Equity Act to because the FDA bill had already passed the House and was supported by the president."

The senator thought about what Rob had said and nodded in agreement. Dezube tried again. "Senator, the Hand Towel Equity Act will help preserve US jobs. It is logical to make it part of a larger bill dedicated to the nation's economy."

The senator looked at Dezube and started nodding at him. I realized that the senator was agreeing with whoever spoke last. At that rate, I was concerned we would be there all afternoon as Rob and Dezube argued back and forth, each one convincing the senator. Worse, I was afraid that Dezube would run out of ideas first and Rob would have the last word. I decided to step in.

"Senator, there are good arguments for keeping the two bills together and good arguments for separating them." The senator looked at me and nodded. "But I think that we should let the FDA bill go through without the Hand Towel Equity Act. You don't want to be accused of jeopardizing the health of American children."

The senator shook his head.

"There will be lots of opportunities to add the Hand Towel Equity Act to other legislation. You and Rob had a great idea adding it to the FDA bill. You now have the attention of the administration and the Senate leadership. It was really a super effort. Now when you add the bill to another measure, everyone will take you seriously. But we should probably not overplay your hand. I suggest you withdraw the amendment from the FDA bill."

Rob frowned. Dezube smiled. The senator nodded. I waited. Finally the senator said, "Rob, you get to work on that." He walked away.

Rob looked at the floor for a minute, then said, "I will call the Senate leadership and tell them about the change of plans. But we will be back on another day."

We thanked Rob profusely and left. Out in the hall, Dezube just shook his head. "We do all their work for them, do you know that? I'm glad they agreed to my change of plans."

"Me too, Doug. Me too."

The next day, Senator Kelly officially notified the Senate leadership of his intention to withdraw the Hand Towel Equity Act as an amendment to the FDA Improvements Act. Within a week, the

FDA bill passed the Senate and was signed into law by the president. Together Sheila Reynoldsen and I called Dr. Garrity to tell him the news. The doctor couldn't believe his ears. He was now sure that I was a miracle worker.

He kept thanking us over and over. We tried to sound humble, but we enjoyed hearing him continue to sing our praises. Finally, my voice full of joy, I said, "Get to work, Doctor. My job is done. Now you have the ball. Run with it. But if your vaccine works, and you are looking for a Latin name to call it, you might want to think about 'Brewsterus.' It has a nice ring to it, doesn't it?" He hung up, laughing.

———————

That very same day, the Senate majority leader approached Senator Kelly. He thanked him for allowing the FDA Improvements Act to pass. To show his thanks, the majority leader offered to help Senator Kelly get one of the 614 bills Kelly had introduced passed by the Senate.

On returning to his office, Senator Kelly called Rob in and told him about the conversation. They were both amazed at the power they had as a result of their skillful use of the Senate rules. They resolved to try it again. That afternoon, while the Senate was debating a bill to fund the Defense Department, Senator Kelly stood and added the Hand Towel Equity Act as an amendment. There was a flurry of activity on the Senate floor and in the halls just outside, until Senator Kelly agreed to pull the amendment off the bill. In return this time, Senator Kelly was promised a ride on Air Force One and was told he could hold a first-class, high-visibility hearing on wasteful government spending.

The next day, the Senate considered a crucial tax treaty between the US and Canada. During the debate, Senator Kelly added the Hand Towel Equity Act as an amendment. All hell broke loose again, until the senator was promised a better Capitol office and he withdrew the amendment. Over the next two months, Senator Kelly added the Hand Towel Equity Act to over thirty bills on the Senate floor. Each time, he was bought off with new goodies. Soon Kelly became a power to be reckoned with, getting his way on a number of issues because the Senate leadership was afraid to see the Hand Towel Equity Act added to another measure.

Having discovered the advantages of manipulating the Senate, Kelly and Rob spent hours learning each intricate, esoteric parliamentary procedure by which the Senate was governed. Senator Kelly became a master of the Senate rules and procedures. He could tie the Senate up in knots for hours, adding amendments to amendments and calling for votes on motions on the Senate floor. Other senators groaned in frustration whenever he appeared. They knew they could not compete with such a master of the rules. They knew they had to accommodate Senator Kelly's wishes or be defeated by use of a little-known procedural loophole.

The president came to rely heavily on Senator Kelly. They became fast friends and loyal allies. Journalists admired him and wrote flattering stories about him, calling him the ultimate inside player. His future as a senator was assured.

As for Dezube, he too gained new visibility and stature. His bill was debated on the Senate floor frequently. Every time it was brought up, Dezube put out public statements and gave press conferences. "Only my good friend Senator Kelly and Congressman Smith understand the issues involved," he said. "He and I are doing the staff work for the entire US Senate." Off the record, Dezube took full credit for Kelly's new prominence. "It was my idea to use the Senate rules to our advantage. I told Senator Kelly that we had to protect American jobs." Everyone smiled at Dezube's boast. But everyone also admitted that there must be a special bond between the two men.

The board of directors of the Hand Towel Association extended Dezube's contract and gave him a big raise. They arranged for him to speak at business and union conventions throughout the country. Dezube became a nationally recognized spokesman on the subject of American jobs. At times he would speak on other subjects, such as how Congress works and how to get along with others. He was enormously successful.

At the pinnacle of his success, he was asked to appear on the *Today Show*. He was interviewed by Katie Couric. Unfortunately, he sweated profusely under the hot television lights, and his hair matted down. His children and close friends had trouble recognizing him.

As he left, he ran into Senator Kelly in the studio. Senator Kelly was scheduled to appear later in the show. When Dezube saw the senator, he stuck out his hand and put on a big smile. The senator shook his hand. "I'm Senator Kelly," he announced.

"I'm Doug Dezube," said Dezube in confusion.

"Nice to meet you, Doug." And he turned away.

The Hand Towel Equity Act never passed the House of Representatives or the Senate. But the bill achieved a level of notoriety that few pieces of legislation ever attain. News stories were run about it, on television and in the papers. It became a symbol of American trade policy and of the efforts to save American jobs.

Although the bill failed to pass, the hand towel industry used it at the center of a new advertising campaign. "The government has failed to protect American jobs," ran the ad. "It is up to you. Buy American hand towels."

The ads were a huge success. Soon every American consumer was buying domestic hand towels. Sales went through the roof. In fact, the industry could not keep up with demand. Secretly, quietly, several of the larger hand towel firms outsourced for towels made in Bangladesh.

CHAPTER XV
BACK AT THE RANCH

At the beginning of October, Congress adjourned for the elections. Following a longstanding tradition, the Washington office of the firm held a party to celebrate our lobbying successes.

As with everything else, the Johnson, Woods & Hart legislative party was over the top. We took over the entire dining room of a prestigious private golf club. The party started at noon, and the bar and the kitchen remained open as long as anyone hung on, ordering more. It included every member of the firm, from the newest messenger to Jason Johnson himself.

There had been rumors that the firm's financial condition would preclude having the party. The purveyors of such nonsense had never reckoned with Jason Douglas Johnson. The party was not only held, it was bigger and better than ever before. From open bars to the seven-course meal, the food and drink were magnificent. One of the many highlights of the afternoon was when three waiters rolled out a huge cart which held an entire roasted pig. They carved the first slices and delivered them with a flourish to Jason. Jason accepted the heaping plate with a bow, and then immediately handed it to a firm telephone operator sitting at his table. She looked up at him with reverence as the rest of us clapped loudly.

It was an unspoken rule, but all the partners knew it was a requirement to be there and make sure everyone else had a great time. We were to put away our differences and present a united front of cheer for our loyal support staff. We all talked extensively about plans for the firm's future. Our manners and presence reassured everyone that our prospects were sound.

We were all there. John Horn did his famous imitations of various judges. Ed Topp explained the communications revolution to three very junior associates, who were terribly bored but afraid to walk away from such a senior partner. Walker Dudley wore a tie with the US Capitol on it. Soon, however, it was covered with pork gravy, which seemed fitting.

But, of course, we were all overshadowed by Jason. He was in his finest form, graciously asking everybody if they'd had enough to eat in a manner that bestowed concern and caring. He laughed and listened to everyone who had a word for him.

When lunch was finally over, he stood and prepared to speak. We all quieted down as he looked over the room. He held our attention for a full minute before he said anything. The room was deadly quiet and serious.

Then he smiled. "Congratulations, everyone," he said.

"Thank you," we all responded, like schoolchildren.

"As always, we had another great legislative year at Johnson, Woods & Hart. Due to our efforts, a number of important bills passed Congress. Important for the country"—he smiled—"and important for our clients."

"If we had any differences," he went on, in a tone that implied that there weren't any, "they do not obscure the fact that we are a firm. We are a group of people who decided to work together to build something great. Less than six years ago, we had twenty total employees. Now we span the country. Next year, we will be overseas. Even today, eight members of the firm are visiting countries in Asia, Europe, and the Middle East. We are growing and going global.

"Soon the election will occur. I don't know who will win, but we have members of the firm working for both sides. Right, Walker?"

"Right, Jason. We covered all the bases, you know what I mean?" Dudley answered, slurring his words.

Jason continued. "I can hardly wait for next year. It will be better than ever. We will grow. We will add new partners and bring in new clients. Next year will be better than ever."

———

As the afternoon wore down, I drifted towards Barbara. I hadn't talked to her since our night in Jason's office. We were both sexual frauds, guilt ridden and embarrassed about it. With fortification from several glasses of wine, I decided to break the silence with her. We weren't destined to be lovers, but we could be friends.

As always, she looked stunning. She had cut her hair and curled it, making her look older, wiser, and more experienced. And when she smiled, there was a hint of sadness in her eyes. She must have seen me crossing the room out of the corner of her eye. She turned and faced me directly, moving away from others around her, and gave me her full attention as I approached. I wasn't sure what I'd say when I got to her.

Fortunately, she spoke first. "I've missed talking to you," she said simply.

"I've missed you too," I admitted.

"Didn't I disappoint you?"

"No, of course not."

"Why not?"

"Why not what?"

"Why aren't you disappointed with me?"

"You mean because you are a cock tease?

"Yes." She said, turning away from me.

I reached out and took her arm. "I was just kidding. I didn't mean it. And even if I did, who am I to talk?" She kept turning away, but more slowly. "Barbara, I'm serious. I am not upset. Not with you." She stopped moving and listened. "Look, you are great. Really. And sexy as hell. But it seems we're both alike when it comes to the sexual game."

"How's that?"

"We are both scam artists." She started to smile. "Of course, you are better than me because you have more potential. I'm just a broken-down married man with three children and an overactive imagination. You could win the Miss Universe contest."

She laughed quietly, not because of what I had said but because I had broken the tension between us.

"You're not so bad," she said. "You are the sexiest man at Johnson, Woods & Hart."

"Who's the competition? Walker Dudley?"

Her laugh deepened. "I don't know, some of those food stains are pretty erotic, if you know what I mean?"

"Hell, if that's what turns you on." I picked an egg roll off a nearby tray and dropped it on my shirt. Then I got us both another glass of wine. "Do you feel better now?" I asked.

"Yes."

"Can we stop avoiding each other?"

"I'd like that. I like hanging out with you."

"I like that, too. It's been a rough and lonely time around the firm."

"I gather. Your scam seemed a bit out of control."

"You have no idea."

———————

The next day, things got a whole lot worse. Jason called me to an emergency meeting of the most senior partners in his office. I had not attained that level of seniority in the firm yet, so I knew I was being singled out. When I arrived, Jason was on the phone. Around his office sat Walker Dudley, John Horn, Ed Topp, and all the remaining senior leaders of the firm. I stood in the doorway as they all stared at me. Jason waved me in and gestured for me to close the door.

When he completed his call, he announced to the room, "That was our lead bank. They are demanding repayment of our loans. It seems they are concerned that collections have dropped off and some clients look like they will never pay us." As he finished, Jason looked right at me.

I saw where this was going. "You mean like the Citizens Against Tax Injustice?"

"You are absolutely right," Ed Topp said loudly. "Are they good for their bills?"

Ed could always get under my skin. "Not right now, Ed. As you know, the government is chasing the client right now. It's pretty hard for him to run his organization and raise money and pay this firm. He has other things on his mind."

"Well, how do you expect us to cover that hole in our budget?" Ed continued.

I was steaming now. "What hole? He didn't put us in a hole. All the bills were for my efforts. I had other clients that covered my salary and overhead. His fees were gravy to the firm, something to throw into the bonus pool."

"Well, now the bank wants its money back. How are you going to pay them?"

"Ed, it's not my fault. I didn't borrow money against those uncollected fees." And there, I had said it out loud. I had blown the cover off the phony accounting that was at the bottom of Johnson, Woods & Hart.

"You know, he's right," said Dudley. "If we hadn't borrowed that money, we wouldn't be in this mess, you know what I mean?"

"If we hadn't borrowed that money and other money against our unpaid bills, you wouldn't have been paid as much this year," said Jason quietly.

"Yeah," said Horn. "We didn't want you to miss a meal, Dudley." The room broke out in laughter.

Now Dudley was defensive. "All I know is that I never trusted that Warren Ford," he said. "I met him early this year and thought he was full of bullshit. I never would have taken him on as a client."

"Even with the problems with Warren Ford, I can't imagine things are so bad that the banks would pull our loans," I said. "There has to be more going on here."

Jason, Dudley, and Horn dropped their gazes to the floor. "Of course, you're right," said Topp, looking at Jason. "It goes far beyond your tax client. We borrowed against good bills, bad bills, future bills. We borrowed against assets we borrowed to buy. The whole firm has been one big Ponzi scheme."

Jason completed the picture. "As long as we kept bringing in money, the banks didn't care. They competed to lend us money. It kept rolling as long as we kept moving ahead. But it seems to have stopped." He looked at me. "With Warren Ford going underground, the banks have started looking at us again. I suspect they were prodded to do that by the feds. But, either way, they are now moving in on us."

"It was only a matter of time," said Topp.

"I don't agree," said Jason. "It was a fragile house of cards, but it worked. And I know that someday, soon, we would have gotten ahead of the bills and been fine."

"Bullshit," said Dudley.

Horn looked at him with disgust. "Walker, when did you ever even suggest that we cut back on our expenses? When did you offer to take a pay cut? Ed is a whiny pain in the ass, but at least he's been saying we should cut back for months. You just keep spending like it is going out of style."

"Bullshit." Dudley seemed unable to come up with a better retort.

"I'm serious, Walker," Horn continued. "I am sick and tired of watching you go off on another $500 dinner with one of your congressional friends who's been out of office for ten years."

Jason stood. "Look. This isn't productive. The banks want their money. We don't have it, and it doesn't seem like we will be getting it soon. We'll have to file for bankruptcy."

When he said that last word, it sucked the air out of the room. Everyone was silent and unmoving. It was even difficult to blink. Finally, the others rose and left the room. I stayed until I was left alone with Jason.

"Did I really cause this?" I asked.

He looked at me in silence for a few long moments. "No. We played with fire for a long time. You were just the one standing there when we got burned."

"God, I am sorry, Jason."

"So am I, Richard. For a lot of things."

In a daze, I walked back to my office and contemplated the harsh realities that I faced. I was thirty-eight, with a wife and three children. I had lived the lifestyle of an up-and-coming Washington lobbyist. And my firm was going under.

I had worked for a large number of paying clients during the year—for nothing. I had embarrassed the president of the United States and earned a special place on the enemies' list of the administration—for nothing. I was under investigation by the FBI— for nothing. I had driven my secretary underground—for nothing. And I had spent the year supporting the growth strategies of Jason Johnson—for nothing. All in all, it was quite a year. And worst of all, I was partly responsible for the wreckage. I felt sick.

———————

The next day, I decided to check on my only remaining source of income. I called Emilio's new phone number. There was no answer. I tried the place where he told me he would start working. There was no answer. I tried calling a number of health clubs around the city. No one had seen him. Steaming with anger and frustration, I called the police and filed a report on him.

As for the rest of the day, we were all in shock at Johnson, Woods & Hart. Jason and the senior partners met privately all day with the bankruptcy attorneys, preparing the necessary papers for the firm to file. Creditors were calling, screaming for immediate payment of their past-due bills. Clients called, wondering who would do their work. Headhunters called, hoping to place attorneys in new firms. Eventually we stopped answering the phone.

The only good surprise I had that day was when I finally took a call from Doug Dezube. He had called several times that day looking for me, and the firm operator finally begged me to take the call to stop him from harassing her. Reluctantly, I picked up the phone.

"Richard Ricardo, why are you hiding from me?" he shouted over the phone.

"I wasn't hiding, Doug, I was working on other client matters."

"Bullshit. I bet you were hiding in your office from your creditors."

I was in no mood for his banter. I tried to get him to the point. "What can I do for you today, Doug? As you can imagine, it's a bit hectic around here just now."

"That's what I understand. So, old Jason ran the firm into the ground. I gather you will have to go somewhere else. And when you do, tell them that you still have me as a client."

"Really?"

"Sure. You treat me like shit at times, but you are one of the best lobbyists in Washington. You are my guy, and I'll stick with you wherever you go."

I was touched. "Thanks, Doug. I appreciate that more than you will know. I half thought you would be telling me that since the firm is going under, you would stiff us on your last bill."

"Wait, can I do that?" he asked with eagerness. *Oh God*, I thought, *I didn't mean to give him the idea.*

"No, you can't. Not if you want me to keep helping you."

"Well, okay, you're my guy and I want you happy. Tell Jason I will pay my last bill."

"Thanks, Doug."

Late that afternoon, I was notified about a partners' meeting. I got a knot in the pit of my stomach. I knew it was the end. Only the timing was unclear. The word sped through the firm with lightning speed. Everyone expected the worst. Secretaries started crying. The partners spent the afternoon talking to each other, in person and by phone. Some still held out hope that Jason would pull off a miracle. Others tried to reassemble a smaller, leaner firm comprised of big producers. Still others pledged undying friendship that would transcend the collapse of Johnson, Woods & Hart. But most of all, we complained to each other. We blamed the demise on Jason, on the malcontents, on the spendthrifts, on the banks, or on the weather. And I complained as loudly as everyone else, although I knew I was more responsible than almost anyone. Jason borrowed the money based on my nonexistent client. We made quite a pair.

At the meeting, we all sat apart from each other. Our emotions were scrambled. We hated the firm and loved the firm. We hated our partners and were saddened by the thought that we would not be working with them anymore. Most of all, we wanted the whole experience to end.

We were introduced to two attorneys who specialized in business bankruptcies. The lead attorney, Mark Karp, looked like Lenin, the Russian leader, but with graying hair. I wondered if Mr. Karp would be as destructive as the real Lenin. He quickly took over the meeting. He spoke in a quiet, calm voice.

"We like to think of this, this project," he called the end of our professional careers, "as if it was a jetliner that had lost its engines. We want to see it coast to a safe landing, without hurting the passengers or the cargo. We want to protect the creditors and see that they get the money they are owed. But we do not want to cause the partners any more financial pain than is necessary."

As he rambled on, carrying the example of the "gentle landing" to an extreme, my mind wandered. I thought about all the good times I'd had at the firm and the friends I had made. I was afraid of losing friends in the unpleasantness that would inevitably follow. My only hope was that as the workout with the creditors proceeded, we would reverse direction and find the will to keep the firm going. Even at that late date, I was hoping that the firm would survive.

"Regarding timing," Karp said loudly, to get our attention back, "I recommend that we preserve the firm's assets by closing the doors sooner rather than later."

"What does that mean?" asked a voice from one of the satellite offices.

"We need to close the firm by Friday at the latest" was Karp's reply. It was Tuesday.

There was a gasp in the room. We heard similar gasps coming from all the other offices. Quickly, before we could think, one of the partners, I think from Nebraska, made a motion to dissolve the firm in less than four days. Usually the debate on such a motion would last longer than that, but on that day, we were all silent. The motion passed without dissent, although many of us were too shocked to vote at all.

It was over. I glanced at Jason. He looked back at me sadly. Topp was staring at me too, with hatred in his eyes. But neither of them said anything. They knew that I was at fault, but so were they— Jason for creating the lifestyle we could not afford, and Topp for not doing more when the firm's finances were spinning out of control. But I thanked them silently for not mentioning Warren Ford, the nonexistent client that brought the FBI and the banks down on the firm.

We sat there for a few moments in silence, but it seemed like a much longer time. Then Karp started talking again, discussing the next steps. No one paid attention. Even he knew that. But I think he recognized the need for all of us to believe that someone with a guiding hand would get us through the mess we found ourselves in. The sound of his voice was soothing. Our pain was dulled.

Karp instructed us not to take any of the firm's equipment or furniture. He explained how the bankruptcy worked and how he would protect us. He advised us not to talk to the press or to any creditors. He was in charge now.

He explained to us that we would pay the creditors out of the collections from our accounts receivable. He pointed out that we had over seventy-five million in bills owed us, and only sixty-two million in debts. If all went well, he said, we would have enough to pay the creditors off without asking the partners to contribute from their personal assets. Of course, I knew that the Citizens Against

Tax Injustice owed one of those bills. I wondered how many other bills were owed by similar clients. I peered over at Jason again. He was staring at the floor.

Karp went on. "However, if we do not collect enough from our accounts receivable, the partners would have to make up the difference. There might be a need for each of you to pay into a central fund to cover the shortfall. But let's not consider that now. Just collect the bills, and you will have no problem." I lifted my head and saw that Dudley, Horn, and Topp were watching me once more. Behind them, out the window, I saw a police car driving down the street. I thought about Agent Kennedy and wondered if he was happy.

CHAPTER XVI
PICKLE IN YOUR MOUTH

One night earlier that year, Elizabeth and I were trying to get the children to eat their dinner. We were having cheeseburgers with all the fixings, including pickles. The children were not very adventurous in their eating habits. They all tasted, and immediately hated, the pickles. Amy refused to eat after the first bite that contained a pickle. The boys opened their cheeseburgers and took out the pickles. Matthew put his on the side of his plate. David waited until Elizabeth and I were distracted and threw his pickles at his brother. Matthew screamed as if he were being beaten, and slugged his brother. Then David started screaming, and Amy, not wanting to miss out on the fun, started screaming too.

From that time on, our family stayed away from pickles. Pickles became an inside joke. After all, Elizabeth figured we would rather have the children call each other a picklehead than a butthead. At any time, in anger or humor, one of us would tell the others to stick a pickle in their mouths. Eventually we made a silly rhyme out of it:

> I went on vacation, and I went away
> Went to the beach and stayed a day
> Got in the car, drove north then south
> And the whole time I had a pickle in my mouth.

We would repeat, "Pickle in my mouth, pickle in my mouth," over and over and over until someone started laughing. Then we would tease each other regarding who had the disgusting pickle in his or her mouth.

During the last three days, as Johnson, Woods & Hart moved towards its end, I was in a daze, trying to figure out what I was going to do and where I was going to be working on the following Monday. Only a few flashes remain in my mind. I remember walking through the ornate offices and halls, wondering what happened. I remember hugging a number of the support staff who came to me crying. I remember calling Jason every name in the book, and then listening to him when he suggested that the two of us open a new office.

"We could make a lot of money together," he told me. "We'll keep the overhead low. We'll stay small and lean. I've learned. Small. That's the way to be a success in the legal profession."

I didn't accept his offer.

On Wednesday, one moment stands clear in my mind from the surrounding fog of the day. I received a phone call from a Detective Wendy Jackson from the District of Columbia Police Department. She called to inform me that one Emilio Ramirez had voluntarily turned himself in.

"Great," I yelled. "Lock him up. Better yet, let him go so I can kill him, slowly, with a bat. With a bat and a knife. With a sharp knife . . ." Then I remembered to whom I was talking. "I'm just kidding," I said.

"Yes." The voice was noncommittal. "It seems that you and Mr. Ramirez have quite a history together."

"He took me for over $10,000, Detective Jackson."

"Yes." Her voice remained calm.

"Are you interrogating him?"

"Oh, yes. Absolutely," she assured me. "He has many things to tell us." The voice remained noncommittal. It angered me again.

"Well, I trust that you will handle the situation," I said in a tone that implied that she would foul it up.

"Believe me, Mr. Brewster, we will fully pursue the matter and will share our findings with the proper federal officials," she replied firmly.

"I just want some justice," I insisted.

"We all do, Mr. Brewster."

"Well, thank you for calling me."

"Yes," she said, her voice still flat.

I hung up the phone, and the fog swept back around me.

At one point, a number of us decided the best thing we could do was go to the Potomac Pub and drink too much. Of course, Barbara Lehman organized the event. "It can't hurt," she reasoned.

"Except we're all broke," I pointed out.

"Not at all," she said, smiling. "The firm's American Express account hasn't been closed yet. I heard two of the senior partners talking about it earlier today. They kept it open so partners out of town could get back."

Laughing, I said, "Then let's get a big group of people." And we did. Even Mark and Brad from the tax section joined us. An hour later, seven of us were sitting in a booth made for four. We were crushed on top of each other. Our suits were wrinkled, and we had managed to spill beer all over the table and the floor.

"I will not hold anything anyone says to me this week against them," said Mark. "No one is in his or her right mind. We are all basket cases."

"Oh yeah?" said Barbara, shooting me a sidelong glance. "In that case, Mark, you are a real weenie."

"Both you tax guys are," I added.

"Oh yeah? Well, to hell with you legislative guys," said Brad. "To call you lawyers is like calling my dog a doctor." He looked at Barbara and me to gauge our reactions, to retract his insult if we took it the wrong way.

We didn't. But devoid of creativity, all I could reply with was "The hell with you."

"The hell with you," all agreed together.

"To hell with the firm," said Mark.

"To hell with the firm," we all agreed.

"The hell with Jason," said Brad. "He ruined everything. It was a great firm, and Jason ran it into the ground. He should have listened to us. We tried to stop him."

"Who?" I asked.

"Who what?" he asked.

"Who tried to stop Jason?" I asked again.

"All of us."

"Bullshit," I said, getting angry. "All of us went along with him like a bunch of sheep. We agreed with every one of his ideas. Hell, we argued in favor of most of them. And we all sure took our salary checks when we knew we were borrowing to cover them. Jason ran the firm into the ground, but he had a lot of help from all of us." Of course, I did not acknowledge just how much help I contributed to the firm's failure.

The table was silent for a few moments. No one was in the mood for introspection.

"Well, I didn't agree to opening the office in Paris," Brad said slowly and defensively. He eyeballed me, waiting for my reply.

As I looked around the table, I decided that I wouldn't force them to face reality that day. I would let them indulge in their anger and bond with fellow victims. "I didn't approve of the Paris office," I agreed.

"Well then, the hell with Jason."

"The hell with Jason," we all agreed.

———————

Friday arrived. The last day of operations for Johnson, Woods & Hart. I felt very sad as I drove to work. At the same time, I was determined to end the day on a positive note. I decided that I would visit all the support staff who had worked for me to thank them for their help. I would go to the offices of the partners and say goodbye to each of them personally. I wanted everyone, at the end of the day, to feel good that they had worked with Richard Brewster.

During the morning, I placed my files in boxes. I still didn't know where I would be on Monday, but I had to take my files with me. As I put them away, I thought about the missing CATI files. I wondered if I would ever see them again.

As the afternoon began, I got ready to make my rounds. Naturally, I was interrupted by a call from Doug Dezube.

"Richard, I need you to see Russ Ratto, in Congressman Conlin's office," he said. "I sent the congressman a letter last week. Ratto has a reply. I need you to read it to see if it says what I want it to say. If it does, send it on to me. If not, try to get Ratto to change it. I need it done this afternoon."

I was about to protest, but he interrupted me. "I know it is the last day of Johnson, Woods & Hart. I am sure you are packing and looking for a new firm to join. I know this is inconvenient. But I need you to do this for me. I've carried this project long enough." He hung up before I could answer.

I had to go get it myself. I couldn't ask the support staff to go, as they were all standing around looking miserable. I couldn't get Ratto to fax it to me as the fax machine and the computers had already been repossessed by creditors. So I got into a cab and cursed Doug Dezube all the way to the Capitol.

Once there, I found Russ and got the letter. It was fine. I asked him to fax it to Dezube. He agreed to do it. Then our business was done.

"How are you doing?" he asked.

"As well as can be expected," I replied.

"Do you know where you are going to work after the firm closes?"

"Not yet. I hope to take a few days to decide."

"I own a beach house up on the Delaware shore. If you want, you can borrow it and go up there to think."

"Is it available now?"

"Sure. It's empty and ready to use. Do you want the key?"

"No. Thanks for offering though."

"Are you sure?"

"I think so." I got ready to leave. Then I remembered I would need a copy of the letter for my files. I asked Russ for one. He went into the back office to find a copy machine. Exhausted from the tension of the previous days, I slumped into a chair in the congressman's waiting room. I was tired from the tip of my head to the bottom of my feet. All I wanted to do was sleep for a week, then wake up and have Jason tell me that the firm was back in operation and the FBI had gone away.

The television in the room was turned to a local station. I watched without enthusiasm as newscasters relayed the stories of the day.

"Can I get you a cup of coffee, or a soft drink?" asked the receptionist. I thanked her and nodded. She went to another room, leaving me alone in the reception area. I slumped lower in the chair.

The television volume was very low, and I couldn't make out any of the words. As I watched, the anchorman started reading a new story. Then the scene switched to the pressroom of the Federal Bureau of Investigation. There at the podium was Agent Kennedy. Behind him were a number of other agents and FBI personnel—and Emilio Ramirez. Next to him, standing arm in arm, was Kathryn

Monroney. Kathryn was crying. I jumped to my feet and turned up the volume. Agent Kennedy was reading a statement.

"Thanks to the cooperation of these citizens," he said, pointing to Kathryn and Emilio, "we have uncovered evidence of extensive criminal activity. We now have definite proof that Warren Ford does not exist. Mr. Ford's existence, and the work of the Citizens Against Tax Injustice, were part of a complicated fraud scheme perpetrated by a local attorney: Mr. Richard Brewster. We expect to bring Mr. Brewster into custody before the end of the day."

Reporters started asking questions. At that minute, the receptionist returned, and I jumped back up and turned off the television set. She handed me my drink. Noticing my look, she glanced around the room.

"Is anything wrong?" she asked.

"Nothing," I assured her, taking the drink with a forced smile. "Thank you."

Russ came out of the back office with the copy of the letter I had asked for. "Sorry I took so long," he said, "but I got distracted by the television in the back office." He handed me the paper.

"It's not true," I said loudly.

"What's not true?" he asked.

"I didn't do anything wrong."

"I didn't say you did. What are you talking about?" Russ was staring at me. So was the receptionist.

"What were you watching on the TV?" I asked.

"It was turned to C-SPAN. They were covering a speech my boss made in the district. Are you all right?"

"Yes," I said, calming down and thinking fast. "It was nothing. I guess the bankruptcy is getting to me. Russ, can I still borrow your beach house?"

"Of course. Here are the keys," he said, handing me a key ring. He crossed over to his desk and also handed me directions on how to get there. "These are for renters," he said. "It's easy to find."

"Thanks. I'll only stay up there a day or two."

"Stay as long as you want. It's empty this time of year. Take care of yourself."

Before I left his office, I borrowed the phone and called Elizabeth at home. Fortunately, she was there.

"Elizabeth, where are the kids?"

"They're all here. We were just getting ready to go out."

"The FBI just announced that they plan to arrest me later today," I said quickly. "We need to get away to think about our options. I've got the key to Russ Ratto's beach house in Delaware. Can you come and pick me up at the Cannon House Office Building?"

"Now?"

"If you wait much longer, you will have to come to the federal building in Alexandria and bail me out of jail instead."

"Seriously?"

"Yes. And we don't have any money left for bail."

"That jerk Jason."

"Will you come get me?" I pleaded.

There was a long silence. Finally, she said, "I have to pack. It will take about an hour. Where should we meet?"

I told her where to find me. I spent the next hour hiding in the lower levels of the Capitol complex. I knew the passages down there better than any FBI agent, and I assumed that the Capitol police were not yet aware of my impending arrest warrant. When the time came, I found my wife and children, and we took off in the car.

We drove through the city. The traffic was heavy, and we moved slowly. I kept scanning for police vehicles. After we had been on the road for an hour, we finally got out of the city and on the highway towards the Bay Bridge to Delaware. The traffic got thinner, and we picked up speed. I began to relax.

"Two FBI agents came to our house after you called," Elizabeth told me. I tensed up again.

"What did you tell them?"

"Nothing. I said that I had not heard from you. I told them I was going grocery shopping."

"What did they say?"

"They told me to have you call them. One of them gave me a card with a phone number on it." She handed me the card. It was Agent Kennedy's.

"He seemed very nice," Elizabeth went on. "He told me that if you cooperated, it would be much better for you."

"I am sure he was nice. What did you expect? If he had been a mean son of a bitch, you wouldn't help him. Instead, you trust him and are trying to convince me to turn myself in."

"Well, what are you going to do?"

"Run away to the beach."

"For how long?"

"Oh, about ten or twenty years. I can't remember how long the statute of limitations is for fraud. I should have taken one of those criminal-law refresher courses. Who says they're worthless?"

She stared at me. "Are you serious?"

"Yes. Why?"

"We can't hide for years."

"Why not?"

"Dad, why are we hiding?" asked David.

His brother answered, "We are hiding so we can go to the beach."

"Oh," said David seriously. "Daddy, why are we going to the beach? It's not summer."

"Daddy said we are going for ten years," answered Matthew.

"We are not going for ten years," corrected Elizabeth.

"Daddy just said we were."

"He was kidding."

"Daddy, were you kidding?"

"I don't know. I just don't know," I answered.

"Don't let them think we're going away for ten years," Elizabeth said heatedly. She turned to the boys and told them, "We are just going away for a special weekend."

"And then Daddy is going to jail," I added.

Both boys started shouting. David was afraid for me, and Matthew thought it was cool. The noise woke up Amy, who had been napping. She started crying. Elizabeth lost her temper. "We are not running away. We are going away for the weekend," she told the kids. She turned to me. "You have to turn yourself in."

"Maybe."

"The FBI agent said he would help you if you turned yourself in."

"Is that why he's been working on the case for several weeks? So he can help me when it's over?"

"We are not going to raise our children as fugitives," she said.

By now the tension was thick. All three children were crying.

David was particularly upset. "Please don't fight," he begged us. "Please don't."

We tried to reassure them even as we avoided resolving the issue before us. Elizabeth unbuckled David's seat belt and pulled him over the seat and into her lap. He stopped crying, but I heard him sniffling for the next ten miles. Finally, I nudged him and started to chant:

I went on vacation and I went away
Went to the beach and stayed a day

At this point, Elizabeth joined in, then Matthew, then David:

Got in the car, drove north then south
And the whole time I had a pickle in my mouth

Then we all repeated loudly, "Pickle in your mouth, pickle in your mouth, pickle in your mouth."

The next morning, I woke up first. I got up and gazed out the window. It was a cloudy, windy, gray day. I decided to go out running. I pulled on my running clothes and left the house without leaving a note. I assumed Elizabeth would figure out what I was doing when she saw that the car was still in the driveway. But I was also not ready to talk to her.

I left the beach house and ran down the main street of the town of Bethany Beach, Delaware. The road hit a dead end at the boardwalk, which ran along the beach for seven or eight blocks. I turned onto the boardwalk and kept running.

The wind cut through me, despite my heavy sweatshirt. Soon I was winded and tired. I had no enthusiasm for running. Gasping for breath, I slowed first to a walk and then sat down on a bench. I stared out into the ocean, trying to decide whether to turn myself in or not. I have no idea how long I sat there.

Along the boardwalk, a few other early risers were walking. I glanced over each of them as they came into view. One man, all bundled up, caught my attention. I couldn't see him well, but he seemed familiar. I decided to wait until he came down the boardwalk to see if I recognized him. In the meantime, I thought about my future. It was bleak. I agonized over whether to keep hiding or to turn myself in, as Elizabeth urged.

Finally, the man got closer. I couldn't see his face clearly. He was in a sweat outfit, with a scarf and a knit hat. He still seemed familiar, but I wasn't sure. He passed me. Still unsure, I said quietly, "Senator?"

Senator Laxalt stopped and turned.

At first he didn't recognize me in my winter running gear. When he did, he gave me a warm smile. Despite the cold, it warmed me immediately. I got off the bench, walked over to him, and shook his hand.

"It's good to see you, Richard," he said.

"Senator, it's great to see you too. How are you?"

"I'm fine. I really like this beach," he said, looking around. Then he looked at me. "How are you? I understand that you are going through some, some . . ." He paused, looking for the right word. ". . . difficulties." That was the senator's understated way of saying that my life was a disaster.

"Things could be better, Senator," I admitted.

"I heard that your firm was in financial trouble."

"It's worse than that. We went bankrupt yesterday."

He looked surprised. "I am sorry to hear that. Are you getting away from the pressures this weekend?"

"Actually, Senator, I am running from the FBI. They want to arrest me for fraud."

Surprise changed to astonishment. "Is there some mistake?"

"Not really."

We stood there in silence. The wind whipped around us. He looked uncomfortable. I knew that I had disappointed him. He had always said that he had high hopes for me. Now it looked like I was going to be the first member of his old staff to go to jail. I tried to justify my actions.

"I never intended for things to get so out of hand. It started as a game, but it got away from me . . ." My voice sounded hollow. He looked puzzled, as he had no idea about the details of the scam. I grew silent as we stood for another minute. Finally I said, "It's a long way from that summer of 1975, isn't it?"

He nodded. I asked, "What should I do? Should I turn myself in or go into hiding?"

"With your beautiful family?" I nodded. "I don't think hiding is the answer." He went on. "Whatever you do, do it with class. We didn't accomplish everything we tried to do in the Senate. But when we lost, we always lost with grace, and we never burned our bridges. Nothing is forever, unless you make it that way. You can always work yourself out of this, this . . ."—he looked for the right word again—"situation, but only if you don't alienate anyone unnecessarily. Always act with style."

Then he gave me another smile, as if trying to chase the troubles out of my life with good humor. Despite my dread, I smiled back. "Thanks, Senator. I guess I'll be back."

"Of course you will."

"Maybe when this is all over, I'll write a book about it. Can I put you in it?"

"Sure," he said, nodding. "Why not?"

"Thank you, Senator."

"Good luck, Richard." We shook hands again, and he continued down the boardwalk. I waited a minute and then started to run back to the house. I got about two blocks before running out of energy again. I walked the rest of the way.

As I entered the house, I found my entire family up and eating breakfast. In her haste to leave, Elizabeth had only packed a box of Fruit Loops. The three children were eating bowls of brightly colored cereal at the table. I popped a few loops into my mouth.

"Daddy!" yelled Matthew as he stood and ran to me. David was right behind him. The boys jumped on me, and we started wrestling. Amy, who was stuck in a high chair, kept calling out, "Daddy, Daddy," demanding attention. Elizabeth looked at me with concern.

"Where is Agent Kennedy's phone number?" I asked her. She rose and found it for me.

"What are you going to do?" she asked.

"I'm going to turn myself in."

"Are you sure now that you are doing the right thing?" she asked.

"No. But I am doing it with class," I reassured her. I met her eyes. "Elizabeth, I know I have been a total ass the last few months. Things got away from me. I thought I could become the master of the city and only proved what an insignificant player I am. I am not sure why I had to prove I was more important than the principal deputy secretary and the academic with the medal by cutting corners. We had a good life, and I threw it away. I was guilty of believing all the DC bullshit."

She smiled sadly. "I was guilty too. We don't need a bigger house or more spending. It isn't worth it." We looked at each other for a while.

I picked up the phone and dialed the number. "Hello," came the sleepy answer.

"Agent Kennedy, this is Richard Brewster."

He was instantly awake. "Where are you?" he demanded.

"It doesn't matter. I'm coming in. Where should I go?"

He told me. I wrote down the information.

"I'll be there late this afternoon," I told him.

"Where are you?" he repeated.

"I'll cooperate with you. You can have a recorder ready when I get there. I'll waive my right to silence."

"We have your files."

"I figured as much. There is not much more information you need. But I will give you the last pieces."

"Where are you?" he asked again, but softly this time.

"I am at a friend's house. I'll be there when I promised. I want to spend the rest of the day with my family. Then I am yours."

"Okay." He was silent for a moment. Then he added, "Have a bite to eat before you come in. It will take us a few hours to process the paperwork."

"Thanks." We hung up. I felt unsteady for a brief second. I had a sour taste in my mouth. I thought to myself, *It tastes like a pickle*.

EPILOGUE

The leather chair wrapped me in comfort. Despite its age, it had the smell of recently cleaned and polished leather. Outside, the sun was shining. The air was cool, and the sky was bright and sunny.

"Would you like a cup of coffee?" he asked me.

"No, thank you."

"It should be coming on anytime now," he said, turning on the television. He flipped through the channels until he found the seal of the Department of Justice. The seal faded into a press briefing room. It was very expensive to get access to all the federal government's internal communications networks, but you never knew when you might need one of them.

On the TV the Justice Department spokesman went up to the microphone at the front of the room and began to make announcements for the day. There were about a dozen members of the press in the audience, taking notes. It was a slow news day, so there were no network television cameras in the room.

A number of routine matters were announced. Those included the appointment of two new US attorneys, the conviction of Ladd Industries in Chicago for violation of environmental and health laws, and the announcement of a number of grants from the Bureau of Justice Assistance. The spokesman then paused. I tensed up. This was the moment I was waiting for.

"I have one further announcement today, before taking any questions," he said. "Attorney General Reno has decided to drop all charges for fraud against Richard Brewster. As you may recall, Mr. Brewster published a newsletter that accused the Internal Revenue Service of arresting a young boy's parents without cause. It turns out that there was no such arrest. In fact, the whole story was a fabrication. However, the attorney general has determined that there was no intent to commit fraud. As a result, she has decided to drop the charges. Any questions?"

The press was all over the last news item.

"I don't understand your reasoning in this case. Could you be more specific?" asked the first reporter.

"If Mr. Brewster had requested money from the public based on the false story, that would have been fraud," the spokesman explained. "He did not. There was no fundraising appeal connected with that particular newsletter. Usually there was, so Mr. Brewster knew what he was doing. But without the request for money, all we had was a lie printed and distributed in the newsletter. The First Amendment protects Mr. Brewster's right to print anything he wants, even if it is in very bad taste."

"Isn't it true that the real reason you are dropping the charges is that the president wants to avoid embarrassment?" another reporter persisted. "I understand that you are afraid that the trial would show how the administration was totally fooled by the story. That is hardly the image the president wants to covey."

"That is incorrect," the spokesman said. "This administration is dedicated to the impartial handling of the cases before it. The case was dropped due to a lack of evidence of intent."

"Are you telling us that Attorney General Reno couldn't find any criminal activity involved here? That she couldn't make a case of conspiracy using other newsletters?"

"The attorney general carefully reviewed the case and found that the interests of justice were best served by dropping the prosecution. This was in agreement with the recommendation of the US attorney."

"Mr. Brewster's case was not handled by a criminal attorney. Instead he used a lobbyist. There have been allegations this decision was made on political grounds. Is that true?"

"Mr. Brewster is free to select the attorney of his choice to defend him. That had no bearing on his case."

"But I understand that Mr. Brewster's attorney placed several phone calls to the White House. Was the attorney general directed to drop the case by the president's political advisors?"

"Absolutely not. This administration does not work that way."

"Mr. Brewster is currently going through a bankruptcy proceeding with his former firm, Johnson, Woods & Hart. Did the attorney general consider that fact? Did she drop the prosecution for humane reasons?"

"No."

"Did Mr. Brewster work out a deal with the Justice Department to provide evidence against Jason Johnson or any other member of his former firm for dropping this case?"

"There were no deals. The department is not currently investigating Jason Johnson or any member of Johnson, Woods & Hart. Their mismanagement of the firm was stupid, not criminal."

"What happened to Emilio Ramirez?"

"No charges have been filed against Mr. Ramirez. He is currently working as an exercise and health trainer for the department."

"Let me make sure I have this right," said the first reporter. "You are saying that there was no political pressure brought to bear on the Justice Department to drop the case by the White House or by Mr. Brewster's high-profile attorney?"

"That is exactly what I am saying" was the patient response.

"If the lobbyist wasn't effective, I wonder if he was paid?" The reporters all started laughing. The press briefing ended. The screen went blank.

Charles E. Nagle turned off the television and looked at me. "I guess that ends that. Now you are free to begin working again."

"It certainly looks that way," I replied. "Where do you want me to start?"

"Touch base with all your clients and tell them of your decision to join me. Then come back and explain to me again exactly how you started your tax group."

"Okay. But why? It ended up a shambles and brought down the whole firm."

"Your problem was that you invented a client. That wasn't smart. But there are lots of people who are willing to pay substantial fees for you to create exactly the same type of organization to further their interests. I have one in mind already. I'll put you on it tomorrow."

"No way," I said quickly. "I want no part of such a deal. I've learned a number of expensive lessons, and I don't want to learn them again."

"Like what?" he said, with real interest.

"I want to work only for clients with legitimate claims, not some bullshit project from someone rich enough to hire us. I want to work within the system, not try to bend it or defile it. If I make less money by limiting my work, I am willing to accept that." At this point, I realized that I was lecturing the premier lobbyist in the city, and my new boss, and decided to drop my judgmental tone. "And I learned never to trust a personal trainer with more than five dollars," I said, smiling.

Nagle smiled back, slightly shaking his head. "You make some interesting points. I'll respect them—"

"Thank you."

" . . . as long as you hold them," he completed his sentence. "In any case, Richard, I am glad you're here. I think you will fit right in."

"I am glad to be here too," I reassured him, wanting to put my demands behind us. "Thank you for taking me in when I was in so much legal trouble. And thank you for handling the matter with the White House and the Justice Department."

"You're welcome. You know, I never lobbied the attorney general directly. She isn't as tough as her reputation."

"She isn't as smooth as you, that's for sure," I said with true admiration.

He stood up. "Well, let's get back to work."

I nodded and got up to leave. As I reached the door to his office, he said, almost to himself, "You know, despite all you went through, I envy you. I always wanted my own scam . . .

ACKNOWLEDGMENTS

Writing a novel is a solitary activity. Getting it published and marketed takes a team. Fortunately, I have a wonderful support group. My thanks to all of them.

I am a lousy proofreader and a marginally better speller. Jane Sargent and Jenny Walker spent hours trying to decipher my words and sentences and correcting my mistakes. Jane especially read the manuscript several times and offered great suggestions.

My current law firm, Akerman LLP—which bears no resemblance to Johnson, Woods and Hart—has been very supportive. My thanks to Scott Meyers and Iris Jones.

The outstanding team at Koehler Books was a dream to work with as they guided me through the process. A special thanks to Anna Torres, Skyler Kratofil, Hannah Woodlan, and John Koehler.

Finally, nothing would be possible without the love and support of my parents, Dick and Jean Spees; my children, Justin, Jonathan, and Emily; and my special angel, Roberta.

CPSIA information can be obtained
at www.ICGtesting.com
Printed in the USA
LVHW110711280822
727027LV00002B/4

9 781646 637478